What is a living person doing in Hell?

He waves, I wave back.

Then he pulls out a gun and fires. It's such a casual movement that I hardly notice it. Don't even react until it's done. My stomach flips; I throw my hands in the air, and stumble backward, then catch my balance on the back of a chair.

The window stars, but doesn't implode. You have more than double-glazing when your office faces Hell.

Through the fragmentation of the glass, I see the "cleaner" frown.

I look at the door; I'm much further from it than the window. If I run that way I'll probably get a shot or two in the back and, while I'm at it, lead him into the office. Enough people have died in here this year already. It seems clear that he's only after me—and if this is about me, I want to keep it that way. Besides, I've taken bullets before and survived them easily. I lift up a chair. Not the throne, that weighs a bloody ton.

He fires again. The window shatters this time, glass going everywhere. The bullet thwacks against the wall behind me. Alarms sound throughout the building and the One Tree's creaking intensifies to a dull roar now there's no glass to block it out. Hell has entered the building.

MANAGING DEATH

DEATH WORKS
BOOK TWO

TRENT JAMIESON

www.orbitbooks.net

Copyright © 2010 by Trent Jamieson
Excerpt from *The Business of Death* copyright © 2011 by Trent Jamieson
All rights reserved. Except as permitted under the U.S. Copyright Act of 1976, no part of this publication may be reproduced, distributed, or transmitted in any form or by any means, or stored in a database or retrieval system, without the prior written permission of the publisher.

Orbit
Hachette Book Group
237 Park Avenue
New York, NY 10017
Visit our website at www.orbitbooks.net

Orbit is an imprint of Hachette Book Group. The Orbit name and logo are trademarks of Little, Brown Book Group Limited.

Printed in the United States of America

Originally published in paperback by Hachette Australia: 2010
First North American Orbit edition: January 2011

10 9 8 7 6 5 4 3 2 1

For Diana

I heard a fly buzz when I died;
The stillness round my form
Was like the stillness in the air
Between the heaves of storm.
EMILY DICKINSON

PART ONE

THE SHIFT

1

There's blood behind my eyelids, and in my mouth.
A knife, cold and sharp-edged, is pressed beneath
my Adam's apple. The blade digs in, slowly.
I'm cackling so hard my throat tears.

I jolt awake, and almost tumble from the wicker chair
in the bedroom. And I really didn't have that much to
drink last night.

Dream.

Another one. And I'd barely closed my eyes.

Just a dream. As if anything is *just* a dream in my line
of business.

These days I hardly sleep at all, my body doesn't need
it. Comes with being a Regional Manager, comes with
being Australia's Death.

And I'm a long way from being used to it. My body
may not need sleep, but my brain has yet to accept that.

But it wasn't the dream that woke me.

Something's happening. A Stirrer...well, stirring.

Their god is coming, and they're growing less cautious,

and more common: rising up from their ancient city Devour in greater numbers like a nest of cockroaches spilling from a drain.

Christ.

Where is it? I scramble to my feet.

Unsteady. Blinking, my eyes adjusting to the dark.

Stirrers, like their city's name suggests, would devour all living things.

They're constantly kicking open the doors between the lands of the living and the dead; reanimating and possessing corpses in the hope that they can return the world to its pristine, lifeless state.

It's the task of Mortmax Industries, its RMs and Pomps (short for Psychopomps) to stop them and to make sure that the path from life to death only heads in one direction. We pomp the dead, send them to the Underworld, and we stall Stirrers. Without us the world would be shoulder to shoulder with the souls of the dead. And Stirrers would have much more than a toehold, they'd have an empire built upon despair and billions of corpses.

But sometimes the serious business of pomping and stalling can get lost in all the maneuvering, posturing and backstabbing (occasionally literally) that modern corporate life entails.

Work in any office and that's true. The stakes are just a lot higher in ours.

My heart's pounding: fragments of the dream are still making their rough way through my veins.

For a moment, I'm certain the monster's in the room with me.

But it's a lot further away.

Lissa's in our bed: dead to the world. I don't know why

I'm surprised at that. After all, me wandering in here drunk an hour ago didn't wake her.

She's exhausted from yesterday's work. That's the downside of knowing how things are run, of having the particular skills she has. I feel guilty about it, but I need her to keep working: finding and training our staff. As well as pomping the souls of the dead, and stopping Stirrers from breaking into the land of the living.

Lissa's heart beats loud and steady. Fifty-five beats per minute.

But it's not the only heartbeat I hear. They're all there, wrapped inside my skull. All of my region's human life. All those slowing, racing, stuttering hearts. They're a cacophony: a constant background noise that, with varying success, I struggle to ignore. Mr. D says that it becomes soothing after a while. I'm a bit dubious of that, though I've discovered that stereo speakers turned up loud can dull it a little; something to do with electrical pulses projecting sonic fields. Thunderstorms have a similar effect, though they're much more difficult to arrange.

Someone dies.

It's a fair way away, but still in Australia. Perth, maybe. Certainly on the southwest coast. Then another: close on it. The recently dead souls pass through my staff and into the Underworld, and I feel a little of that passage. When I was one of the rank and file it used to hurt. Now, unless I'm doing the pomping directly, it's only a tingling ache, an echo of the pain my employees feel. So that I can't forget, I suppose.

At least Mortmax Australia is running smoothly. Though I wish I could take more credit for that. Our numbers are low after the bloodbath that occurred just two months ago. But with my cousin Tim being my Ankou, my second-in-command, master of the day-to-day workings of the business, and Lissa running our HR department and leading the Pomps in the field, our offices have reopened across the country. It seems there are always people willing to work for Death. And we've found many of them. Some from the old Pomp families, distant relatives or Black Sheep who've decided to come back to the fold. But most of them are just people who had heard things, whispers, perhaps, of what we're about.

Who'd blame them? The pay's good after all, even if the hours can be somewhat...variable.

It used to be a family trade. Used to be.

I leave Lissa to her sleep, stumble to the living room, down a hallway covered with photos of my parents: smiling and oblivious to how terribly it was all going to end. My feet pad along a carpet worn thin with the footsteps of my childhood and my parents' lives. This was their home. I grew up here, moved out, then my house exploded along with my life. Now I'm back. They're dead. And I'm Death. It's pretty messed up, really. *I'm* pretty messed up.

My mobile's lying next to a half-empty bottle of Bundaberg Rum.

I grab my phone and flick through to the right app, marked with the Mortmax symbol—a bracing triangle, its point facing down, a not-quite-straight line bisecting its heart. I open up the schedule: the list of all deaths to be in my region. Technically, I don't need to look anymore; all of this comes from within me, from some deep knowledge or force gained in the Negotiation. Regardless, it's reassuring to see it written down, interpreted graphically, not just intuitively.

It was definitely a death in Perth. One of my new guys, Michio Dugan, is on the case. There's another, in Sydney, and two in Melbourne. A stall accompanies one of those. The stir that necessitated that was what woke me.

I close my eyes, and I can almost see the stall occurring. The Stirrer entering the body: the corpse's muscles twitching with the invader's appropriation. Eyes snapping open, my Pomp on the scene—another new one, Meredith—grimacing as she slashes her palm and lays on a bloody hand.

Blood's the only effective way to stall a Stirrer (though I once used vomit), and it hurts, but that's partly the point—we're playing a high stakes game of life and death. No matter how experienced you are, a Stirrer trying to reach into the living world is always confronting. And my crew are all so green.

I feel the stall that stops the Stirrer as a moment of vertigo, a soft breath of chilly air that passes along my spine.

The Melburnian corpse is just a corpse again.

I dial Meredith's number. I have all my staff's numbers, though I rarely call.

"Are you all right?" I ask before she can get a word in.

She's breathing heavily. My breath syncs with hers—it's part of the link I have with my employees. "Yeah. Just surprised me."

I wonder, though, if she isn't more surprised that I rang her. I know I am. I must still be a bit drunk.

"Stalls get easier," I say, though in truth they do and they don't: a Stirrer is always a bugger of a thing to stop. "You didn't cut yourself too badly?"

"No... Maybe... A little."

They all do when they start out. There's a good reason

why we call our palms Cicatrix City. The scars that criss-cross them chart our passage through this job.

"Get to Number Four and have it seen to," I say.

"I'm a long way from the office, maybe—"

"No maybes." I've seen the schedule. Meredith's a ten-minute drive from the Melbourne offices, at most. Every state and territory capital has an office, a Number Four, and medical staff on call. "I pay my doctors far too much not to have them see to you."

"OK," she says. "I will."

"Good work," I say, then worry that I'm sounding patronizing.

"Thanks," I can hear the smile in her voice—maybe I'm not. "Thanks a lot, Mr. de Selby."

"Mr. de Selby? That's what they called my dad, and he didn't like it either. Steven's fine."

"OK, Steven."

"Now get to Number Four." They're all so new. It's exhausting. "If I hear that you decided to tough it out I'll be very pissed off."

I hang up. Slip the phone in my pocket. Then open the bottle of Bundy and sip my rum. I'm all class, Dad would say.

Another five pomps and one stall, across the country, in quick succession. All of them done in time.

Five heartbeats gone from the pool. And another monster stopped.

It's nothing, right? But I hear them all. I ache with their urgency and their passing. There are always new heartbeats as well. One of those falters after a few minutes.

Another successful pomp.

Life's cruel. Life's what you have to fear.

Death. All we do is turn off the lights and shut the door and if we need to bolt it, that's none of your concern.

I briefly consider going into the kitchen, making a cup of coffee. But I don't like spending time in there at all. Mom and Dad loved to cook; somehow the skill passed me by. And that space drives it home. Lissa and I eat a lot of takeaway.

What's more, my parents were killed in the kitchen. That was where most of the blood was. I miss them so much. I miss their guidance, their laughter. I even miss their bickering. Their bodies, Morrigan's Stirrers inhabited those. The last time I saw my parents as flesh and blood they were being used to try and kill me. That was how far Morrigan had fallen.

Yeah, the bastard was a regular puppet master. He still haunts my dreams. He was directly responsible for starting a Schism, and the deaths of almost every Pomp in Australia. Nearly killed me too. I wish I could say I'd survived because of my tenacity and bloody perspicacity. Truth is, I was lucky. Lucky to have Lissa around. Lucky to have brighter, more able friends.

Sure I'd beaten Morrigan at the Negotiation and become RM—on the top of the One Tree, the heart of the Underworld, where his and my future, our very corporeal and non-corporeal existences were decided—but even that had been more through luck than design.

Two months ago I was just a Pomp—one of many—drawing souls into the afterlife.

Now I'm so much more, and I hate it. Morrigan even killed my border collie, Molly Millions. Until very recently, I imagined seeing poor Moll out of the corner of my eye, several times a day. And every time I did, it knocked the wind out of me. Another casualty in the minefield that is my life.

I could try and sleep. But even if I did, I'd wake just as weary.

And the nightmares. They drive into me even when I'm awake. I close my eyelids for more than a second and there they rush, blood-slicked and cackling. I'm clambering and running over screaming faces. Torn hands clawing and scraping, and these aren't the dead, but the dying, and they're dying because of me. More often than I care to admit, I'm enjoying the madness: reveling in it. Sometimes there is the scythe, and I'm swinging that thing, loving its heft and balance, its never-dulling edge, and laughing.

No sleep. No rest. Not when that's waiting. And a man shouldn't wake with an erection after such a dream. How can that arouse me?

I dig out something doleful and rumbling from my CD collection. A little Tindersticks, some Tom Waits. Let the music dim down the roar of a nation's beating hearts. But no matter what I choose tonight, the volume refuses to drown out the sound—and I don't want to wake up Lissa. I sit there restless, Waits crackling along like bones and branches breaking.

I work on finishing the rum.

What the hell, eh? Drinking's easy at any time once you start. Easier if the right music's playing. Tim once told me that music was the perfect gateway drug. He's not wrong. Finally the rum and the music start to work. Not a lot, but enough.

Twice I stumble into the bedroom to check on Lissa, and to marvel that I didn't lose her when I lost nearly everything else, that she's sleeping in my bed. All I want to do is hold her. There was a time that I couldn't, when to touch Lissa would have banished her from me forever. I went to Hell and back to find her, I pulled an Orpheus Maneuver. Not even Orpheus managed that one, but where he failed, I succeeded. If one good thing has come of this, it's Lissa.

She snores a little.

It's endlessly fascinating the things that you find out about your partner when you can't sleep. The sounds, the unaffected routines of their bodies. The way a person's eyes trace their dreams beneath their eyelids. There's more truth in slumber. Perhaps that's why I feel so unanchored. It's a space lost to me.

What a whiny bastard I've become.

Sometimes Lissa wakes screaming from her own nightmares. She never tells me what they are, claims she can't remember them, but I can guess.

There's not much of the Bundy left come first light. And there's been seventy-five more deaths, two of them followed by Stirrers stirring.

Seventy-five more successful pomps and two stalls and the day hasn't even properly started.

I never wanted this. Nor was I supposed to have it.

For Death, it never stops. It's a twenty-four-hour, seven-day-a-week sort of thing. When I was a Pomp, out in the field, I had thought I understood that.

Well, as it turns out—as it turned out for a lot of things—I'm completely clueless.

2

I'm making coffee, trying not to think about my parents (where they were sitting, what they were saying) when Lissa stomps into the kitchen. She's dressed in her usual black: a neat blouse, a shortish skirt, and a pair of purple Doc Marten boots, at once elegant and perfect for kicking in the heads of Stirrers. Around her neck is a silver and leather necklace from which hang rows of black safety pins leading to a Mickey Mouse charm at the bottom. Early *Steamboat Willie* Mickey, grinning like mad. I can't help but roll my eyes at that. Only Mickey's smiling, though.

"Do you know what time it is?" she demands.

I shrug.

"Seven," she says. "Someone switched off my alarm."

I pass her a cup. Surely you can't stay mad at someone who's just made you coffee. I lean in to give her a kiss. Lissa screws up her face. "Christ, Steve. Just how much did you have to drink last night?"

I wince, slipping on a pair of sunglasses. It's bright enough inside the house, and the cruel sun of a Brisbane summer waits outside. "Maybe more than was good for me."

"More than was good for the both of us. Again. Try not to breathe in my direction, will you?"

Seven in the morning. The sun is already high and bright, the air-conditioning throbbing, like my head, though the hangover's fading. One of the upsides of being RM is that I heal faster than I used to. Regional Managers are considerably harder to harm or kill than your average Pomp, though I've seen it happen. My predecessor, Mr. D, died beneath the wheels of an SUV, but by then he had lost the support of his Pomps. Most of them murdered. He looks pretty good considering all that, but you have to go to the Underworld to see him. I try and avoid it if I can.

I grab the car keys from the bowl on a table next to the front door. Lissa snatches them from my hand.

She glares at me. "Don't even think about it. Turn off the aircon and clean your teeth. I'll be waiting in the car."

I'm quick about it. Lissa looks very pissed off. For no good reason, as far as I can tell. Hey, I haven't been drinking *that* much lately. She offers the barest hint of a smile as I get into the car, hardly waits for me to sit down before we're going. The little multi-colored Corolla's engine bubbles along. This car predates air-conditioning. There's a bead of sweat on Lissa's lip that I find endearing. I reach over to touch it with my thumb, and she pushes my hand away. Ten minutes of silence. Out of the 'burbs and onto the M3 Motorway.

"You really should be practicing your shifting." Lissa says at last. The traffic's already creeping, the highway burdened with even more cars than usual; it's a matter of days until Christmas.

"Yeah, but I like coming to work with you." That's only partly true—certainly not today.

Shifting hurts, I really haven't mastered it yet, and I don't like the pain. I'm sure I could handle it if it was the same sort of agony each shift, but it's not. Sometimes it manifests itself as a throbbing headache, others as a kick to the groin, or a hand clenching my guts and squeezing. There's usually a bit of gagging involved.

Lissa grunts. Changes lanes. I reach over to turn on the stereo and she slaps my hand again. This is the real silent treatment.

"What did I do wrong?" I shake my stinging fingers.

"It's what you haven't done," she says, and that's all I can get out of her, as she weaves her way through the traffic.

What the hell *haven't* I done? It's not her birthday. And we've only been together for two months, so there's no real anniversary to speak of. I try to catch her eye. She ignores me, contemplating her next move. Changes lanes again.

We cross the Brisbane River on the Captain Cook Bridge, crawling as the Riverside Expressway ahead becomes anything but express: choked by a half-dozen exits leading into and out of the city. I can feel the water beneath us, and its links to the Underworld and the Hell river Styx—all rivers are the Styx and the Styx is all rivers. When I was a Pomp it was just murky water to me, a winding thread that bound and separated the city, east from west, north from south. Now it hums with residual energies, it's like stepping over a live wire. My whole body tingles, the hangover dies with it—down the river and into the Styx, I guess. A smile stretches across my face. I can't help it.

Lissa doesn't seem to appreciate the grin.

She clenches her jaw, and swerves the Corolla into a gap in the next lane barely large enough. A horn blares behind us, Lissa holds the steering wheel tight, the muscles in her jaw twitching.

I settle in for one of the longest fifteen minutes of my life. The only noise is the traffic and the thunk of the Corolla's tires as it passes over the seams in the unexpressway. I can't find a safe place to look. A glance in Lissa's direction gets me a scowl. Looking out over the river toward Mount Coot-tha earns me an exasperated huff so I settle on staring at the car directly in front of us, my hands folded in my lap. It's as contrite a position as I can manage.

At last Lissa belts into the underground car park of Number Four, off George Street, pedestrians beware. She pulls into a spot next to the lift, turns off the engine and stares at me. "So, even after that drive you've got nothing to say for yourself?"

"I—" I give up, look at her, defeated. I can feel another grin straining at my lips. That's not going to help. Lissa's eyes flare.

"Look," she snarls, "we've all lost people that we care about, but you—"

"I've what? What do you think I've done?"

"Oh—I could just—no, forget about it." Lissa yanks her seatbelt free, storms out of the car and is already in the lift before I've opened my door.

I have to wait for the lift to come back down. The basement car park's full. I can see Tim's car a few spots down. I'm last to work, yet again.

I could shift up to my office from here. But I don't reckon it's worth the pain.

The lift takes me straight up to the sixth floor. Everyone's a picture of industry when the doors open, and no one gives me a second glance. Which worries me. Where are the usual hellos? The people wanting to talk to me? Why hasn't Lundwall from the front desk hurried over to me with a list of phone calls that I'm not going to bother returning? I look around for Lissa. Nowhere. No one meets my gaze.

"OK," I mumble. If that's how everyone is going to play it…I mean, I haven't come to work drunk in over a week.

I amble over toward the coffee machine in the kitchen. The tiny room empties out the moment I walk in. I don't hurry making my coffee, then stroll into my office, taking long, loud sips as I go.

"Nice to see you've made it," Tim says. Tim's trying so hard to hold it all together. I used to be able to tell, with a glance, what he was thinking. Now, sometimes I can't even meet his eyes. He's developed movements, tics and gestures, which are wholly unfamiliar to me. He's sitting on my desk—his bum next to the big black bakelite phone—carefully avoiding the throne of Death. I understand why. It exerts a pull. I'm sure he feels it, too. How it does it is beyond me, it shouldn't. It's not particularly imposing, merely an old black wooden chair. There are thirteen of these in the world, made for each member of the Orcus. Just a chair and yet so much more. I cannot stand in here without feeling the scratching presence of it. I know I could lose myself in it, that I'm perhaps losing myself already. Sometimes I wonder if that wouldn't be so bad. Then I wonder if that's what the throne wants me to wonder. If a chair can really *want* anything.

In one hand, Tim's clutching the briefing notes that I should have read about three weeks ago.

"Yeah, isn't your office across the way?" I ask.

Tim folds his arms, says nothing.

"So who's stealing paperclips this week?" I force a grin. Honestly, that *had* been a major issue last month. Paperclips and three reams of A4.

The door bangs shut behind me. I jerk my head around, and Lissa's standing there, her arms folded, too. Ambushed!

"What the hell is this? Look, those Post-it notes on my desk are all accounted for."

She's not smiling. Neither is Tim. Christ, this is some sort of intervention.

"Do you know what today is?" she asks.

"The 20th of December." Sure, I have to look at my desk calendar for that.

Tim snorts. Pulls the bookmark out of the briefing notes. A bookmark whose movements have been somewhat fabricated—damn, I thought he'd swallowed that one. He slaps the notes. "If you had actually read these, you'd have an idea, you'd probably even be prepared."

"Look, I've got work to do. The Death Moot's on the 28th and I—"

"Absolutely. What do you need to do?"

I shrug.

In a little over a week the Orcus, the thirteen Regional Managers that make up Mortmax Industries, will be meeting in Brisbane for the biannual Death Moot. With just two months in the job, I'm expected to organize what my predecessor Mr. D once described as a meeting of the most bloodthirsty, devious and backstabbing bunch of bastards on the planet.

"You've got no fucking idea, have you?" Tim says.

Lissa touches my arm. "Steven, we're worried about you."

Tim doesn't move. His eyes are hard. I can't remember seeing him so pissed off. "Mate, I like to have a drink as much as anyone, but I have responsibilities. And you do, too. To this company, to your staff and your shareholders, and to your region. You're an RM. You're one of the Orcus!"

"I know, I know," I say. How the hell did I ever become one of the Orcus? Me being RM was just a massive mistake, a joke played out by the universe. I'd fought for this role, only because I'd had no choice. Death for me, and death for my few remaining friends and family—or fight and live. I'm about to mention my call to Meredith when Tim laughs humorlessly. My cheeks burn.

"Then start acting like it," he says.

I walk past him, drop into my throne. For a moment, there is no argument. Lissa and Tim fade away. It's just the throne and me. The throne deepens and broadens my senses, brings the living/dying world even closer to the fore. In this chair I touch not only the land of the living but the land of the dead as well. Traffic is moving nicely in both zones, which is really rather remarkable. The throne is opiate, CNN and 3D extravaganza rolled into one. I have to concentrate to manage that sensory overload. Part of me doesn't want to; the effort of it burns a little behind my eyes like the seed of a migraine. How the hell am I expected to handle all this? And it's not getting any easier.

I open my eyes. Oh, yes, the "interventionists" haven't left. How much have they seen?

"You don't have a clue how hard I work," I say, but they do, and they're right.

"That's just it," Lissa says. "You're working so hard at avoiding everything that you're going to avoid everything out of your life. You've come unstuck, you're drifting, and you haven't even noticed it."

Tim's nodding. I glare at him.

"Steve, you're even more disengaged than you were when Robyn left."

Now, that's just too low. Robyn's my ex. She couldn't handle me being a Pomp and it took me years to get over that. It took Lissa, and the loss of nearly everything that I cared about. Surely I'm not… "That's bullshit!"

"What's bullshit is the amount of work Lissa and I have had to do to cover for you. When was the last time you spoke to another RM?"

I'd initially tried really hard to keep in touch with them. To start a discussion about a global response to the Stirrer god. Nothing, silence. The global response had been for every RM to ignore my emails and my calls. If they weren't going to speak to me, I wasn't going to speak to them. "They're all pricks and backstabbers," I say.

Tim nods. "Exactly, and you've left us to deal with them. The whole Orcus, and no RM to bat for us. Thanks a lot, mate."

"Well, you're my Ankou."

Tim nods. "And I'll watch your back. But I'm not here to wipe your arse. If this keeps going on… we're both out of here."

Lissa's face is as resolute as I have ever seen it. "Do you know how hard I've been working? Hunting down new staff in Melbourne, Perth, Mount Isa, Coober Pedy?

I've run around this country, God knows how many times, trying to find you people who at the very least have a chance of not dying on the job. And you're hardly interested. Have you spoken to any of them after their interview? Have you made yourself available to any of them?"

I open my mouth to speak: what about Meredith? But once, just once, isn't enough of a defense. They're right. I know they're right, but if they could sit in this throne... dream my dreams... They're right. "So what do you want me to do?"

"Today?" Tim asks. "Or from now on?"

"Both."

Tim beams at me. "That's what I want to hear. A bit more enthusiasm would be nice, though."

I lean back in my chair. "All right. All right. Where do I start?"

Lissa unfolds her arms, walks to the desk and takes up another chair. "The Death Moot. Let's start with that. The business we can get to, but the Moot is a priority. You've got to find the Point of Convergence."

"Can't we just book a hotel?"

"Ha! This is Mortmax Industries," Lissa says. "Things don't work that way. It's revealed through some sort of ceremony, although I'm not sure what it entails. And Tim can hardly go and ask anyone else. How do you think the other RMs would take that?"

"Bad. It would be bad," I say.

She pats the black phone on my desk. "You're going to have to speak with Mr. D. And after that you're going to have to start paying attention to the business of being RM."

I pick up the heavy handset. "Do I have to call him now?"

Lissa starts to fold her arms again. Tim's face is settling into a scowl. "It has to be done. And today," Lissa says. "In some ways we've been as bad as you. We should have done this sooner. Today's the last day you can perform the ceremony."

More than a twinge of guilt hits me at that. They've been putting this off and putting this off, hoping I'd come good on my own. I can't help feeling I've let them down. The business I don't care about, but Lissa and Tim are the center of my world.

Yet there's part of me wondering how they could have let this get so far. Ah, more guilt! I put the phone to my ear.

"I was wondering when you would call," Mr. D says, without the slightest pause. There's a large quantity of affront in his voice. Maybe the bastard has some feelings after all. I certainly didn't witness them when he was alive.

"Are you in on this, too?" I ask.

"Mr. de Selby, I have no idea what you mean."

"I need to talk to you."

"Yes, you should have been talking to me for some time, but you haven't. Oh well, it's never too late to start." He chuckles. "Until it's too late. And you are running out of time."

"I'll be there soon."

"Don't keep me waiting."

I put the handset back in the cradle. "There," I say.

Both Tim and Lissa stare at me.

"Don't you two have work to attend to?"

Tim smiles thinly. "Of course we do." He's out of my office without a backward glance.

Lissa stays a moment, touches my arm. "It had to be done," she says. "I'm sorry."

"Don't be. You're both right." I grab her wrist as she pulls away, and squeeze it gently. Flesh and bone. I doubt I'll ever get used to being able to touch her. "I'm just happy that you care enough to do this." I'm not sure that I sound all that convincing. I've got to see Mr. D. I've suddenly got work to do.

Lissa bends down and kisses my cheek. "Dying isn't the only way a girl can lose someone," she says.

I want to ask her if that's a threat, or a fear, or a promise. Talk of Robyn has got my head in something of a spin. I could do with a drink.

Instead, I get to my feet, prepare myself for my shift into the Underworld and say, "Don't worry, you haven't lost me yet."

I let go of her wrist and, looking into her eyes, I disappear—or she and the office do. I'm not sure which it is. One reality is exchanged with another, the air folds around me, changes density, and taste. Light, sound, all of it is instantly different. I'm bathed in the red glow of the Underworld.

The shift is hard. This one makes me sick, literally. Mr. D pats my back until the vomiting stops. "You do understand that it gets easier the more you practice?"

I wipe my mouth with the back of my hand. "Yeah, but it's the practice that's so hard." He passes me a glass of water, obtained from a small tank by his chair. I gulp it down, and take in my surroundings. This is Hell of course, but what a view. I'm standing on one of the uppermost branches of the One Tree. The Underworld equivalent of the city of Brisbane is beneath us, suburbia stretching out to the dark waters of the Tethys, the CBD's knuckles of skyscrapers constrained as Brisbane is bound up in a ribbon of river. The air is loud with the creaking of the One Tree. It permeates everything in the Underworld. The One Tree is the place where souls go to end their existence. It draws them here from across the Underworld and absorbs them, down into its roots and into the great secrets of the Deepest Dark. It's a Moreton Bay fig tree, bigger than any city, with root buttresses the size of suburbs. It's also where my old boss hangs out. Dead but not dead, he waits here to act as my mentor in all things RM.

There's a cherub by the name of Wal fluttering about my head. He looks a little plumper than I remember him, but I wouldn't say that to Wal. He's rather sensitive, comes from spending most of his existence as a tattoo on my arm. In fact, it looks like he's already pissed off. His Modigliani eyes are narrower than usual. It's been a good couple of weeks since I was in the Underworld, and it's only here, or close to it, that he can manifest. He gets rather shirty if he can't spread his wings. I do my best to ignore him. I only have enough strength for one intervention today.

"You know why I'm here?" I ask Mr. D.

"It's the 20th of December. Must be getting hot up there. I was always fond of Christmas in Brisbane. Are the cicadas singing? Have they put up the Christmas tree in King George Square?"

"Yes, but—"

"It can be very lonely in Hell," Mr. D says, and his face, which notoriously shifts through a dozen expressions in a second, grows even more furious in its changes. "Particularly when you are in someone's employ. Specifically to advise that someone. To steer them through the roughest channels of their job away from the snares and the rocks of Orcusdom. To save them making the same mistakes you did. And yet, they never visit you. Never call. Never ask for advice." He nods to his armchair, the single piece of furniture on the branch, and the stack of old science-fiction novels beside it. "I'm running out of things to read, and without you I can't even go fishing. When did you last drop a mercy pile of books down here? When did you last reply to one of my invitations on Facebook, or comment on an update? You're not even following me on Twitter."

"He really is rubbish, isn't he?" Wal says to Mr. D. "I can't fly, can't do a thing when I'm stuck on that arm. And would it hurt to use a little deodorant, mate?" He lands heavily on my shoulder. Talk about the weight of opinion. And I'm not too happy about being that close to all that pudgy nakedness.

I raise my hands in supplication and defeat. This all would have been a lot easier if I'd had something to drink beforehand. "You're right. Both of you are right. I'm sorry. I'll do better. I have to."

"I forgive you," Mr. D says, grinning a dozen various but magnanimous grins. "But you owe me."

I clench my jaw, try not to make it obvious. "Yeah, I owe you. But, finally, I'm here to make you work."

Mr. D dips his head knowingly. "Yes. You need to find the Point of Convergence. Without it, you can no more have a Death Moot than you could hold the Olympics *sans* stadium. And without the Point of Convergence you cannot engage the Caterers."

"I thought we could just hire someone from a restaurant."

Mr. D chortles, exchanges an amused glance with Wal. "And they would be able to enter the nexus between the living and the Underworld, how?"

Wal's laughing too, holding his belly. "Oh, he's beyond bloody naive!"

"Yeah, beyond naive," I say, feeling sick. Which is either the residue of the shift, my embarrassment at not knowing this and the fear of all the other things I don't understand, or just possibly the throbbing filament of rage that is firing up in my brain at all this mockery. "And I will continue to be beyond naive if you do not educate me."

"Right," Mr. D says, "the Point of Convergence is revealed through a ceremony. This is what you need to do…"

By the end of his instructions, I'm less than pleased.

He gives me a hearty pat on the back. "You'll be fine, son. Be careful with those Caterers, though. You don't want to piss them off. Oh, and the canapés, you want them to do the canapés—they have this thing they do with an oyster…"

Son? Mr. D never calls me son.

Maybe boy, or Steven, or de Selby. Just what is he up to? This is why I've barely used him as a mentor. Too many riddles, too much in the way of diversion—and I don't think he even realizes he's doing it.

He hands me a piece of paper and a pen. "Oh, and I need you to sign this."

"What is it?"

"A release. A legal and magical document. It allows me at least a modicum of movement. Sometimes I would like to be able to visit my friends. Aunt Neti is down there, as are the markets. How am I supposed to sample the Underworld if I am trapped here on the branches of the Tree?"

Seems fair enough. Maybe a little *too* fair.

I glance at him suspiciously and he smiles, almost looks innocent, but for the tumble of faces that follow. Mr. D can never settle on just one.

Still, out of guilt at my neglect of him, I sign it.

"Don't be a stranger," he says, and looks at his watch. "You better get going. I can't believe you've left it so late."

Neither can I. The one thing I don't want to mess up is a Death Moot. Ruin this, and I'm on my own. And that Stirrer god is approaching. The End of Days is approaching, and it seems I've gotta jump through a whole lot of bloody hoops to stop it.

"Oh, and next time? Some books, please," Mr. D says. "Now shoo!"

Another shift.

Back in my office.

I take a deep breath. Maybe it is getting easier. Then I throw up in my wastepaper bin, noisily and messily. *Bloody shifting.* I rinse my mouth out with cold coffee, put the bin as far away from the desk as possible, to be dealt with later, and walk out into the open workspace of Number Four. People are busy coordinating pomps, getting the right people to the right place. The floor beneath us would be just as hectic, though they deal with the business end of Mortmax: the stuff that finances all of this. Our shares are doing quite well at the moment, so Tim tells me.

I knock on Tim's door.

"Enter," he says somewhat officiously.

I poke my head in. Tim's having a smoke. He juts his jaw out, daring me to comment. I don't take the bait.

"Lissa out on a job?" I ask.

"Yeah. There's a stir expected at the Wesley Hospital." I remember the last time I was there. Seven Stirrers and me, one of the few Pomps left alive in Brisbane. Still gives me the shivers.

"I miss her when she's not around."

Tim snorts at that. "Ah, young love. Give it time. The missing goes, along with all the sex. Believe me." Yeah, right, I know how much he misses Sally. Young love, indeed.

"OK, I just wanted to tell you that if anything goes wrong with this whole Convergence Ceremony thing it's your fault."

Tim stabs the cigarette butt into his ashtray. "That bad is it?"

"I have to see Aunt Neti."

Tim smiles wanly. Aunt Neti freaks him out. Maybe it's the eight arms, or the murderous glint in her eyes. "You going now? Do you want someone to come with?" It's the least earnest sounding offer I've ever heard. But no surprise there. Our first meeting had been rather memorable, Aunt Neti's predatory eyes focused on the both of us as she recounted tales of particularly bloodthirsty Schisms. She'd been very annoyed when Tim didn't finish his scones. His joke about avoiding carbs had fallen curiously flat, and the air in Neti's parlor had chilled considerably. I thought she was going to tear his head off.

"Yeah, I'm going now. Better to get it over and done with, obviously. And thanks, but I need to do this one alone. I want to." At least I can manage to sound like I mean it.

"OK." Tim can't hide the relief in his voice. "On the plus side you've only got a short walk."

A short walk to Hell; well, a particular part of it. "I'll talk to you when I get back. I'm going to need your help with the ceremony," I say. "I'm sorry. I didn't realize how badly I'd let work slip."

That's not true. I knew, but I just couldn't find a way out. Can't say that I have yet. But at least I'm trying.

"We were never going to let you fall too far," Tim says. "We love you too much. Now be safe."

"I will." I shut the door behind me. If I really wanted to be safe there's no way I'd do what I'm about to do.

There's a doorway—and though its door is very heavy, it's never closed—that leads to a hallway, which in turn leads to Aunt Neti's parlor.

Every region's headquarters has one. As I walk toward the portal, conversation in the workspace dies down. I straighten my back, check my hair in a mirror near the door. I sigh. It'll have to do. Still no one has said a word. I turn around: a dozen pairs of eyes flick this way and that.

"Don't you all have work to do?"

A phone rings. Someone starts typing away furiously. A stapler snap, snap, snaps.

I enter the hallway, suddenly I need to pee. But I can't, I have to stay on the path.

No turning back now.

3

The hallway creaks and groans, echoing the One Tree. Two, three steps in and the sounds of phones ringing, the beating of hearts, the snap of staplers grow muted. Then there's just silence, but for that creaking and groaning. The brown carpet ripples in sympathy with a floor that buckles with the stress of keeping a link between dimensions. It's hard to stay on your feet here, but I do my best, and I don't need to grab a wall to steady myself.

My right biceps starts burning. I take a few more steps and Wal pushes his way out from under my shirt sleeve. He flaps his wings and grins at me.

"Hello again," he says, then his eyes widen. His little head swings from left to right. "Bugger, wasn't expecting this." His voice is low and quiet.

Neither was I. The last time I walked down this hallway, about a month ago, Wal didn't appear. Something's happening that shouldn't. Just another thing to disturb me. At least I have company. Wal settles down on my shoulder and considers the walls and the rippling floor, his face pinched with distaste.

The closer I get to Neti's door, the heavier Wal gets. There's a subtle hint in the air of scones freshly baked; of butter, jam and cream. Aunt Neti's expecting company.

I reach her front door and lift my hand toward the brass knocker which is shaped like a particularly menacing spider.

The door swings open.

"Good morning, dear," Aunt Neti says. Her eyes dart toward Wal, and the little guy almost topples from my shoulder. "Oh, and you've brought a friend with you, and not your rude Ankou, this time. How sweet."

Seeing Neti is like looking at an iceberg and knowing there are immeasurable depths beneath it. More than nine-tenths, I'm betting. And she's terrifying enough as it is. Aunt Neti is all long limbs and bunches of eyes—eight of each. A purple shawl is wrapped around her shoulders. She straightens it a little, with a spare hand or two, and bends down to peck me on the cheek. Her lips are cold and hard, and the peck so swift and forceful that I'm sure I'll have bruises tomorrow.

Aunt Neti bustles me inside, all those hands patting and pushing and pulling at once, so I'm not quite sure what she's touching, just that I'm being moved from doorway to parlor and that my pockets hold no secrets from her. Her nails are black and sharpened to points, and they click click click with her pinching and prodding. It's all done before I can even put up a struggle. I've gotta say it's not that much of a stretch to imagine that's how a fly would feel as it's spun and bound in spider's silk.

She shuts the door behind her. Wal's keeping away

from those hands, though at least a couple of her eyes follow him. And I'm making the decision that you always have to make when you're talking to her: which eyes do you look at? I choose a bunch in the middle of her face. The ones with the most smile lines. They're crinkling now.

"Sit down, sit down." Neti gestures toward one of a pair of overstuffed chairs set across from each other, a low table between them.

As we sit in her parlor, I keep to the edge of my seat—as though that would save me. The room is tiny and cozy, the walls papered with an old damask design. The paper's peeling in one corner and a tiny spider has webbed the gap between wall and curling edge. I can't shake the feeling that it's staring at me. And those eyes are no less hungry than Aunt Neti's.

There are two plates on the table. On both there are crumbs, and butter knives, covered with jam as red as arterial blood. And my seat is warm. Someone was here, only moments ago. I look around, wondering if they've really gone. But there's no one. I look down at the plates. There's no hint there of whoever I've displaced, just crumbs and jam.

Aunt Neti picks the plates up and slides away to her kitchen with them, saying, "Plenty of visitors today, my dear. But none as special as you."

Wal raises an eyebrow at me. Neti is one of the two caretakers of the interface between the living and the Underworld. The other one is Charon. Both have their unique ways of running things. Charon with his boats; Neti with her residence, which, like a web, is connected to everything. She lives in these few rooms: a parlor that intersects every office of Mortmax in the living world. Like Charon, Aunt Neti's an RE, a Recognized Entity.

And despite appearances, she's not that fond of me at all. Mr. D tried to explain why a few weeks ago. Something about the Orpheus Maneuver that I pulled to get Lissa back from the Underworld, and how I should have gone through her, not Charon. At the time I thought I'd had no choice. Seems I did, and it's made me an enemy—no matter how unknowingly on my part.

Aunt Neti comes back into the parlor, walks past me to a tall cabinet. It's covered in scrollwork and seems to be carved out of the same black wood as my throne. Several of her hands apply pressure to different bits of the cabinet, a palm in one corner, a finger tapping on a carving, another hand applying pressure at its back.

A door slides to one side. Aunt Neti reaches in and pulls out two stone knives that I'm all too familiar with. She grins at me, revealing a mouth full of crooked black teeth, and drops the knives on the table before me.

"You'll be needing these," Aunt Neti says.

I pick them up. They're perfectly weighted and heavy. They mumble and hum.

I used these on the top of the One Tree in a place the Orcus call the Negotiation, to "negotiate" my way into the position of RM. It had been a bloody reckoning between me and Morrigan—once a family friend, a man as dear to me as any uncle. These knives had slashed his throat and blinded his left eye. They'd cut his soul away from existence itself.

I need these knives for the Convergence Ceremony but seeing them, holding the damn things in my hands, is terrifying.

"Now," Aunt Neti says, laying down two clean plates, "be careful for goodness sake, or you'll cut yourself. That's for later."

I hold them away from me gingerly, my hands tight around the stony handles. Until this morning, I hadn't expected to see them again for a very long time, had hoped that it would be even longer than that. They whisper to me.

Hello.

Hello.

"Put them down," Neti says, and slaps my wrists. "Put them down."

I drop them back onto the table, cracking one of her plates with a knife hilt. My breath catches. The stony knives grumble.

"That'll cost you." Neti's laugh is shrill and horrible. "Oh, it starts with plates, and before you know it, you're putting a vast crack in the world."

"Sorry," I say.

"Never you mind, Mr. de Selby. Never you mind. Was just having a joke at your expense. I've a room," she jabs a thumb at a door to the left of us, one of many, "a big room crammed floor to ceiling with others, just like them. I make them from the bones of the dead—it's a hobby. You'd be smashing plates from dawn till dusk for a century or more before you'd put a dint in the size of my collection. And how many have I used in all these ages? Just a dozen or so." She smacks her lips. "Now I trust you will indulge me, and have a scone."

I do, and it's delicious. As long as you don't think too much about where it's come from. There's something too sanguine about that jam. But it's sweet, and it's no real trouble to have another one.

Neti looks at the knives. "You know what you have to do with those?"

I nod. "Yes, I have been given instructions."

Neti sniffs at that, and I wonder if I haven't fucked up again and offended her. "You'll have them back before three, thank you."

"You could always come with me." It doesn't hurt to offer an olive branch.

Neti grins wryly. "Oh, to walk the streets of Brisbane again. To terrorize and shop. Hm, what sort of parasol is in fashion these days?"

I start to frame an answer and she laughs. "Mr. de Selby, these rooms and my gardens are enough. But I appreciate the offer. Besides, what you need to do is a private thing, and best shared only with your Ankou. That is, if you trust him."

"Of course. Absolutely."

Neti swings a set of eyes toward the grandfather clock that takes up a large chunk of wall space between two doors. "You're best away. You don't have much time."

I wipe my lips with a linen napkin on which little black spiders have been stitched, far too realistically. I stroke one for a moment, and I swear its legs flutter. I drop it, pick up the knives and leave Neti to her parlor. I feel every single one of her eyes watching me as I walk back down the hallway.

"She's not kidding," Wal says, his eyes fixed on the Knives of Negotiation. "You be damn careful with those."

"I will," I say, but he's already a tattoo on my biceps again. And it's just me and the knives.

I walk through the offices, the naked blades in either hand. I've got nowhere to put them and they're certainly not the sort of thing you slip in your pockets. My staff keep their distance. Maybe it's the slightly manic expression on my face. No, it's definitely the knives. It gives the concept of staff cutbacks a certain, well, edge. I feel every eye on me and I try not to look menacing, but with the Knives of Negotiation it's impossible not to. The knives, too, seem curious. They're mumbling and somehow staring at everyone and everything. I can feel that rapt attention running through my wrists. They want to jerk this way and that. I don't let them. Though part of me wants to. Part of me knows how easy it would be to re-create my dreams of blood and cuts.

Once ensconced in my office, I take a deep breath and call Tim.

Tim regards the knife in his hand with a look that tells me he's wishing he was back working in the public service. "So, how do we do this?"

We're standing in the middle of my office. My back's to my throne, but I can feel it there, the bloody thing a constant presence.

"I know you haven't done a lot of pomping, but the cut has to be shallow and long. Just like you would if you were stalling a Stirrer."

Tim hasn't stalled anything since we faced off against Morrigan's Stirrer allies in these very offices a couple of months ago. I've kept him away from all of that. He's much better at administration, at getting people to do what needs to be done. Lissa's the opposite. She leads by example; people follow her because she gets down and does it, too. I've fallen down on the leadership front, but that's going to change now.

Tim's knife hand shakes.

"I wouldn't ask you to do this," I say, "if I didn't need you, and believe me there are much more confronting ceremonies than this one in a Pomp's repertoire." I remember the binding ceremony I'd once performed with Lissa's ghost. That had involved arcane symbols and a few good dollops of semen. "From what Mr. D says, the knives will guide us."

For a moment I feel sorry that I've pulled Tim into all this. But then he grins at me, and it's just like old times.

"Fuck it, let's do this now."

I find myself grinning back. "Pub afterward?"

"Absolutely."

As one we slice our hands. My cut burns, a flaring burst that wrenches its way up my arm. These are the Knives of Negotiation, after all, they are edged in a multitude of ways and all of them are cutting. The blade bites deeper than I intended. Blood flows thick and fast. Tim reaches out his bloody hand, and I grip it.

And then.

Tim's eyes widen, in sync with mine, and we realize what we are about to do. Both of us struggle, but the ceremony is driving our limbs now. There are no brakes that we can apply to this.

We slam the knives point first into each other's chest.

4

I die for a heartbeat then.

So does Tim. I can feel it.

I cry out, but my lips don't move. The air tightens around us. The One Tree's creaking becomes a roaring. Great dark shapes loom and cackle. Then, out of nowhere, I see the Kurilpa Bridge. Its tangle of masts and wires. Mount Coot-tha rising in the northwest. Lightning cracks, a luminous finger trailing down.

And then the knives are back in our hands, bloodless. The wounds gone.

Sometimes I would like a job that involved less stabbing.

Tim coughs, his fingers scramble desperately over his chest. "What the fuck was that?" He waves the stone knife in my face. "Christ. Christ! *Christ!*" I snap my head backward to avoid losing my nose.

Then he seems to realize what he is doing, breathes deeply, slowly, in and out, and puts the knife down carefully on my desk, as though it's a bomb.

And it is, I suppose. I follow suit, and the knives mumble at the both of us. They sound happy.

"Shit, I don't know," I say. "It wasn't what I was expecting."

"Wasn't what you were expecting? What the hell were you expecting?" Tim's looking down at the front of his shirt.

There's no blood. I haven't bothered checking, I'm an old hand at these sorts of things now.

"No one told me that would happen, believe me. Not Mr. D or Neti."

"I can see why." Tim drops into one of the chairs at my desk. He grins a little though, surprising me. "It was a bit of a rush."

"So Kurilpa," I say.

"Yeah, the new pedestrian bridge."

Kurilpa Bridge sits on the curving Brisbane River just on the edge of the CBD. It's a wide footbridge; steel masts rise from its edges like a scattering of knitting needles, and between them are strung thick cables. You either love it or hate it.

Can't say that I love it.

"How do you hold a Death Moot on a bridge?" I move to sit in my throne, shaking my head. The moment my arse touches the chair the black phone on my desk rings. I jump then look from the phone to Tim.

"Well, I'm not answering it," he says.

I snatch it up.

This is no regular phone call. Down the line a bell is tolling, distant and deep. I keep waiting for some slamming guitar riff to start up.

Instead a thin voice whispers, "You have engaged us,

across the peaks and troughs of time. And we will serve you."

There's a long pause.

"Thank you," I say at last.

"We are coming," the voice says. "The bridge has been marked with your blood. The bridge has been marked and we are coming. Oh, and there will be a set menu. And canapés."

The line goes dead.

"They're coming," I say, looking at the handset.

"Who?" Tim looks at me blankly.

"The Caterers."

"Excellent," Tim says, taking this whole being-stabbed-in-the-chest thing very well.

"Oh, and there will be canapés."

"As long as there aren't any of those little sandwiches, then I'm happy."

"But when do these guys arrive? I forgot to ask."

"That I know," Tim says. "Four days from now. We'll take them out to the bridge then." He gets to his feet. "Well, that's that. The Death Moot has begun. Pub?"

I shake my head. "You and Lissa are right," I say. "I need to start actually being here. I need to make sure that I'm ready." I pick up the knives. "And I need to get these back to Aunt Neti. They're much too dangerous to leave lying around."

Tim grins at me. "Nice to have you back."

There's an angry bruise on the horizon when I get home. It's six o'clock and a storm is coming. I feel virtuous, and pleased that, after two visits in one day, I won't have to speak to Aunt Neti for some time. The Knives of

Negotiation are safe. The Caterers are on their way, and the Death Moot has a venue. Not bad for a day's work. I've texted Lissa, told her I'll be waiting at home.

I'm determined to show her I can do this. That I'm not dropping out, and that she isn't losing me.

She's right, I do need to practice my shifting, and I want to read as much of Tim's briefing notes as I can before she gets home. Here, where I'm relatively free from distractions. I've been drifting. Dad once said that pomping is for Pomps and that business is for dickheads. Of course, it didn't stop him being very good at both. Pomping's all I've ever known, but managing a business is uncomfortably new to me. I like people, but I'm not sure I can tell them what to do. After all, I spent a lot of my time as a Pomp arguing with management. The shit I gave my immediate superior Derek…I almost miss the guy.

Tim's last words to me this afternoon, after a very quick beer, were: "Meeting tomorrow morning at 8:15. Cerbo. Do not be late. And you would be better off for reading my notes." Faber Cerbo is Suzanne Whitman's Ankou. I've not had much to do with him. I wonder what he wants?

Tim's notes are extensive, and amusing. He knows his audience, I guess. And I can understand why he might be hurt that I haven't read them yet. He's obviously put a lot of work into making it de Selby digestible.

By the time Lissa pulls into the driveway, I'm a third of the way through the notes and aware of various allegiances within the Orcus or, as Tim has subtitled his report, Who Hates Who. The most prominent allies on the list surprise me: Neill Debbier, South Africa's RM, and Suzanne Whitman, the RM of North America. Between them they seem to wield the most influence.

It's fascinating. As is the fact that Cerbo is Mortmax's resident expert on the Stirrer god. I should have been pushing for a meeting earlier. Tim's notes suggest that now, with the Death Moot so close, the lobbying is going to start in earnest. Hence my meeting with Cerbo, I assume.

I watch Lissa get out of the Corolla. Her face is pinched with the weight of a day's work. She pomped five souls today. I felt them all, as I did the stall she performed at the Wesley Hospital.

There's a bandage wrapped around her hand, and she's bending over to pick up some groceries. I leap down from the front steps and run to carry them for her.

"You don't have to," she says.

"Bullshit." I take the bags from her. "Let me look at that hand."

"It's nothing. Dr. Brooker's seen to it. Says to say hi."

Dr. Brooker's the Brisbane office's medico. He's tended to that office since before I was born.

I take her bandaged hand and kiss it, gently. Wrap my arms around her, and hold her tight. Just liking the way she feels. The corporeality of her.

The storm's coming, dark clouds boiling, dogs howling and barking in response to bursts of thunder. The rain sighing, exhaled from above and beating down on a thousand suburban roofs not too far away. The air's electric and, with it, my region's heartbeats are shed from me like a cloak. Steam rises from the road.

Bring on the lightning. Bring on this moment of peace.

"Let's get inside," Lissa says.

And we do. Just before it starts pissing down.

I lug the groceries to the kitchen and I'm a few minutes putting stuff away. Looks like there's cooking going on tonight. For the first time that feels all right. I grab a Coke from the fridge for Lissa and a beer for myself, and we sit out on the balcony. It's too hot inside.

Lissa holds my hand and we sit there, drinking our drinks, sweat cold against our skin, and watch the rain fall.

Storms build slowly but pass too quickly, and soon the pulse of the world is back.

"What are you cooking for dinner?" I ask.

Lissa arches an eyebrow.

"What are *we* cooking for dinner?" I offer.

"You'll find out."

"I'm sorry I've been such an idiot lately."

"I think the correct word is dick," Lissa says, and kisses me hard. Apology accepted.

After dinner I walk into the bathroom and my good mood evaporates at once. The walls are covered with blood. It's a typical portent for a Pomp but this is the worst one I've seen in a while. A stir is coming, and a big one.

We need unity in the face of the Stirrer god, and that's not going to happen unless my Death Moot goes off without a hitch. With the exception of the odd alliance, regions keep to themselves outside of these biannual meetings, partly because the work load for each Death is phenomenal and mainly because most of the RMs don't trust, and/or actively hate, each other. I need the Death Moot to succeed.

I try to be quiet about it, cleaning furiously at the

walls—all tiled because my parents were Pomps, too, and no one wants to make work for themselves—but Lissa catches me in there.

"Oh, no," she says.

"Yeah."

She looks so tired. I don't let her help, she's worked hard enough today, and she needs her sleep.

Bad shit's on its way. That's what this wall is telling me. The blood dissolves easily enough with soap and water and scrubbing. It's not the real stuff, but an ectoplasmic equivalent. Regardless, it takes me a good half-hour to clean it all away, and clean myself up.

When I finally get to bed, Lissa's asleep.

I lie next to her for a while, but don't close my eyes. I wish I could follow her, but I can't. I've no desire for nightmares tonight. After all, I've already faced some of them today, and been reminded of others.

People die as I lie there. Heartbeats stutter and fail.

Then my eyes shut. *Wham.* I'm back in that madness of knives and laughter. And then the scythe. My hands clench around its snath, the blade humming at the other end. Two hundred people stand before me, their eyes wide, their mouths small Os of terror. And I start swinging.

I jolt awake. Only a moment has passed.

I pull myself from the bed, pick up Tim's notes and finish them off.

I also started on another bottle of Bundy.

5

I open one eye a crack. There's half a bottle of rum settling uneasily in my stomach. I'd fallen asleep again. Well, I don't know if you could call it sleep, but I was definitely unconscious.

My mobile phone's ringing.

The clock radio gives out a hard red light: 2:30 in the am. Bloody hell. Lissa nudges me with an elbow, soft, then not so. When did I come back to bed?

"Going to answer that?" Her voice is a late-night mumble, with just a hint of edge to it.

It's the first night in two months that I've actually fallen asleep—totally by accident, Lissa's head on my chest—and someone calls.

At least they dragged me from that cackling nightmare. The swinging scythe, though in this version it was in time to Queen's "We Will Rock You." Maybe I was awake before the phone started ringing, just trying to pretend I was asleep. Either way, I'm awake now.

If this is Tim calling, drunk and doleful, from the

Regatta in Toowong, there are going to be serious words. Particularly after his and Lissa's intervention.

Another elbow nudge. She's going to crack a rib at this rate. "Well?" Lissa says.

The sheets tangle as I try and get up. Lissa grabs a handful, tugs, and I'm free enough of the sheetly bonds to move. I scramble for the phone on the bedside table. It's the brightest (loudest) light source in the room, so it's easy to find. Still, 2:30! And it keeps on ringing. Who'd have thought a Queen medley ring tone could get annoying?

Not Tim. Caller ID sets me straight on that.

Suzanne Whitman.

Mortmax Industries' North American Regional Manager. What the hell is the U.S. Death doing calling me now?

"Hello," I croak.

"I'm sorry, did I wake you?" She sounds surprised. Sleep is hardly de rigueur in the RM crowd.

I pause, long enough to get my game voice on—sort of. "Not at all. Just came back from a run."

"At 2:30 in the morning?"

"My personal trainer's a bloody bastard. What can I do for you?"

Lissa sits up next to me and mouths, "Who is it?" I shake my head at her. She frowns. If there's one thing that Lissa hates, it's secrets. She'll have to wait.

"It's not what you can do for me, Mr. de Selby, but what I can do for you—and it's quite a lot," Suzanne says, somehow sounding both threatening and sexy at once. "Meet me in the Deepest Dark in an hour."

"An hour?"

"I assume you're going to need a shower after your run." She hangs up.

I drop my phone back on the bedside table, and pull myself completely out from under the sheets. Lissa's bedside light switches on.

She looks at me intently. "So . . . who was that?"

"Suzanne Whitman."

Lissa's face tightens. "Her. Why now?"

"She wants to see me in an hour, in the Deepest Dark."

"Death Moot?"

"What else would it be?" The ceremony has set more than just the Caterers in motion.

"You want me to come?" Lissa asks.

"You know you can't go there. There's no air, for one, none that you can breathe, anyway." I drop back down next to her, rest my chin on my hand. "Are you concerned about me spending the wee small hours of the morning with another woman?"

Lissa purses her lips. "No, of course not, but the Deepest Dark's a bloody odd choice."

Lissa's been there. She wasn't alive at the time. I don't know how much she remembers, but she certainly doesn't look too keen to return.

I shrug. "It was her decision."

"Don't let Suzanne Whitman make your decisions for you."

"I won't. No one makes decisions for me but me. You're starting to sound like you don't like her."

"I don't."

"And why's that?"

Lissa rolls away and pulls the sheets over her head.

Then reaches out and switches off the light. "I need to sleep," she says.

The shift to the Deepest Dark is a blazing supernova of agony in my skull.

It's *really* that bad.

I arrive bent over and coughing. Desperate as I am not to show any weakness, it's as good as I can do.

It's a moment until I'm aware of my surroundings.

The creaking of the One Tree permeates everything because, in a way, the One Tree *is* everything in the Underworld and the Deepest Dark. The sound rises to us through the dark soil beneath our feet, it builds in my bones. To say that it is loud is to emphasize one aspect of it to the detriment of everything else. It is a sound against which every other sound is registered.

And this place is hardly silent. The dead whisper here, a breathy, scratchy, continuous whispering. They release their last secrets before ascending into a greater secret above.

Up and down are relative in the Deepest Dark. Around us, through dust and soil that comes directly from the Underworld, wend the root tips of the One Tree: each is the width of my thigh. In the Deepest Dark we are beneath Hell itself. The air smells of blood, ash and humus. It's a back of the throat kind of bouquet. Not the best thing when you're already gagging.

Suzanne doesn't speak until I'm standing straight, and I've wiped a hand across my mouth. "You're late."

I make a show of peering at the green glowing dial of my watch. "I'd hardly call thirty seconds late." I'm being deliberately provocative. I find it helps when people think you're stupider than you are. It's about the only advantage I have.

Suzanne smiles thinly. Her dark eyes regard me impassively.

Suzanne's got a Severe—yes, with a capital S—sort of Southern Gothic thing going on. Her hair is cut into a bob. A black dress follows sharp lines down her lean body. Pale and muscular limbs jut from the sleeves. It's certainly not sensible garb for the cold fringes of the Underworld. She could be going out for the night, or about to chair a meeting. If she could get away with it in the Deepest Dark, if it wasn't so dark, I guess she'd be wearing black sunglasses. She glances at the tracksuit pants and tatty old jumper I'm wearing beneath my dad's old duffel coat, and sniffs.

"So, Suzanne, just what is it that you can do for me?"

She smiles condescendingly. "I chose this place because it is important to you."

Above us the sky is luminous with souls, glowing faintly red, heading out through the ether to wherever souls go once life and the Underworld is done with them. It should be peaceful except there's a great spiraling void, like a photo negative of a galaxy, eating up one corner of the sky, and it's getting bigger. The Stirrer god.

In the distance, maybe a kilometer away, is Devour, the Stirrer city. Its high walls glow a color very similar to my watch. I rode a bike through there a few months ago, fleeing for my life and for the life of the woman I love.

That Stirrer god, though, is hard to ignore. It's a sinister dark stain on the pants front of Hell and it's getting bigger. Sometimes it's a great eye, as I remember it, sometimes a million eyes, staring down. Leering at the Underworld.

I've felt the weight of the god's vast and angry gaze upon me, and I've stared back at it. So I've a personal stake in all of this, but then when that god arrives, life itself, from bacteria up, will be under threat. It's amazing, though, just how much people are pretending that it isn't going to happen. RMs, my colleagues. People who should know better.

"You chose this place because you knew it gives you an advantage over me," I say.

"What a cynic."

"I prefer to call it realism." I point toward the dark god in the sky. "Maybe it's just too big. Maybe it's something that we can't do anything about at all. But we have to try."

"What do you know about that thing up there?" she asks.

"That the Stirrers worship it and that it's drawing closer. What else is there?"

Suzanne waves her hand dismissively, as though the Stirrer god was nothing more than a buzzing insect. "Look, I want to offer you a deal. Think about all the resources you would have at your disposal. My offices, my staff—they're much bigger than yours. And that difference in staffing is even larger now after your little problem."

The "little" problem she's referring to, the one that led to my promotion, wiped out Mortmax's Australian offices and, almost, due to a minor Regional Apocalypse, Australia's living population. Workplace politics can be genocidal in my line of business. And when things get that way they have a tendency to spill out into the world. The Spanish Flu, the Black Death—they were both preceded by "problems" in my industry.

"You let that happen, too." I glare at her. None of the RMs stepped in to help. In the end it had been left up to me. "All of you are guilty of that."

Suzanne's eyes narrow just enough that I know I've got to her. "You know the rules," she says, "our hands were tied. Morrigan manipulated us."

Morrigan manipulated me more than anyone. But I'm not going to let Suzanne get away with her comment. "Excuses aren't going to save the world. Morrigan was small time compared to *that*." I point at the Stirrer god amassing on the horizon.

Suzanne raises her hands placatingly. "I have my best people working on it," she says. I open my mouth to speak but she jumps in first. "But that's not why I'm here. You need me."

"Like a coronary." My turn for a condescending grin.

Suzanne grimaces, though I can see that I've amused her, which makes me a little grumpier. "Try not to be so aggressive. Yes, this is scary for you, Steven, I understand that. You're a newly negotiated RM, in the process of building up your Pomps. It's going to be years before you're at full strength. You're vulnerable. You can barely shift without throwing up."

Fair assessment so far. But I can't let it lie. "I'll get better."

"Of course you will," she says, "but I can help you. I can ease the transition. I can lend you more Pomps, for one thing." She reaches out, squeezes my hand. Her fingers are warm. I pull away, and Suzanne frowns, but not with anger. She dips her head, even manages a smile. "I understand exactly what you're going through. I can guide you."

"I've already got Mr. D for that."

Suzanne's face tightens, her smile attenuates, whatever humor there was in her eyes leaves with it. I'm familiar with that expression—I tend to bring it out in people, and Mr. D was even better at it than me.

"Mr. D was never one of us," she says. "You want a second-rate mentor? You stick with that idiot. I'm giving you a chance." She bends down, grabs a handful of the dust which coats everything here, and lets it fall. Only it doesn't. The dust drifts around her lazily, glowing in all the colors of a particularly luminous acid trip. It spirals around her head creating a halo, and beneath it she's all shadows, sharp angles and full lips. The darkest points of her face are her eyes. When she smiles, her teeth are white and straight. "No one understands this place, this job, like I do. Just consider it. That's all I'm asking."

"And what do you get out of it?"

"I get an ally, Mr. de Selby, and one who is aware of his powers and limits, one who doesn't go off rushing madly into things, making it difficult for everyone. Mr. D isolated himself. He never really bothered with us. Sometimes I think he delighted in making enemies. When you think about all the people who died—all that you've lost—remember who let it happen. Morrigan had the schemes, but Mr. D allowed him to flourish in your branch."

She has a point.

"Steven, I liked your family. Michael and Annie were good people. The things your father did for Mortmax... He even lifted our profits in the States."

I can imagine Dad rolling in his grave at that. He'd always been slightly embarrassed by his business acumen. All he'd really wanted was to be a Pomp. Now Dad, if pressed, would have made a great RM. Mom, too. I wish they were here. I wish I knew what they would do.

Suzanne shivers. It's cold here, and I doubt she would ever show such vulnerability willingly, but my father raised me this way: I shrug out of my coat and put it around her shoulders. She's wearing Chanel No. 5, my mother's favorite perfume. I remember coming home, after my parents had died. The house had smelled of it and it was the first time the reality of their deaths really hit me. It was also the first time that I wondered if moving into their place was a mistake.

I pull away. Suzanne doesn't notice, or pretends not to, though she does look at me oddly. "You are a gentleman, Mr. de Selby."

I open my mouth to speak, but she's already gone. "Hey! What about my coat?"

All I have to answer me is dust falling to the ground again. I crouch down and scoop up my own handful. In my palms it's just dust, gritty and gray. I open my fingers and it drops. Only the souls in the sky, and the nearby city of Stirrers, offer any light.

My right biceps tingles, then burns. Ah, finally. Wal crawls out from under my shirt and stares up at me.

"I don't trust her," Wal says. No surprise there, that's Wal's standard response, though it's been proven remarkably accurate.

"Where were you?" I ask.

"Stuck to your arm," he says, looking more than a little chagrined. "She stopped me, I don't know how. But she did it well."

I grin at him cruelly. "Ah, so there are things, very *useful* things, she could teach me."

Wal slaps me across the face with all the force of a handful of tissues. "You shut your mouth."

He actually looks hurt.

A dim hooting comes from the city of Devour—like a parliament of malevolent and fractious owls. Bells ring and, all around us, the dead whisper their brittle, final whispers before drifting out of hearing and further into the Deepest Dark.

The air chills. Both of us feel it. I don't have my coat anymore, but Wal is the only one who is naked.

He shivers. "I don't like this place."

He's not the only one.

6

I can't believe I'm going to be late!"

Most of my clothes are in piles in the bedroom. But my suit, one of eight I own, hangs in the wardrobe. A Pomp never leaves their suit on the floor. Never. And I'm RM now, I have to set the standard. I slip into it like a second skin. It's Italian, and cost me three weeks' salary—and that's my current salary. This meeting with Cerbo is formal; tracksuit and jumper just isn't going to cut it. Lissa watches, then hits me with the most deafening wolf whistle. I can't understand how she finds this body attractive. OK, maybe a little, I do work out. And the suit looks pretty fine. But still, I feel my cheeks flush at Lissa's scrutiny.

I knot my tie, straighten everything, and even I have to admit that I look good.

Though not nearly as lovely as Lissa. I want to be back in bed with her. We never seem to spend enough time together. A moment apart is an ache in my chest. Tim might be right, new love and all that. But I never felt this intensely for Robyn. And Lissa is the only woman I have ever pursued to Hell.

"Maybe I should call off this meeting, spend the morning with you. You're not working till late, I've seen the schedule. We could..."

Lissa appears to give this some serious thought. "No, Tim would kill you, and me. Not after all we've done trying to get you engaged with the business again. The Moot's a week away. You've got to—stop that!"

She doesn't push me away, though, as my lips brush her neck. Then—I feel her body stiffening with the effort of it—she does, and I'm backing off the bed, away from the intoxicating smell of her. "You'll crush your suit, or, at the very least, stretch the front of those pants."

"Oh." I look down. "I see what you mean."

And I'm blushing once more. Lissa grins at me wickedly. I straighten my suit again.

Yeah, new love. Such new, new love.

"How do I look?"

"You're the bomb," she says.

"The bomb?"

Lissa laughs at me. "Just get out of here. Or your cousin will have an aneurism."

"How's the hair?"

She squints at me. "Still thinning."

"I hate you."

"No, you don't."

I kiss her again, and then I shift to Number Four.

It's another body punch of a shift. I miss my office by about fifteen meters. End up at the reception desk. Lundwall blinks at me.

Number Four. This is Australia's Pomp Central, and

the major node in the southern hemisphere's Underworld–living world interface, which makes the architecture interesting in a multi-dimensional kind of way. Outside one part of the building, Brisbane is in the middle of a boiling, sweating summer. And outside another part, Hell is going through a rather mild spring. The seasons rarely correspond. In here, the air is loud with the hum of air-conditioners and the creaking of the One Tree.

Phones ring throughout the office. People are working busily and trying hard to ignore me and my clumsy entrance. I get the feeling that Tim has been doing a fair bit of storming around this morning. Tim is great at his job, but you don't want to get him mad. He says it doesn't help that I'm so casual about the whole thing. Well, I think we balance each other out perfectly.

But I *would* think that.

I stumble over to Tim's office and open the door without knocking. He's stubbing out a cigarette when I appear and looks guilty.

"Gotcha," I say.

"What if I was having a wank or something here?"

I smirk. "Hardly. If you had to choose between smokes and masturbation there's no contest."

"Ah, your deductive capabilities astound me, Holmes."

Other than the ashtray heaped with cigarettes, Tim's room is as neat as an anally retentive pin. I'm more than a little envious of his work ethic. His inbox and out are emptied throughout the day and there's a well-marked year-planner on one wall. Seven days from now, on the 28th of December, the Death Moot begins. He's circled that day, and the two that follow it, in thick red marker. I've a year-planner somewhere under the mess on my desk.

This was once Morrigan's office. Tim hasn't changed it that much, apart from the photo of Sally and the kids next to his keyboard—I bought him the frame. He's even using the same daily desk calendar, the one with the inspirational quotes. Everything from Dorothy Parker to Sun Tzu is in there. He and Morrigan shared a deep commitment to work, a fastidiousness about everything in their life, and a love of beer, though Tim has never tried to kill me. But the way he's looking at me, maybe that's all about to change.

Then the pain of the shift hits me in a residual wave.

Tim waits politely until I finish dry heaving before he starts taking strips off me. "Jesus, mate! Could you at least have a shower before coming to work?"

I shrug. No point telling him how hard it was to leave Lissa this morning. Then I see the bandage on his left hard. "Not like you to be out with the Stirrers. Was it a hard stir?" Sometimes a Stirrer will require more blood than usual to stall it.

Tim shakes his head. "I wish, it'd mean I was out of the office more. No, the door's being particularly demanding today." Number Four may be the only place that demands— well, not so much demands, but takes—a blood sacrifice of its staff on entry. RMs are exempt, most of the time, something I'm pleased about. For me, it's usually only a tiny pricking of the thumb, and weeks may go past where it asks for nothing. I wonder if the ferocity of Tim's sacrifice has anything to do with the massive portent I spent part of last night cleaning from the bathroom.

Tim throws me a small spray can of deodorant. I manage to catch it before it hits my head. Then he hurls a pack of breath mints. Not so lucky with those, they skitter all over the desk. I scoop up a few of them.

"I'm guessing you didn't clean your teeth before you headed over here," Tim says.

"You guessed wrong. Anything else?" I pop a handful of mints into my mouth, regardless.

"Oh, I haven't started yet." His hands rest on his hips. "You cut it this fine again, and you can find yourself another Ankou."

"Where am I going to find one as good as you?"

"Exactly. Which is why you are never going to do this again. Now, I've been thinking about this Death Moot—"

"Is Cerbo here?" I interrupt.

"Not yet. Wonder of wonders, we've actually got five minutes."

"Good. I had a meeting with Suzanne Whitman last night."

"And you have only told me this now because...?"

"Look, it was late. I didn't want to wake you. At least you can sleep."

"Still having trouble, eh?"

"Shit, Tim, I've been whingeing about this for a month."

"Pardon me if I've been too busy to notice." And as if to prove his point, his mobile starts ringing.

He looks at it. "It's only mildly urgent," he says. "I'll call them back."

Tim slips his phone into his pocket and smiles at me. "Now, this is interesting, *really* interesting. If the U.S. RM is so keen to negotiate, the others can't be too far behind. What did she want?"

"She said she wanted to help."

Neither of us successfully choke down the laugh that follows.

"Said I could do with an ally."

Another snort.

Tim checks his watch. "We'd better get to your office. Cerbo will be there in a minute." We walk past the desks of Pomps and the hallway that sits in the middle of the office, the one that leads directly to Aunt Neti's parlor. She's baking scones or muffins or biscuits; the smell drifts down the hall. Probably expecting a visitor. I can't help wondering who.

My office is a bit stuffy. I switch on the lights and the aircon. It's your basic sort of corner office, except for Brueghel's painting, "The Triumph of Death" against one wall (not a copy, the real thing, all those skeletons bringing on the apocalypse, herding the living to Hell) and the throne, of course.

I drop into the throne, and my region immediately grows more vital around me. The beating hearts, the creaking tree.

Sitting in my throne I feel what Tim's reports can only tell me. We're stretched painfully thin. My Pomps are struggling out there. It might be a picture of industry in the offices, but it's little more than a veneer painted over chaos. I've been ignoring this for far too long.

"We need more staff," I say to Tim.

"Lissa's doing the best she can," he says irritably. "It's not exactly easy to advertise for Pomps. There's a whole bunch of stages that we have to steer people through. I think it's remarkable that we have as many staff as we do."

"We've got to do better."

"You could take a more active role. That might help," Tim says sharply.

"I'm doing the best I can," I say, mimicking his tone.

Tim groans, shakes his head. "How about a unified front?"

"Yeah, how about it?"

"Sometimes you piss me off, de Selby."

I grin at him. "That's what family is for."

"Maybe that's why I decided to become a Black Sheep."

"Nah, you can't escape it no matter what you do. As long—" and I stop myself there. I was going to say as long as there is family left, but there isn't that much family remaining. There are some things neither of us are ready to joke about.

I'm almost relieved that Faber Cerbo shifts into the foyer at that moment. Apparently Ankous can do that, if their RM is sufficiently skilled. Morrigan could, and it didn't seem to hurt him, either, the prick. Cerbo's appearance is presaged by a slight pressure in my skull. His heartbeat, a sudden addition to my region, is loud—like you'd expect from an Ankou—even louder than Tim's, and at a steady sixty beats per minute.

I glance at my watch. He is exactly thirty seconds late, and I can't help feeling that Suzanne is making a point. Lundwall—heartbeat ninety-three bpm, up from seventy, now that Cerbo has appeared at his desk—leads him into the room.

Faber Cerbo, like any self-respecting Pomp, is in a suit. We all are, here. As though Death was truly like any other business. Well, we can pretend. The real reason is the vast number of funerals we attend and morgues and mortuaries we visit. In those places a suit makes you virtually invisible—even in Brisbane on a forty degree day. Unlike Tim and me, Cerbo is wearing a hat, a bowler. That, and the pencil-thin mustache, make him look like a mash-up of a

British accountant from the thirties and the filmmaker John Waters, and are completely at odds with his Texan accent. I've never liked wearing hats, they mess up my hair. But it suits him, somehow. Gripped in his left hand, his nails coated with black nail polish, is a brown leather folder.

Cerbo doffs his bowler, and rolls his shoulders. Bones click with the movement.

I don't get up from my throne, in fact I make a point of swinging back on it, looking as casual as I can. After all, here I am in the seat of my power, so to speak. It is poor form to neglect it.

I nod at Cerbo and gesture to one of the chairs in front of the desk. He gives a swift and slightly mocking bow— well, I think it's mocking, and if I can't be sure, the odds are high. My rise to RM was something of a shock to a lot of people—myself included—and I'm not treated as seriously as I could be. But then again, it fits into my tactic. Just grin and let them think you're stupid.

Tim shakes his hand. Cerbo gives him a warm smile then sits down, so lightly it's as if he's hardly sitting at all. He puts the folder on the table.

"My mistress says she met with you last evening, Mr. de Selby." He gives Tim a pained look, and Tim nods sympathetically. I wonder what Ankous say about their bosses when they're not around. Hell, Morrigan ran over Mr. D with an SUV. Maybe we push them to it.

"Yes, we had an interesting chat."

"Unfortunately, since I have not been apprised of your *chat*," another pained look in Tim's direction, "I can only tell you what it is that I was briefed on, and hope that our topics of conversation are in some way sympathetic."

He opens his folder, extracts a single sheet of paper, and slides it toward me, pushing aside a half-dozen unopened envelopes, a Mars Bar wrapper, and a scrunched up packet of salt and vinegar chips. We all jump back a little when a cockroach scurries out of the chip packet. Tim whacks it with a packet of envelopes, misses, and the insect's off and running toward a distant corner of the room. Tim glances at me. OK, so I need to clean up a little. Cerbo doesn't say a word (his pursed lips and raised eyebrows are enough) and deposits the sheet of paper in front of me.

The number 10 is written across the sheet in black marker.

I look from it, to Cerbo, then to Tim, then back to the paper. I shrug. "And this means what? You're shifting to the metric system?"

Cerbo gives out a rather theatrical sigh, as though it's painfully obvious what the number represents. "That, Mr. de Selby, is the number of Pomps Ms. Whitman is willing to add to your ranks from her own."

I raise an eyebrow and lean across the desk, my elbow crunching down on the chip packet. "And what is expected of me if I accept?"

Cerbo clears his throat, makes a little nervous gesture with his hands as though he's shooing away flies. "Time, Mr. de Selby. You are to give her your time. An hour for each Pomp. Ten hours, in total, of your undivided attention, before the Death Moot begins."

"It's a generous offer," I say.

Cerbo's lips curl in a grimace. "It is more than generous. Ms. Whitman doesn't want you to fail in your work. Power vacuums are something of a danger in this business."

"And what do you think the odds are of that?"

Cerbo doesn't answer.

"I'll consider it," I say.

I get the feeling that he was expecting a response, and an enthusiastically positive one, at that. But I'm not ready to answer, and Cerbo can tell. He's disappointed, and not all of that seems to be about going home to his RM empty-handed.

He dons his hat. Slips his folder beneath his arm, and stands. "Don't be *too* long in considering it. That may be regarded as an insult."

I nod. "I am aware of that. Believe me, I've no desire to put anyone's nose out of joint. But this is my region, and I'll take as long as I need."

He glances at Tim. Tim shrugs and gives him his most "my boss is crazy" look. Cerbo sighs again. "Good day, gentlemen."

He shifts, and there's nothing but air filling the space he's left. The sheet of paper flutters on my desk, the Mars Bar wrapper falls to the floor.

"How the hell did he do that?" Tim asks enviously.

"I don't know." I throw my hands up in the air, and the throne tips. Both it and me end up on the ground.

Tim laughs.

My face burning, I get to my feet. The chair looks very smug. Bloody throne. I drop back in it, heavily. "You told me you'd do the talking."

"Sometimes listening is better than talking."

I want to say that he knows nothing of listening, that he knows nothing of the things I can hear, of the things bodies tell me—beating hearts and closing veins, the stealthy drift of a clot toward the brain. But I'm just not that petulant.

"You did good, I think," Tim says. "The game's started. Opening gambit, all that shit."

"Whose game are we playing?"

"It was never going to be ours, at the beginning. Someone else had to make the first move. We're too new. We don't even know what pieces we've got, or what the game is."

"Ten Pomps. We could do with ten Pomps," I say.

"But they wouldn't really be yours. They'd be doing her bidding."

"But they'd *know* what they're doing."

Tim gets to his feet. "That's what worries me." He glances at his watch. "Shift change. Things are about to get crazy. We'll discuss this tonight, eh?"

"Yeah. Holding off until tomorrow is long enough to piss her off, but only a little."

"Annoying people isn't the greatest tactic, Steve."

I grin at him. "You use what gifts you're given."

"Oh, you use that one all right, and it's a rough instrument." He closes the door behind him.

"I didn't get this job because I was subtle," I say to the door. "I got it because I was stupid."

The chair beneath me shivers, as though it is dreaming. Three people die in a car accident. Someone clutches at his chest. His heart beneath races, shudders, halts. I look at the corner where the cockroach ran. There's been enough death already. I let it be.

I'm Death, not an exterminator.

7

With Tim and Cerbo gone I get to work.

Well, I try to.

First I pick up the chip packet and toss it in the bin. The chocolate wrapper goes the same way. I straighten a few papers, open some letters, but I'm not really reading them. I switch on my MP3 and listen to some Black Flag. Henry Rollins gets me in the right head-space today.

Complacency's a killer, Morrigan used to say. He should know. He used it to kill most of Australia's Pomps. But it took him down, too, in the end. He certainly hadn't expected me to win the Negotiation.

If I'm honest, neither had I.

Here I am sitting in the throne. An RM with all the responsibilities that entails. Staff beneath me, a region and a world to save from Stirrers, as well as a commitment to good returns for our shareholders.

I think about those ten Pomps and just how helpful they would be, not to mention Suzanne's knowledge. The black bakelite phone sits there. This is the sort of thing Mr. D could advise me on. But I need to start making my own decisions. I'll talk to him this afternoon, once I work out exactly how I feel about this offer.

I type up a couple of emails, then text Lissa: *Interesting morning, how about you?*

No response. So I send another one, creaking backward and forward in my throne: *Wish you were here. Naked.*

No response. I play the crossword in the *Courier-Mail*—only cheat half the time.

Then I consider the paperwork on my desk. There's a whole bunch of stuff I sign off on.

A car accident on the Pacific Highway chills me with eight deaths. It's just a gentle chill, but their deaths come so suddenly—I worry that there is no one there to facilitate their way into the Underworld. That there is, and that it is done, brings a tight smile to my lips. A seventy-five-year-old woman in her garden in Hobart clutches at her chest and tumbles among her rhododendrons. Two children jump off a bridge in some northern New South Wales town: only one surfaces. Someone takes a hammer to their husband, claw end first. Death. Death. Death. And my people are close by at every one.

It sounds terrible. But there's life before those endings, and existence after. It's not the world ending, but lives. The world's ending, though...I need to find out more about that Stirrer god.

Still no response from Lissa, so while I work I follow her via my Avian Pomps.

A crow witnesses her stalling a Stirrer in the Valley—the corpse had somehow escaped the Royal Brisbane

Hospital. She lays the body gently against a bench and makes a call. An ambulance will be along soon. They'll ship the body back to the morgue and it will be as though it never happened. She binds the wound in her palm quickly and efficiently.

A sparrow watches as she eats a kebab for lunch, sitting in a mall, just a few streets from where she laid the body down. I can almost smell the garlic. I want to reach out and touch her, and the sparrow, misinterpreting this desire, flies at the back of her head. I manage to convince it otherwise an instant or two before contact.

An ibis ostensibly digs in a bin as she attends an open-air funeral service and pomps a soul, that of an elderly gentleman, whom she charms utterly. I can see his posture shift from scared, to guarded, to a chuckling disregard as she reaches out to touch his arm. He is gone in a flash—I feel the echo of the pomp through me. And Lissa is standing there, on the very fringes of the funeral service, alone.

Lissa's the ultimate professional. She talks to the dead so easily. Knows how to bring them around from loss to acceptance. She is the best Pomp I've ever seen.

After a while, she walks up to the ibis. I stare at her through its dark eyes. "Steven, I love you, but this is creepy. Don't you have work to do?"

I'm out of there in an instant, my face flushed.

I get out of my chair and, as I do every day about this time, pull open the blinds to the rear windows. These face the Underworld. My office is immediately lit with a reddish light. The One Tree isn't far away. Down below, the traffic of the Underworld moves slowly, in a stately reflection of the living world's traffic. The various bends of the river that I can see are busy with catamarans and ferries. Traffic, cars and buildings are almost identical to the living city, except everything is that little bit ornate. Mr. D says that's his fault. I haven't bothered to change it, yet. I'm not sure how, but I'm certain it's a lot of work.

With the blind open, the sunlight and unlight battle it out over my desk. They're equally matched. Where they strike my desk there's a patch of gloom, neutralized only when I turn on my lamp. I've read that the living and the dead worlds occupy the same place, but I don't really understand how that's possible. I prefer to think of them as two skins of the same onion.

A shrill screech startles me. I flinch, then glance over at the window leading to Hell. Someone's hanging from a harness and cleaning the glass from the outside with one of those big plastic squeegees. He's slowly sinking into view. This is a first. He's a big fella, pale skin, long black hair pulled back into a ponytail, a strong jaw marked with stubble. The harness digs into his shoulders. What is a living person doing in Hell?

He waves, I wave back.

Then he pulls out a gun and fires. It's such a casual movement that I hardly notice it. Don't even react until it's done. My stomach flips, I throw my hands in the air, and stumble backward, then catch my balance on the back of a chair.

The window stars, but doesn't implode. You have more than double-glazing when your office faces Hell.

Through the fragmentation of the glass, I see the "cleaner" frown.

I look at the door; I'm much further from it than the window. If I run that way I'll probably get a shot or two in the back and, while I'm at it, lead him into the office. Enough people have died in here this year already. It seems clear that he's only after me—and if this is about me, I want to keep it that way. Besides, I've taken bullets before and survived them easily. I lift up a chair. Not the throne, that weighs a bloody ton.

He fires again. The window shatters this time, glass going everywhere. The bullet thwacks against the wall behind me. Alarms sound throughout the building and the One Tree's creaking intensifies to a dull roar now there's no glass to block it out. Hell has entered the building.

My arm tingles, then burns. Wal extrudes from my flesh. He pulls the most impressive double-take I have ever seen, his wings fluttering madly.

"What the hell?"

"Gun!" I shout. "Assassination attempt!"

"Right, then. Shouldn't you be running the other way?"

"Shut up and help!" I yell.

I charge toward the gunman, the chair gripped in my hands as though it's some sort of medieval weapon. Here's a guy with a pistol, and me with something that I bought from IKEA. My boots crunch over glass, a big chunk of which slides through the side of my shoe and into my foot. It should hurt more, and it will, I'm sure, but right now all it does is make me angry.

I jab the chair at his head. He leaps back with all the grace of a gymnast. Fires again.

Misses.

But not quite, my ear stings. I resist the urge to slap a hand over the wound. It hurts more than the last time I was shot.

Wal's already buzzing around the bastard's head, and

the gunman slaps him away easily, but Wal is back just as fast.

The gunman arcs out on the end of the rope, a pendulum packing a pistol. As he hurtles back in, I hurl the chair at him. He struggles to weave out of the way and the backrest hits him in the head with a sickening crunch. He swings in, then out, and in again, hanging limp.

I hobble over to him and reach out, but suddenly he falls, a long tail of rope following him. I peer down into the Underworld and watch him tumble, his limbs twitching. It's a bit of a mess when he hits. The mess itself is gone a moment later, back to the living world. He wasn't from the Underworld, that's for sure. Someone's just received a very nasty, splattery surprise.

"Watch it!" Wal yells. "There's someone on the roof!"

Who the hell is that? I swing my head up—stupid, stupid, that's the best way to lose your face, but I have to look—and someone ducks for cover. But I catch a glimpse of the stork-like beak of a plague mask.

I jerk back in from the window, and shake my head at Wal, who grimaces and then shoots up past me, hurtling toward the roof. He's gone a moment, before swooping back. He tears past me and hits the carpet hard, but is back in the air almost at once.

"Shit," he hisses. "That hurt. Not enough Hell here for me to fly properly."

"Did you see who it was?"

"Oh, yeah, I'm all right. And no, I didn't, they were gone."

Then the first bastard's soul arrives, lit with the bluish pallor of the dead. I'm the nearest entity capable of pomping him. I should have expected him.

He blinks—like the dead do, and his death was more sudden than most—surprised, perhaps, at who he's ended up with. He snarls at me, his every movement a blur, as though he can't find traction here. There's a terrible weight of anger in him. It's holding him here where his lack of flesh can't. I try to use it to my advantage.

"You're not going anywhere until you tell me who sent you."

"You'll find out soon enough." His voice is quiet, controlled, and then he's running at me, a final act of defiance, and one I'm not expecting. I can't stop the pomp from happening. He tears through me, a scrambling fury of claws. This fellow didn't expect to die, and he's mad about it, but not enough to betray his boss. In fact, I can tell he blames me. After all, I didn't die and I was supposed to.

Well, he doesn't have my sympathy.

The pomp is painful, but fast, then he's gone, and I'm left standing, feeling dizzy. Rubbing at my limbs. No one should die with such rage inside them. It leaves me hurting, and angry. Dissatisfied on every level.

"You really should clean up in here," Wal says, picking up another chip packet.

"Don't you start," I growl.

My mobile chirps. I drag it from my pocket. It's a text from Lissa: *Of course you do.*

What?

My office door swings open and Wal slips from air to arm. The ratio of earth to Hell has shifted in earth's favor. There are shouts, another ringing alarm, and Tim and a couple of the bigger guys from the office rush in. They look at me then at the broken glass. All this mess. It's the first time I have a real excuse for it.

"Naked." I lift the phone up in the air. "Of course!"

"What the—Steven, are you right?" Tim demands, then his eyes widen. "What the fuck happened to your ear?"

Oh, I'd forgotten about that. I reach up and touch it. My fingers come back bloody. I'm aflood with wooziness. *Jesus.*

"Someone just tried to kill me. And a second someone killed them, from upstairs, on the roof—Hellside, but you should check the real roof, just in case . . ."

Tim looks at the men with him, nods, and they run off. Leaving him, me and the phone.

I sway near the broken window. Perhaps I should move away from that drop. "Sorry about the mess." And then I remember the glass in my foot.

"Watch your step," I say, as darkness swallows me.

8

I'm rushing through the creaking, mumbling dark.
Knives whisper and flash around me, winding and
slashing at each other. In their wake, smoke trails
and bodies fall where there were none—as though the
knives have knitted their victims' existence and demise in
the same instant.

My boots crunch on ash and bone.

A man gibbers on the hill. He sees me, comes rushing
down. I stand and wait, uneasy, my belly cold. But I will
not run. I recognize him at last.

Morrigan.

"You didn't think you had it that easy, did you?" he
says.

The earth is a mouth, a great swallowing mouth. Morrigan tumbles and is gone.

I am rushing through the dark. The knives a circle of
stone around me.

A hand closes on mine and I can't get free.

Another hand, and then another grabs me. Someone

pulls out my index finger, and cuts. Severs the digit from the palm.

"One by one. That's how it works." It's Morrigan again. He brings his face close to mine. *"You never should have won. The job's too big for you. Your feet are too small for the boots you're clomping in."*

I push him away. He slashes out with a whispering knife. Another finger falls.

I'm awake. I check my fingers.

All there.

Someone is stitching up my foot. There's that uncomfortable sensation of skin being pulled tight, without the pain. Not that I want the pain, but my body is all too aware it's going on somewhere, that trauma is being had whether I can feel it or not.

I'm lying on a bed in Brooker's room, which has to be the best fitted-out sick bay in any workplace in Australia.

"I don't remember Mr. D ever getting into this sort of trouble," Dr. Brooker says, looking at me over his glasses. Brooker's work as Mortmax Brisbane's physician usually means the occasional bit of stitch work, a few prescriptions and a lot of counseling. He's very rarely in Number Four—which is what saved him during Morrigan's Schism—but he's available most of the time. I've known Dr. Brooker since I can remember, before memory, in fact. He was the attending doctor at my birth. Yeah, and I get about as much sympathy from him as anyone in my family would have given me. I suppose I could take that as a compliment. I called him the "good Doctor Brooker" once and got a cuff under the ear. His mood hasn't exactly improved since.

I grimace. "Mr. D had been doing this a century or two before you were even born. He'd gotten the trouble out of his system."

"Nevertheless...you really need to concentrate on your job, not this messing about with guns. People always get hurt." He jabs a gloved finger at my foot. "You're an RM. You're not about hurting people."

"*He* had a gun. *I* had a chair, and believe me, he ended up much worse than I did. Ouch!"

Brooker harrumphs and pulls a stitch tight. "Keep still. You were much better when you were unconscious. You'll be all right. Quite frankly, I don't know why anybody even bothered trying to shoot at you. Waste of time—you can't be killed that way."

"Maybe they just wanted to see if they could hurt me?"

"Well, they can hurt you all right." He smiles broadly. "But not as much as me if you don't keep still."

"Where is everybody?"

"Does this look like a party to you?" Brooker rolls his eyes and finishes his stitching with a neat knot—he's done an awful lot of those over the years. "They're waiting outside, where I told them to wait."

Yeah, I might be RM, but in this room Brooker is king.

I clear my throat softly. "Can I ask you something?"

Brooker looks at me. "Shoot. No pun intended."

"Did Mr. D ever talk to you about his dreams?"

Brooker shakes his head; I can tell he thinks the question has come out of left field. "Steven, I hardly ever spoke to him at all. Don't tell me you thought otherwise. He was a peculiar man." Brooker squints at me. "To be honest, I like you much more."

I don't tell him that Mr. D is still very much around.

I remember how Mr. D died. Bones crunching as the SUV rolled over him. He certainly ended up in a lot of trouble. But then again for the majority of us that's all we can expect. Time and the world are hard and grinding. Bones and flesh are soft.

"Now, these dreams…"

I sigh. "They're nightmares really. Nasty as hell nightmares."

"Everyone has bad dreams," Dr. Brooker says. "Particularly in your job, and mine."

"That's not the problem," I tell him. "It's just that I rather like them." My face flushes.

"How much?"

My face is burning. "A lot."

"Hmm." He squints at me like I'm some kind of thermometer. I don't know what sort of reading he gets but after a while he turns away. "Don't get caught up with dreams. Sometimes that's all they are."

We both know that isn't true. Brooker looks worried. "See me in a day or two—this really isn't my specialty. Now isn't the best time, you've been through a bit of trauma. And I'm sure that hasn't helped."

"It'll heal," I say looking at my foot.

"I wasn't talking about that. The way all this happened— the way you became RM, and the betrayals you faced— none of it was good. Steve, I lost a lot of dear friends that week. You lost more than that. It takes its toll."

But is that really a good enough excuse for the number of times I've shown up at work drunk? Or just not bothered to show up at all? When you don't sleep there's an awful lot of time you can spend drinking, even if it's not filling up the hole left by all that loss, and the guilt that I'm letting those nearest to me, and equally wounded, down. Which, of course, leads to more drinking. It's how I've dealt with all the major dramas of my adult life.

Home and work, everywhere I look there are gaps. Reminders of friends and family gone, snatched away by the chaos of Morrigan's Schism. And as for the work itself, I don't know how to lead people. Where do you learn that? Where do you pick up all the arcane and complicated tricks required in the running of a business like mine? Despite Tim's notes there's no manual. I have Mr. D, but I don't know what questions to ask, and he isn't that great at answering the ones I do. I'd suspect him of being deliberately evasive, except he's always been that way.

And Lissa. Where do you go after what we've shared? Surely happiness of the forever-after sort is deserved. I'd settle for a few years of it, but there's no prospect of that. We've a dark god coming.

Suzanne's offer is looking very attractive. Maybe it's not too late to fix this. To be what I need to be.

Brooker works in silence for a while, cleaning then binding the foot. "All done," he says at last. "You'll need to sit on your chair for a while."

"My throne?"

"Don't start putting on airs and graces. When I was a kid we called the shitter a throne." He sighs. "But that's the one. It'll heal you much faster than you can on your own."

There's shouting outside. It's an achingly familiar voice, an achingly familiar heartbeat, even if it is racing. My ears prick up. Dr. Brooker grins. "I'll just get her for you."

The door flings open and nearly bowls him over. Dr. Brooker doesn't even bother calling her on it. He knows better than to get between us. She's in her usual black get-up: a Mickey Mouse brooch on one collar of her blouse. I don't get the appeal of Walt Disney characters—give me Bugs Bunny any day—but I'm so happy to see her.

"Are you OK?" Lissa asks. She grabs me tight enough that my ribs creak.

"Yeah, I am." I groan in her embrace. "Well, I think I am."

Brooker nods. "He's fine." He's already packing up his bag: good doctors are always in demand. "As far as I know, nothing can really hurt him, just slow him down a little."

"Define hurt. My foot's throbbing!"

"Well, the glass was part of Number Four, I'd say that's why it hurts you so much." He rubs his chin thoughtfully. "Or it could be that your body is still getting used to what it has become. The pain may just be old habits dying hard."

I wish they'd die a little more easily.

Lissa pulls back, looks at me, and winces. Oh, I'd forgotten about the ear. It starts to sting, but now no more than a scratch might. The top of the ear is already growing back.

Tim peers through the door. Dr. Brooker delivered him as well. "He OK, Dr. Brooker?"

"Nothing a bit of rest won't fix. He's an RM: both wounds will heal quickly, not like the rest of us idiots." Dr. Brooker looks at me. "Just be careful."

His phone chirrups, signaling another emergency, or a game of golf. He merely looks at it, grunts, and with a curt nod, leaves the room.

I glance over at Tim. "OK, we're six hours into the working day and I've already been shot at. I want to know why, and I want to know now."

"I'm already on it," Tim says, pulling his phone out. "I'll call Doug at my old department." Doug Anderson is a good choice. The man has more fingers in more pies than anyone we know. He took up Tim's role as policy advisor and head of Pomp/government relations. "The last time this happened..."

Call me a pessimist, but I have a terrible certainty that this is going to be worse.

And why's Morrigan in my dreams again? He's gone, and there's no coming back for him. As Mr. D said, after the knife fight of the Negotiation, Morrigan's soul was obliterated.

I can't be feeling guilty about that, surely?

9

Seems I'm stuck in my office. Despite her concern, Lissa couldn't stay long. Her hand is bandaged again, another cut, another stir. And she's always on the hunt for potential Pomps. That's hard work. Like Tim said, we advertise, of course, but that's not easy either. The job titles are deliberately vague, the interview process detailed and convoluted. None of us earlier generation Pomps ever had to interview for the job. Our families had all worked for Mortmax for generations, probably since the last Schism.

There's just too much work to be done. People never stop dying, and there are not enough of us to make sure the transition is smooth.

For all its healing attributes, the chair itself really isn't that comfortable. Not enough lumbar support or something. I'd rather sit in a recliner, but no recliner I know is going to knit me back together as quickly. A fella could go mad with all this sitting, *Rear Window* style. I'm used to being on my feet, out and about: pomping the dead, and stalling Stirrers.

I keep having to remind myself that that is in the past now. The first thing I can do is check on my staff. Make sure I'm not letting them down anymore.

I close my eyes; connect with all my Pomps, the 104 people that I have working around the country. My other Pomps, my Avians—the sparrows, crows and ibis—work as good eyes but they are hard to control and their "process" in stalling a stir involves a considerable amount of pecking. I find directing them gives me a migraine which makes practice somewhat unappealing. Generally they're left pomping the spirits of animals, those big-brained enough to cage a soul.

The window's already repaired, and the floor has digested the broken glass. I wonder what else it might just eat. The building is self-healing; the glass had apparently grown back within a few minutes of me blacking out. Looking at it, the glass appears thicker—dark filaments line it, some sort of reinforcement, I guess. Number Four has grown paranoid.

A familiar face pokes around the door wearing a big grin that fails to obscure the concern behind his eyes.

"Don't people knock anymore?"

"What a mess," Alex says.

"No, this is what my office usually looks like bar the blood and paper." I glance around; the glass has already gone. "In fact it looks a little neater than usual."

Alex is dressed in his uniform. He is a Black Sheep but, unlike Tim, I couldn't lure him back into the fold. He lost family like the rest of us in the Schism. His father Don saved my life and Alex kept up the tradition. He got me out of town when the worst of the Schism was going down. He saved me later, too, when I came back from

Hell, thinking I had failed in my Orpheus Maneuver, and lost Lissa. Without his help, Australia really would have sunk into a Regional Apocalypse. I feel a bit guilty that I haven't been keeping in touch with him nearly enough. But seeing him always reminds me of Don, and my parents, and Don's girlfriend Sam. I can't help wondering what he thinks when he sees me. He's my link into the Queensland Police Force. I trust him almost as much as I trust Tim.

"So this is the first time this has happened?" he asks.

"Well, not exactly." I glance at Alex, we've been through a few bad times together. He knows that I've been shot at before. "Not since October, and the Schism."

"Two months." He shakes his head.

"Yeah, no wonder I was getting used to not being shot at."

"You're understandably shaky."

"No, I'm pissed off. It happens whenever people start shooting at me. Bloody hell, Alex, don't pull this shit on me. I don't need you telling me I'm all right feeling nervous. I need to know what's going on."

Alex sits down. "I'm more worried about this than you could believe. People shooting at you tends to lead to scary places." Right now, the way Alex grits his jaw brings Don back to me. I miss the old bugger. I miss them all. "You've an alarming tendency to draw trouble to you, Steven."

"I'm trying not to make it a habit."

"Yeah, I know. I want to help you with this but I've been told explicitly that this isn't my area. They've got someone else in mind. The moment Tim called for help—"

"What? Tim called who?" He was only supposed to call Doug. I guess he's just used to thinking for me.

"Me, but once he did, I had to alert my bosses. Major incidents are flagged, and someone trying to kill the current RM is a major incident, now." Alex sighed. "I know you like to sort out your disputes inhouse. But after Morrigan... Well, you know, the rules have changed."

"So who are they sending in?"

"A new group, federal not state. Still police, though. I hadn't heard about them until about an hour before I came over here." Alex scowls. "They're called Closers. Seem to know an awful lot about you."

So, another government department. I'll get Tim to do some digging.

There's always someone poking around here. Unofficially, of course, because the work we do at Mortmax can't be official. Unofficially we could tell them to piss off, but unofficially they could cause a lot of trouble for us.

"I hate this," I say. "Bloody governments."

"They're not too fond of Mortmax, either. Look, the paint hasn't even dried on this department yet. None of them will have much experience in dealing with the things that are dumped on their desks."

"So why aren't people like you involved?"

"Why do you think?"

"You're regarded as compromised? Guilt by association." I frown. "Don't they trust you at work anymore, Alex?"

Alex scowls. "If you were doing your—"

"What? If we were doing our jobs properly? Is that what you're saying?" I look at my ruined office, the blood, the paper blown everywhere. He kind of has a point. "I'm not here to bend over for every government department."

Alex grins. "Not every department, mate. Just one from now on." His face grows more serious. "Steven, be careful. People aren't over the moon with what's happening here. I've been hearing things."

"You can't be serious. Morrigan was responsible for all of it." I fix him with as severe a stare as I can manage. "What sort of things?"

"Nothing specific. Just that no one was happy to have a Regional Apocalypse at their doorstep. They're blaming you."

"I had nothing to do with it." I straighten in my throne, slam my foot down on the floor and remember why I'm sitting here in the first place. *Fuck, that hurts.*

"Doesn't matter, Mortmax did, and you're running the Australian branch. You're responsible as far as people are concerned. And they don't think you're doing such a great job."

"If they want to have a go at running death, let them." My bluster is just that, though, and Alex knows it.

"Perhaps you shouldn't be so bloody glib, mate."

"Yeah, well, I've got eight stitches in my foot, and a bit of my ear is missing. Inappropriate glibness is all I have." We glare at each other.

There's a knock on the door.

A man peers through at Alex and me. An Akubra hat obscures his features. Most people can't pull that look off, but he manages it, somehow. It's the broad shoulders, the skin just on the flesh side of leather. He doffs the wide-brimmed hat, scratches his head. The hair beneath is clipped to within a breath of shaved; a band of sweat rings it. Dark eyes peer at me through thickish metal-rimmed glasses. I can't tell what he's thinking, but his heart beats slow and steady.

"Can I join the party?" he asks, and smiles warmly.

Alex glances at me, gives me a we'll-talk-later kind of face.

"Yeah, absolutely," I say. "There's room for everyone. Once I know just who they are."

"Of course, of course. I thought you knew I was coming. Detective Magritte Solstice," he says. "I'll be running this investigation." He shakes my hand. It's one of those firm but slightly threatening grips that suggests a lot more strength could be applied—if needed.

"Can't say I'm pleased to meet you."

Solstice's laugh is warm and deep. "No one ever is under these situations." He looks over at Alex. "That's all for now, Sergeant."

"Yes, Sergeant," I say. "It's time for the grown-ups to talk."

Alex nods, gives me a little (and very ironic) salute and gets out of there.

Solstice shuts the door behind him. The smile slips a little. "Now, to get the shit out of the way before it stinks up the room, if you have any problems you call me. I know he's your friend, but this isn't Alex's specialty." Solstice hands me a card with his name and number on it, and a symbol of three dots making an equilateral triangle. It reminds me of the brace symbol we use to block Stirrers. "My group runs these investigations."

"You're the Closers?"

Solstice blinks at that. I'm happy to wrong-foot him

a little. "Yeah, it's our job to close doors that shouldn't have been opened in the first place."

"A bit poetic, isn't it?"

Solstice grimaces. "I didn't come up with the name. Our job is to work with organizations like yours, off the public record, of course."

"Well, off the record, what do you really think you're doing?"

"Fixing your fuck-ups."

"That's good to know," I say. "Puts everything into context."

"All right. So where did it happen? Scene of the crime and all that."

"You're looking at it," I say, waving at the room. Solstice lifts an eyebrow.

"I'm sorry, but the window's self-healing. The body's missing, too. It went back to wherever it came from. It was a professional hit, but it didn't work out too well for the professionals."

"At least no one was hurt."

"Much," I say.

He looks at me.

"No one was hurt *much*," I say.

"What's wrong with you?" Solstice asks. "You look fine to me."

"Yeah, now I do."

"Stop your complaining."

I frown at him.

"Oh, sorry. Stop your complaining, *sir*." Solstice walks around my desk and stares at "The Triumph of Death." It was Mr. D's particular obsession: death at war with life, a vast wave of skeletons breaking over the world. Mr. D said he found it soothing. I don't know about that, but it is something. "Isn't *this* a bit much?"

"Look, I didn't buy it." (Actually, I don't think Mr. D *bought* it, either.) "But you have to admit it's funny in this context."

Solstice peers at all the mayhem on the panel. "If you say so." He walks to the window and pushes his face against the glass. "So the body fell...? Where am I looking?"

"That's Hell," I say, pouring myself a glass of rum. "You're looking into Hell."

Solstice blinks. "Remarkable. It's not exactly what I was expecting."

"It never is." I offer him a drink.

He shakes his head. "On duty, and all that." He goes back to peering out the window.

He jabs a thumb down. "So the body struck the ground and it disappeared?"

"Yeah, someone cut the rope a few moments after I'd knocked him out."

Solstice looks at me. "You knocked him out?"

"I got lucky."

"Very lucky." He scrawls something in his notebook. "So someone cut the rope. Are you sure you weren't that someone?"

"Very sure. I wanted to know what he was doing. Why he was there, and how."

"Couldn't you have just asked his ghost? Maybe killing him was an easier, safer way of getting the information you required."

I shook my head. "It doesn't work like that, not as neatly anyway. I pomped the soul, and the body returned to wherever it was when it entered Hell."

"You didn't think to ask the spirit any questions?"

"Oh, I tried, but with a death that violent, the soul just usually blazes through. I didn't get much more than rage and anger at being betrayed, I guess, and then I was losing consciousness myself."

I hobble over to the window beside Solstice. Stare down. "What I want to know is how a living person ended up out there."

"Is it really that odd? I mean, I'm here right now, aren't I?"

"It's remarkable, all right," I say. "In here you're not really in Hell, just a point that juts into Hell, and even that involves quite a bit of power. Two worlds are mixing here, and it's not a very good mix. A lot of people have trouble with this room; they get all sorts of migraines, dizzy spells. It's why we do our job interviews here. If you can't cope with the energies in this room, you really shouldn't become a Pomp. You're handling it very well, Detective."

Solstice rubs the bridge of his nose. "Hm. I do have a bit of a headache, but that could be just the condition I suffer from."

"What's that?"

"Hypochondria."

Yeah, funny guy. I point down at the footpath. "Down there. To get down there with the possibility of returning involves serious pain. The Underworld doesn't like life, just afterlife. Its barriers are permeable, but not without incredible effort, arcane knowledge, and a lot of blood."

"Blood?"

"Yeah, you need to die and not die. It's about as easy as it sounds, believe me."

Solstice's pen gets to work again in his notebook. He

has a swift, neat writing style—a dot-the-"i"s-cross-the-"t"s sort of thing. "Well, he didn't stay living for long." Solstice scratches the bridge of his nose. "But then that seems to be something that happens to people who spend any time with you, doesn't it?"

"What are you implying?"

Solstice grins. "Nothing at all."

"I honestly don't know how you're going to uncover anything," I say. "There's no body that we could find. Who knows where it is? Number Four is healing itself, and we've never used closed circuit TV here."

"You leave that to me," Solstice says. "There's a body somewhere. And there will be a gun."

"I don't know about that—oh, sorry, Detective, just a condition I suffer from."

"Yeah, and that is?" he asks.

"Pessimism."

"I like you already," Solstice says, patting me on the back. His rolled-up shirt sleeve slips back to reveal a rather large tattoo.

I get a good look at it before Solstice pulls down his sleeve in what must be an automatic gesture. I'm not sure how they regard tatts in the force.

"You'd make a good Pomp," I say, nodding at his arm.

"What? Oh, yeah." Seeing no point in hiding it, he grins a little crookedly and pulls up his sleeve to reveal more. A dragon extends all the way along his forearm, the tail disappearing under the fabric. Its scales are a luminous green, narrow red eyes stare at me, and a tiny puff of smoke curls from its nostrils.

"Nice work isn't it?" Solstice says. "Guy who did it won a lot of awards."

"Yeah. Your own design?"

Solstice dips his head. "A little bit Tolkien, a little bit Chinese. I call it Smauget."

I'm not about to compare tatts. Wal isn't quite as fierce, and his creation was less considered, more alcohol-fueled.

Solstice peers at his phone. "No bloody signal."

Closers certainly don't have access to a phone network as good as ours.

Solstice reaches over to the black phone in the middle of my messy desk. "Mind if I make a call?"

"Not with that, you won't." I lift up the tattered end of the phone cord, bits of rusty wire jutting out.

"What is it then, a paperweight?"

"Internal line," I say with a lame grin. I'm not about to tell him it's a direct line to my old boss, Mr. D. The fewer people who know, or even suspect, that he's still about, the better.

Solstice nods his head and glances at his watch. "I'm going to have to leave. Believe it or not we have more than one case."

"You Closers," I say, "you're a big department?"

"Big enough."

"Why haven't I heard of you until today?"

"You've never needed to." He glances at his card on my desk. "You call me if anything happens."

"I will."

He slips on his Akubra. "And try not to give us any more work."

10

Tim and I meet at a park in the leafy suburb of Paddington, near enough to some decent pubs if we feel so inclined. It's a meeting place that we use if we want a little privacy. And I'm not sure who I can trust in the office right now; most of my staff are brand new. But last time we met here I was on the run for my life and Lissa was dead, so things could be much worse. Silver lining, right?

After two months of being ignored, the afternoon had seen a flood of RM visitors. I'm not sure if it was because I've finally peformed the Convergence Ceremony, or that I was shot at by an unknown assassin, but they certainly didn't talk much about the latter.

China's RM, Li An, was the first to visit. He surprised me; just sat down across from me and didn't say a word. His eyes fixed on me.

I didn't know what to say, I just stared right back. Finally, after twenty minutes, his lips just hinting at a smile, Li An nodded his head and stood. I shook his hand. It was dry, and just a little cold.

"I think she made the right choice. It was a pleasure getting to know you, Mr. de Selby," he said. Then he shifted out before I could ask him what he was talking about.

East Europe's RM, Madeleine Danning, came and gave me a pot of daisies. "They'll look good in the corner, over there. But you mustn't forget to water them. I always thought they'd cheer this place up."

England's RM, Anna Kranski, wanted to talk early Hitchcock films, and was mortified that I hadn't watched *The 39 Steps*.

No one suggested any deals. Not Kiri Baker from New Zealand. Not Devesh Singh from India. No one made any offers. I didn't know how to take it. This was the Orcus. These were the Deaths of the world, and I was treated with nothing but the utmost politeness.

Those who did talk were anxious about the Death Moot. Had the Caterers hinted at what they were doing this time? Was the bridge prepared? Which bridge was it exactly?

The fact that it was a footbridge seemed to impress Japan's RM, Tae Sato. "A good omen," he said. "You'll find it to be a good omen."

Charlie Top, Middle Africa's RM, was also pleased.

All this RM happiness. And there I was with that image in my head of them at the Negotiation: the hungry gleam, bordering on naked bloodlust, in their eyes.

The only two RMs who didn't visit were Neill Debbier and Suzanne. I didn't know what that meant, but by the time I was ready to leave my office I was tired and didn't really want to know.

"You're one of the club now," Tim says leaning back on the bonnet of his car. "It's a good thing."

He passes me a beer, and I twist off the cap. "Yeah, but none of them wanted to talk about the attempt on my life."

"Maybe it's more common than you think."

"No, Mr. D would have mentioned it." *Or would he?*

The sun's set, but the night is slow in cooling, the air close and thick. We used to sneak off to this park and smoke. Tim's furiously working his way through a packet of cigarettes between mouthfuls of VB. I'm not such a fan of the beer—I like my Fourex—but at least it's cold. Our stubbies are beaded with beerish sweat. I could do with something stronger though.

"So who do you think's responsible?" Tim asks. "Stirrers?"

"No, I'd have sensed them if it was. We all would have."

Tim nods. You can smell and feel a Stirrer from a long way off. Their presence pulls at the throat, burns the nose like a bad chemical. There's been enough Stirrers rising to get us far too used to the sensation.

"I've been dreaming about Morrigan, lately. Maybe..."

Tim leans in toward me, eyes hard. "No, he's gone. You told me that yourself. He's deader than dead." His voice is strident, but he looks like he needs reassurance.

"Yeah, I saw him die. He's gone. Would have been easier though, knowing it was him."

Tim shakes his head, jabs his beer in my face. "Morrigan was a devious, murdering prick. Don't you dare wish him back on us!"

I draw back at his vehemence. "No, they were just dreams. That's all, they can't be anything else. So where does that leave us?"

"One of the Orcus, then?" he suggests.

"But which RM wants me dead? All the RMs are capable of it, but I don't think it's one of them. And certainly not after this afternoon. It's in the Orcus's interests to maintain stability. And I think if one wanted me dead, well, they wouldn't screw it up so badly, and they wouldn't be so underhanded about it." I glance at Tim. "Do you think Solstice will have any luck?"

Tim shrugs. "Those guys know less about our organization than we do."

I fix him with a stare. "How long have *you* known about these Closers?"

"Not too long. Actually, I thought they were a bit of a joke." Tim takes a slow mouthful of beer. "What they've done is built on an idea I had years ago at the department— a group to actually work in tandem with Mortmax, to help out if the Stirrers ever became too much of a problem. I thought it would be a good thing, maybe increase the flow of information between both sides, and reduce some of the fear. But they've started it too late."

"You didn't think it worth your while to give me a heads-up about it?"

"Like I said, I thought they were a bit of a joke, though I've changed my mind, now. A scared government is a dangerous government."

I glower at him. It's bad enough feeling the scrutiny of the Orcus without knowing the federal government is looking into us, too. There was a time when no government would even consider questioning our actions. Trust them to decide otherwise when I'm in charge.

Something crunches in the undergrowth close to us. Tim and I spin toward the sound.

"Down," I say, and Tim drops behind his car.

I can hear a heartbeat. It's racing, and it's not Tim's. I grab the only weapon at hand, my stubby. The heartbeat is coming from behind a nearby tree. Taking a deep breath, I rush toward it and catch sight of a dim shape there, a large figure, hunched down.

There's a flash. I hurl my stubby at the form. Beer splashes back at me. Glass shatters.

There's no detonation of a gun firing. No bullets penetrating my thick skull. The heartbeat is gone. I scramble around the tree.

Nothing. Just a torch, its beam directed at my feet—the source of the flash, I guess. I can feel the residual warmth of a body from where it had leaned against the tree, and the slight electrical residue of a shift. It's less than the memory of a ghost post-Pomp.

Whoever was here is good. They know how to hide their movements, even if they're heavy on their feet.

"It's all right," I yell at Tim, holding the torch in the air.

He gets up and curses. Seems he threw himself onto his packet of cigarettes. Every single one of them is bent or broken.

"At least you're not drenched with beer," I say.

Tim grins staring at the mighty stain spreading across my trousers. "Are you sure that's beer?"

I give him the most sarcastic smile I can. "Who the hell was that?"

"Now, *that* could have been one of the RMs, or an Ankou. Spying on us, maybe wondering why the hell we were out here."

"They know how little we know then, if that's the case."

After another drink we've relaxed a little, and the beer down the front of me has evaporated. I might smell like a brewery but at least I'm dry. I've had two texts from Lissa, asking where I am, and I'll respond to them soon.

"We're going to need someone to watch your place," Tim says. "You'll want Lissa close."

"What about you?" I ask.

"I'll organize some security for us all." He straightens a cigarette.

"Just how effective can security be if whoever is after me can shift?"

"Look, we don't even know if these two incidents are connected. If they were, why didn't they just shift into your office this morning? A bit of protection is better than nothing. And trust me, the guys I've got in mind are *far* better than nothing. They're prepared for this sort of thing."

"Really?"

"You're so used to dealing with this through Mortmax that you've forgotten that other people work to fill the gap. These guys are like this. I've used them before—my old department had the occasional bit of trouble."

"If you say they're good enough. I trust you. I just wish—"

"What are wishes going to get you?" Tim asks. "This is happening. You are who you are, and you have to act appropriately."

"Sorry," I say.

"For what?"

"For bringing you into whatever the hell this is."

Tim shakes his head. "Steve, you didn't bring me into the last Schism. This is as much a part of my heritage as it is yours. I may have turned my back on it, but it wasn't you who forced me to return. That bastard's dead, dreams or no dreams." He pats my arm. "How are you coping?"

I want to tell him that I'm not, that I'm drowning in my responsibilities and inadequacies, and now someone is trying to kill me as well. That when I close my eyes, dreams pound into me like the laughing waves of some gore-soaked sea.

"I'm doing OK." I grin. "Hey, I'm head of an Australia-wide branch of an international company, and a profitable one at that."

"Yes, we're living the dream," Tim says sardonically. He picks out the least damaged cigarette. "God help us." He lights up. "I've got to get going. Sally has bridge tonight, I have to look after the kids."

"Be careful," I say.

"If the last few months have taught me anything, it's exactly that." He smiles. "I'll be careful, and you, too. Don't go running into anything without letting me know—and even then, maybe think before you run."

11

Tim's bodyguards stand outside my parents' place. Dad wouldn't have tolerated this. Mom would have laughed, maybe made a reference to Whitney Houston and Kevin Costner.

They're two burly guys who Lissa tells me are called Travis and Oscar. Both of them arrived about twenty minutes before me. Tim doesn't mess around. I rather suspect he had this organized well before he broached the subject with me. They are armed and stationed at opposite ends of the house. Oscar's at least my height, and nearly that wide, but it's all muscle. Travis is even bigger. I'm not too sure about all this, having guns in and around the house—they're nothing but trouble. Dr. Brooker's right about that much.

I've drawn enough souls, who were killed by guns, to the Underworld, been nearly killed by guns myself. But this time I suppose they're a necessary evil. Doesn't mean I have to like it.

We've just finished dinner, and I'm on my third beer,

helping with the washing up (Dad didn't believe in dish-washing machines) when Lissa fixes me with a peculiar, disappointed stare. "When were you going to tell me about Suzanne's deal?"

I lift my foot with exaggerated care, even groan a little, but it doesn't cut it as a sympathy maker. Lissa's hands are on her hips now, and she's scowling at me.

I drop the scrubbing brush into the sink and stop myself from asking who told her. "Look, I've been a little distracted of late."

"I know, but this is big. You're talking about the most influential member of the Orcus. What does she want with you?"

"She's going to give me ten Pomps to supplement our numbers, and all I have to give her is ten hours of my time."

"I don't like it. Suzanne could do a lot with ten hours."

"Not nearly as much as you, my dear." I know I've said the wrong thing at once. I narrowly avoid a tea towel in the eye.

"She has a reputation, you know."

I feel my face flush. "You've got nothing to worry about."

"Don't tell me what I do and don't have to worry about."

"Hang on, you wanted me to get involved, to work harder. And that's what I'm doing, isn't it?"

"I don't trust her, and you shouldn't either. The woman's a scheming bitch!"

That vehemence in Lissa's voice gets my attention. *What has Suzanne done to her?*

"Think about it," she says. "They're pushing so hard.

The phone call at 2:30 in the morning. The meeting in the Deepest Dark. Cerbo's offer—and then someone starts shooting at you."

"Lissa, they're Americans. They're brash, they're proud."

"Exactly. And who loves guns more?" She hangs up the tea towel.

"No, I'm willing to accept that they're playing at something, but the shooting, it's got to be a coincidence. Maybe it's something to do with the Death Moot. Maybe it's something to do with the Stirrer god—perhaps it has other agents here. What I know for certain is that we need more Pomps. Look at what it's doing to you. Look at your palms."

I know how much they must hurt. When Morrigan started his Schism, and as the Stirrers stepped up their invasion, my hands became open sores. And then there was the consequence of pomping itself—the psychic pain and damage. With every pomp it built until you felt as though you were being scratched from the inside out. Things weren't that bad, but they could be better.

"I'm all right," she says. "Things are improving."

I lean in to kiss her but she pulls away.

"I don't think you should do it. Just tell her to piss off."

"I'll take that into consideration," I say.

Lissa scowls at me. "RMs are devious, and she's worse than all of them combined."

I need those Pomps. Ten more workers could make a real difference. Lissa can obviously see me thinking this; I'm certainly not one of those devious RMs. She takes a deep breath.

"Look, I'm serious, that woman slept with my father.

It's all I can do not to hit her when I see her. It didn't stop Mom."

"*What?*" Seems Lissa's just as good at keeping secrets as I am.

"It's a small world in any corporation. It happened twelve years ago, at a Death Moot in San Francisco. Steven, it nearly destroyed my parents' marriage. It certainly scarred it. I don't want that woman having anything to do with you."

"But you can't think—"

Lissa glares at me.

"I mean, I love you. I'd never do anything to jeopardize that. But—"

Lissa's glare burns into me like the light of a very attractive but blazing sun. I'm withering beneath it.

"OK," I say. "I promise I won't agree to her offer without letting you know."

That seems enough for now. I hobble to the couch with her and we snuggle and watch a DVD. She's asleep before the first scene is even finished. I stroke her hair for a while, she snorts in her sleep, and I ease myself out from under her. I'll wake her in an hour or so. I switch off the DVD, surprised that the sudden silence doesn't drag her from her dreams.

I'm in trouble. I need those Pomps and I need what Suzanne can give me: her experience. Mr. D isn't enough, already he is distanced from the game, and from what I've read, and Suzanne's comments, he was always a little isolated. If I don't know what I'm doing, and why, there's no way that I'm ever going to run my region well.

But I don't want to hurt Lissa. She stirs in her sleep,

frowns as though my plans are already upsetting her. My heart twists in my chest. There has to be a way I can keep this from her, and reduce the capability of Suzanne's Pomps to spy on me. The new ten could service some of the regional areas, with a couple more surreptitiously inserted into the Sydney and Perth offices. Those are the two that Lissa knows least of all. If I can keep them out of Brisbane I should be all right.

And Lissa has been on at me to keep practicing my shifts. It's not as though she can tell where I'm going. With the preparations for the Death Moot, I'm going to have to be moving about.

Yeah, I think I can do this.

I grab my mobile, fast, before I can change my mind and text Suzanne: *Yes.*

A text hits my phone.

Suzanne Whitman.

No time 2 waste. We might as well start now.

"I can't see why not," I say out loud.

"I thought you'd say that," Suzanne says from behind me.

What? I spin and face her. Her presence strikes me hard, burns into my skull.

I glance over at Lissa—still sleeping on the couch, thank Christ. In fact, she's rolled away from Suzanne like a sleeper might from a cold draft.

"Get out of here, now," I hiss, nodding toward Lissa.

Suzanne smiles. "Keeping secrets, eh?"

"Deepest Dark, ten minutes."

Suzanne is gone.

I walk over to Lissa, crouch down and shake her, gently.

Her eyes open.

"I have to go out for a little while. Didn't want you to panic if you woke up and I wasn't here."

She yawns. "What?"

"I have a meeting."

"With who?"

"Cerbo." Well, that's almost the truth.

"What does he want?" Her eyes narrow.

"That's what I'm going to find out. It'll be about Suzanne's offer at a guess."

She purses her lips. "Don't trust her, or him. Never trust another RM or their Ankou. There's always a bigger game at play."

"I know."

I lift her up gently, she rests her head in the hollow of my neck. All I can smell is her hair. How does it always smell so good?

"I love you," she says into my shoulder.

"Love you, too," I whisper. She's already asleep, poor tired baby.

I carry her to the bedroom, pull the sheets over her, and set the ceiling fan on high. After a quick peck on her cheek I direct a crow to circle above, to monitor the front and the back of the house. Oscar and Travis are still there. Neither seem to have noticed Suzanne's sudden appearance. I really wonder how effective they are going to be.

At least the contact with my Avian Pomp hasn't given me a migraine this time. Must be getting better. Of course I'm probably heading into a much bigger headache with Suzanne.

12

The Deepest Dark is just as cold as the last time we met here. We're a little closer to the city of Devour. Lights are flashing there, and it's toward them that Suzanne is staring as I arrive. This shift is a particularly bad one. I'm a few minutes catching my breath. But at least there's no vomit. Gotta love that.

"Something's happening over there," Suzanne says. She's wearing my duffel coat. I can't quite bring myself to ask for it back.

"That's usually a good thing isn't it?" I watch the lurid fires burn. "If it's happening here, it's not happening in the living world."

"You'd think so, but their focus is only on our world. Anything happening down here has consequences for up there."

"What do you think it is?"

Suzanne shrugs. "I have my spies and, of course, I will inform the Orcus of anything that they uncover."

"Spies?"

Suzanne smiles. "This is your first lesson, I suppose. The Underworld is more permeable than you might think. Stirrers can enter our world through the agency of a corpse. Well, we can enter theirs, too. It doesn't always work, but I have received some very good information before my spies have been discovered. And they always are. Just as a Stirrer takes a while to get used to a human body, a human takes a while to get used to a Stirrer's."

"You're telling me they actually enter a Stirrer body?" All bony limbs, cavernous eyes and sharkish teeth; what would it be like to inhabit such a form?

"Yes, remarkable isn't it? And you're already learning something."

"What's it like?"

"Horrifying. It changes people. The ones I've managed to bring back, anyway. They're different, life becomes less appealing to them, more wretched. Let me just say that they don't tend to stay in the organization for very long."

I try and imagine how it must be, trying to make a life in that city. Being so deep undercover that the very smell and essence of life disgusts you. Does the reverse happen? Do Stirrers learn to love life as we do? I've not seen it.

I wonder if she mightn't also use those spies for assassination attempts. Say, on RMs. I'm starting to feel a little uncomfortable out here in the open. If keeping face weren't so important I'd be away in a shot.

"And what happens when they're discovered?" I can't imagine ever sending anyone down there.

"The ones we get out? Well, they survive. But the others…" Suzanne shrugs. "Something horrible, I suspect. They don't get to make a report afterward, Steven. This is the Deepest Dark, after all. You don't play around down here unless you're hungry for pain or retribution." Suzanne touches my arm. "You should understand that."

"Is that what you do?" I ask. "Play around down here?"

"It's much more serious than that. I'm as concerned by the Stirrers' plans as you are. Things are in motion, believe me. But we'll leave that for the Death Moot, not now."

Where her fingers touch me is the only warmth in this place, and she leaves them there too long. I pull away, but perhaps not fast enough. Hell, I shouldn't be worrying about what is fast or not. I should be focusing on her conversation. She's watching me, waiting for a response. And I already feel outplayed. "I'm not one for waiting."

"Six days isn't very long." Suzanne's tone suggests she's talking to a five year old, any more patronizing and she'd be handing me a lollipop. "Now, let me say how horrified I was to hear of the attempt on your life." She closes her eyes a moment. The air glows, dust swirls around us, becoming a round table and two chairs. She gestures at one of the chairs. "Sit, sit."

I touch the chair tentatively. It feels solid enough. I sit down and it takes my weight. I want to ask her just how she does this, but now isn't the right time. There are more important things before us.

"Steven, you made a lot of enemies when you performed that Orpheus Maneuver of yours."

"I had a lot of enemies already."

"But these are of greater consequence. You broke rules, you performed the impossible, and that scares people. Does the name Francis Rillman mean anything to you?"

Rillman. Where have I heard that name? "It sounds familiar."

Suzanne nods her head. "It should. He was Australia's Ankou before Morrigan, and a major embarrassment to Mr. D. His disgrace is an important, some might even go so far as to say tragic, part of your corporate history. It's what allowed Morrigan to do what he did. Certainly gave him ideas."

"Maybe that's why his name only sounds familiar. Morrigan didn't like to share information, not the important stuff anyway."

"Yes, well, he was partly involved in Rillman's downfall. And his downfall certainly led to Morrigan's rise." Suzanne sighed. "Francis Rillman, like you, performed an Orpheus Maneuver after his wife died. Only he failed, utterly and terribly. I thought he was dead, but the name's been surfacing lately. And more often than not it's been around you." She sighs. "I rather believe that Rillman wants you dead."

"Why? Why would someone I don't even know want me dead?"

"Because you did what he couldn't, and Rillman is a bitter creature."

"I'll dig around in the files," I say.

Suzanne clicks her tongue. "I hate to say it, Steven, but Mr. D should be educating you more thoroughly. Take this to Mr. D. He's the only one 'alive' in your organization who knows the full story."

The next hour or so is taken up with a series of lessons echoing Tim's briefing notes: short histories of my fellow RMs, things I should have known, things Mr. D should have taught me. I'm wary though, this is only Suzanne's perspective. After the Moot, when I have time (ha!) I'm going to talk to each and every RM, draw out their stories, and put what Suzanne has told me into context.

The lesson's interrupted by a cry from the Stirrer city. A packed-stadium sort of roaring—if a stadium was full of meth-addicted berserkers. Suzanne and I both turn toward the sound.

Suzanne shakes her head. "OK, looks like class is over for the night. Do you want to check that out?"

"Why not?" We get up and the table and chairs return to dust.

She holds my hand. "Don't pull away," she says. "I thought I would spare you the pain of a shift."

"I can do it myself." But we're already there.

So that's how it should feel. I think I can copy that, model my own shifts on it. Suzanne nods at me. "Get the basics right, and everything else will follow."

We're at a point just outside Devour's walls. The city didn't have these when I was last here—riding a whispering bike on my way to find my lost love—but the Deepest Dark, like the Underworld, changes fast.

I place a hand against one of the huge stone blocks. It's cold and shuddering in time with the Stirrers' yells. I realize Suzanne's still holding my hand. I try and pull away. "Not yet."

Another shift. We're on the walls, all that juddering stone beneath us.

We crouch down and stare into the city, which is really the wrong term for the spaces open before us, though there are structures analogous to our cities. It's more of a nest, a nexus of hunger. Below us, hundreds of Stirrers have gathered in a circle, their teeth-crammed mouths chanting in utter synchronicity. They're as identical in appearance as ants, which is why the Stirrer in the center of the circle stands out. Its face warps, or unwarps, grows human. It is a face wracked with agony.

Suzanne squeezes my hand.

"One of yours?" I ask.

She nods.

I look around for some way to get down to her spy and for a possible escape route once we do. "We have to get him out of there."

Suzanne shakes her head. "We can't do anything, not here. Not now." She lets go of my arm. "You need to leave."

"What are you going to do?"

"Bear witness." She glares at me. "Go."

The man in the center of the circle screams, and I feel a force push at me: Suzanne. I give in to it. But not before seeing the man's long limbs torn from him and thrown out into the crowd. The Stirrers howl.

The shift to my parents' living room is easier than I was expecting, but I bring that howl with me. I blink, let my eyes adjust to the light, and slump into the couch.

Poor bastard.

Oscar's standing out the front. I can hear Travis's heartbeat coming from the back. The pair's heartbeats tell me all I need to know. Nothing has happened since I left. Still, I go and check on Lissa.

She's sleeping.

Then I call Tim.

"Do you know what time it is?" he grumbles.

"Yeah, I'm sorry, but I've got a lead."

"And Lissa's obviously sleeping." He yawns. "So what's this lead?"

"Francis Rillman. Mean anything to you?"

"Not a thing." He sighs. "Actually…It does sound familiar."

"It should. He used to have your job."

"Ministerial advisor?"

"No, your job here." I run through what Suzanne has just told me.

"Really? Shit. *Now* I remember the name. Something my dad used to say when I was grumpy. Don't chuck a Rillman. Never understood what it meant. Let me Google him." He sighs again. "So how do you spell Rillman?"

"The usual way," I answer.

Tim groans. "Don't be a smart-arse."

I spell it out. "Anything?"

"Nothing, but give me some time. If he's out there, I'll find him. Keep safe."

"You too."

I hang up; make my way back to the bedroom.

I need Lissa. Right then I need her more than anything. I kiss her. Gentle and hard on the lips, her mouth responds. Her tongue searches mine. I slide a hand down her neck, slowly, and she pulls me in close. Eyes opening.

And for the first time in what feels like weeks, we really connect.

"What was that about?" she asks when we're finally still, sweat-drenched.

"I love you."

"Well, duh." She stretches, and I can't help but stroke one of her breasts gently with a fingertip. She pushes my hand away—after a while. "How was your meeting?"

"Informative."

"And Suzanne's offer?"

"I don't know." The lie sticks in my throat.

"Suzanne is like that. She has a way of confusing the issues." Lissa clicks her tongue. "Are our heavies still outside?"

"Yeah."

"How long is this going to go on, Steve?"

"A while, I think. I've got a bit of a lead though, someone by the name of Francis Rillman."

"Did you say Rillman?"

"Yes."

"It can't be him. I pomped him two weeks ago."

"Are you sure?" I slide out of bed, disappointed. Rillman looked promising, and I want this over with.

"We had a chat. He's an interesting character. You know he tried an Orpheus Maneuver once. His wife, he lost his wife. And he failed to bring her back."

"I'm aware of that."

"Maybe, but did you know he failed because Mr. D stopped him?"

I nod toward the kitchen, slipping on some boxers. "Coffee? I think I need to be properly awake to get my head around this."

Lissa laughs. "You're supposed to offer that *before* the lovemaking." She gets up and pulls a dressing gown around her shoulders.

The kitchen is quiet but for the heavy breathing of the espresso machine. I pour two cups. Why is Suzanne so sure it's Rillman if he's dead? Where does that leave me? I've got two suspects as far as I can see: Rillman who is dead, and Morrigan who is beyond dead. It's easier to believe that Suzanne is trying something.

Shit, I am so bad at this!

Lissa watches me as I set the cups down on the table.

"So Rillman, what'd he look like?" I ask, pushing her cup toward her.

She brings it to her lips, sips contemplatively. "Nothing much. Bland, unmemorable. I know that sounds glib, but..." She furrows her brow. "Tired, he looked tired, washed out. His hair was short, parted to one side. Wait a minute, there was one thing." She reaches up and touches my nose. Her fingertips are warm and I blink at the contact. "His nose was broken, not badly, but you could tell someone had given him a mighty whack once."

"Maybe Mr. D?" Though I can't imagine Mr. D ever hitting anyone.

"Yeah, possibly. He asked about you. Seemed very interested in what you did. Hey, I might have a photo!"

Lissa runs out of the kitchen. I hear her digging around in the bedroom, then a cry of triumph. She comes back holding a photo album, open to a page. "Here, here they are! Mom, Dad and Rillman."

Lissa's description is apt. He's plain, all right, not unhandsome, I suppose. But in this photo he's smiling, and there's not a glint of murderous intent. His arms are around another woman, tall, dark hair down to her shoulders. She's smiling, too. Happy days.

"Is that his wife?"

"Yes," Lissa says. "I can't remember her name."

No one remembers names, just the tragedies. What must it be like to fail at an Orpheus Maneuver? Not just fail, but be stopped? I understand him a little, I think. Suddenly I have to hold Lissa. I kiss her hard.

"What was that about?" she asks when I let her go, but I know she gets it too. She has to, right?

I look back at the photo. "Did he seem angry at all?"

"No, more resigned. I got the feeling the angry part of him was long gone. And you know how souls are, they're a bit insipid, bloodless."

I reach across the table and touch her arm. "You weren't."

Lissa smiles. "But that's just me, I'm special."

"You are. You don't know how much you are."

Lissa shakes her head, but she isn't one for false modesty. "I should have paid more attention to him, but it was a busy day. I think I must have pomped eight people that afternoon. Rillman was the last."

"I'd have been the same. Strange, though—-everything that I've been hearing seems to suggest Rillman could be behind the attack."

"Where'd his name come up?"

"Something Mr. D said," I lie, and it's easier than I thought it would be. Like shifting, I'm getting better with practice.

"Really?"

"Yeah, why not? He's *supposed* to be teaching me something."

"It's just...Mr. D doesn't like to talk about Rillman. It's a generational thing, none of them did. Rillman apparently put Mortmax Australia about ten years behind the rest of the world." She grins. "Oh, yeah, he also ruined a Death Moot."

"I like the sound of this guy."

"It was quite the scandal."

"Well, the chances of it being Rillman are pretty slim," I say. "You don't come back."

Except we both know that isn't true. It makes me

uncomfortable to consider it, but somehow Rillman's death, his interest in me, make me certain he is the one responsible. That he has come back somehow. It feels right. It terrifies me. Before tonight I didn't know that humans could inhabit Stirrers. What's a little moving between worlds compared to that? Like Suzanne said, the Underworld is more permeable than I had thought. Who and what else might be coming through?

Lissa picks up her coffee cup and walks it to the sink. I can see her thoughts in the slope of her shoulders as she rinses the cup.

"It's OK," I say, kissing the back of her neck.

"I'm so sorry." She places the cup in the drainer. "Sometimes I think all this is my fault. If I hadn't—"

She's mirroring my thoughts. This isn't her fault, it's *mine*. I think about what Suzanne said. About the enemies I've made, and all because I fought to stay alive and honor the memory of my family, and because I loved someone enough to chase them through Hell and bring them back.

We saved each other. Whether it was the right thing or not, it was the only thing either of us would have done. And hang the consequences.

13

The office is quiet, predawn. I've a stack of files before me: Rillman, everything I could find on him. Which is virtually nothing. Who the fuck is Francis Rillman? What did he become?

Solstice had left a message on my phone, asking just this question, which is worrying and encouraging. Solstice obviously knows his job—and mine.

There's another half-bottle of rum sitting in my stomach. My head's spinning a bit. The throne might heal my wounds but it doesn't seem to do too much with alcohol until I stop drinking. I'm in my suit, my second-best one. I keep telling myself the drinking's not a problem when you're in a suit.

Fifty-nine people have died across Australia in the last hour. My ten new Pomps have taken some of the workload off my crew—Suzanne was exceptionally quick about organizing that—but the work is still constant. People are always dying.

And the phone calls have been pretty steady, too. RMs

or their Ankous. All of them wanting a piece of me, some favor, or their seat moved in the grand marquee of the meeting room.

I look at the calendar on my desk, pushing the rubbish off it. The Death Moot's drawing ever nearer. The catering's organized at least, and the location.

Of course, I could be dead by then.

I grab a sheet of paper, write *Francis Rillman?* in thick black pen. Then scrunch the sheet up and hurl it at my bin.

I'm going to have to go to the source for this one.

I pick up the handset of Mr. D's phone. Even though the line's dead I can feel the presence listening in on the other end. I play with the phone cord that spirals down to nothing, kind of a nervous thing.

"We need to talk," I say.

No response, but I know he's heard me.

"Now. We need to talk now."

"My boat," Mr. D says, his soft voice coming through like a slither of ice in my ear. There's slight irritation in his tone and I know that I've interrupted his reading. Well, too bad. His novels will be waiting for him when he gets back.

There's a click, and silence again. Seems I'll be fishing, literally and figuratively.

I send Lissa a text, tell her where I'm going. Then I take a deep breath, close my eyes and shift to Mr. D's boat.

Mr. D raises a hand in frustration as I throw my guts up over the edge of the rail—the other is gripping his fishing rod. "You're not practicing. You've got to keep practicing."

"I'm not enough of a masochist."

"Really?"

I hobble over to Mr. D across the broad wooden deck of his boat, the *Mary C*. My foot's throbbing. The wound's healing fast, but it still seems to be a case of my mind catching up with my body. My nose burns with the salt of the sea of Hell, which is better than the taste of vomit. "And I have been practicing!"

"Yes, well, this is the second time you've seen me in three days. One would think you were having troubles." He hands me a fishing rod. Wal's already holding his, knuckles white. He got it almost the moment he peeled from my flesh, seems to be enjoying the novelty of it all.

"Suzanne's made me an offer."

"An offer, eh?" Mr. D's eyes narrow as he connects the rod to a belt around my waist.

"I've taken it. Ten Pomps for ten hours with her. Ten hours of mentoring, of course. Nothing else, completely above board."

Mr. D stares out at the choppy water. I can't tell if he's hurt, or being melodramatic. His shifting face doesn't help either.

"We're stretched to capacity," I say.

"I don't need your excuses and you don't need her advice."

"Where the fuck am I going to get it?"

Mr. D rounds on me. "That hurts. That really hurts. I've been an endless fount of—"

"Bullshit."

Wal shakes his head at me sternly. Since when did these two become so pally?

"Sometimes I could just slap you, de Selby," Mr. D says.

"It doesn't work. Believe me, mate, I've tried it," Wal says.

"I'm not surprised," Mr. D says.

Yeah, the Steven de Selby fan club is in session. "Look, I don't really have time for this," I say between teeth so tightly clenched they're squeaking a little round the molars.

Wal rolls his eyes. Considering he doesn't really have any, it's impressive. "Christ, Steve, would you look at where we are?"

A long way from shore, I think.

Mr. D casts his line into the sea of Hell. The sinker plonks and plunges down, down, into what Mr. D calls the deep tract depths. Great shapes roll out of the luminous water: proto-whales and megalodon mainly, long ago extinct, but this is Hell, and Hell teems—there's really no other word for it—with such things. Extant memories, the seething echoes of other ages. I just wish that all the teeming stuff wasn't so bloody huge.

Mr. D assures me we're safe. After all, I'm the big boss around here. "Unlike those above, these seas are yours."

One of the perks of being RM. Nothing in Hell can touch me. But I'm not about to go for a dip. Wouldn't if you paid me, wouldn't if you gave me a cage to swim in.

I glance back across the bay toward the coastline, salt still stinging my eyes and burning my lungs. The One Tree rises on the distant shore, its great branches extending like a leafy mushroom cloud over the entire Underworld echo of Brisbane. But out here I can almost imagine that it's just a regular Moreton Bay fig in the distance. I peer over the edge of the boat, my free hand gripping the icy stainless steel rail.

A great sharky eye looks up at me. I swear it winks as it glides past.

I step away from the rail. "Um, pass me a beer…and maybe a bigger boat."

Mr. D digs around in the esky. "How many times do I have to tell you, de Selby? You're perfectly safe here on the *Mary C*." He slaps a cold one in my hand.

"You think you should be having that?" Wal asks, his lips pursed.

I shrug. "Hair of the dog."

Wal casts his line into the sea, his tiny wings flapping furiously. "Hair of the dog, my arse."

As usual I can see rather too much of his arse. His chubby baby fingers grip his fishing rod, and he hovers like an obese hummingbird. How's he going to cope if a fish takes the bait?

This is all looking like such a bad idea. I take a mouthful of whatever brew Mr. D could get on sale in Hell, some sort of generic brand that I've never heard of—Apsu Gold. It goes down pretty rough and bitter and tastes of ash in my mouth. Still, it's beer.

The boat rocks, shivers, judders, messes with my already impaired sense of balance. I swear it's moving in a dozen different directions at once. One of Charon's pilots is behind the wheel. Even he's looking a bit green. Of course, he's used to river traffic.

Mr. D has returned to his chipper and annoyingly distracted state. He sips on his beer politely and eats tiny sandwiches, cut into triangles. His rod is lodged casually under his right armpit. I've never known a more capable man who somehow manages to look like he doesn't have a clue.

Something tugs and I let it feed out, give it plenty of line. Mr. D doesn't mess around with his fishing gear. His beer might be cheap, but this is top-of-the-line Underworld equipment.

"So what has she told you? What has she said that has led you to me, your old boss, your *current* mentor?" Mr. D asks. I'm almost shocked by his directness. Finally.

"Francis Rillman," I say. "The name keeps cropping up."

Mr. D shakes his head. "That is one person I will not talk about."

"But he—"

"That bastard crossed me. He tried to tear down everything I had built and all…all for a woman."

Mr. D had a terrible track record with his Ankous. After all, Morrigan followed Rillman.

"I think he's trying to kill me. Suzanne says it's because I managed to pull off the Orpheus Maneuver."

Mr. D checks his line. "It may have drawn his attention to you, but Rillman, I doubt it. He's an idealist."

"And what does he want?"

"An end to death itself," Mr. D says as though it's the most amusing and obvious thing in the world. "And, ironically, me dead. I told him at the time that he couldn't have it both ways." I can see him inhabiting that moment. Something passes across his faces, an old hurt—a bitterness—and the amusement is replaced with an emotion more resolute. His lips tighten, he plays out more line. "That is all I will speak of him."

An end to death! As if that is possible, or even preferable. Death is pervasive and necessary: it is the broom that sweeps out the old and allows the new to flourish. Sure, I would think that, but I can't see why Rillman would want this.

My fishing rod dips. I let out a little more line.

And then something is more than tugging—there's a wrenching, hard against me. "Hey, I—"

And then I'm plunging into that brimming-over-with-monsters sea. The line didn't feed, and that line is connected to me. I'm being dragged down.

The water's cold and slimy. It snatches the breath from me. I'm tangled in the rod, and I'm going fast. Already the water pushes hard against my ribs.

Should be no problem. I should be able to shift myself out of here. Only it isn't working. What should feel like an opening out, a broadening of perspective, mixed with the snapping of a rubber band against my back brain, is nothing but a dull ache. I can't shift. Interestingly, my hangover's gone. You've gotta take the good with the bad.

I look up. The *Mary C*'s hull is a tiny square on the surface. It winks out of sight; something big has passed between the boat and me. Something huge. It's several seconds before I can see the bottom of the boat again, and it's barely a square at all now.

I think I see a pale shape dart in the water, but it's more likely the spots and squiggles dancing before my eyes. I'm still going down, and fast. I grab the pomping knife from my belt, start cutting at the line. It should be easier than it is, but I'm not surprised that it isn't. Finally the line snaps. My lungs burn. Great dark shapes are circling.

I feel a pressure on my shoulder, sharper than the water, and ending in five points, each digging into the muscle of my shoulder.

I whip my head around—no one, nothing—but the grip, if anything, grows more certain.

A whisper, straight into my ear, no wet gargles. Just a voice as sharp as that grip: "You're in danger."

No shit.

I thrash in the dark. The last bubbles of my breath escape my lips. This shouldn't be happening. This is no earthly sea. This is *my* domain. Damn it, I'm the RM of this entire region of the Underworld. Nothing should be able to touch me here. But something has—is. And not just touching, but squeezing. I wonder for a moment if this isn't some elaborate initiation ritual.

No breath now. All I have is a mild discomfort, a soft dizziness running through me, and that insistent voice, and it's permeating me more completely than my blood.

"You fall, but not alone, and in the falling, darkness waits."

Darker than this? I doubt it.

"And then you will be alone. Everything dies, by choice or reason. There is meaning in the muddle. There is blood and crooning in the mess."

I'm not finding much sense in the mess presented. I struggle in the grip, but it's unyielding.

"Oh, but there's a long drop for you."

"Let. Me. Go." I swing my head toward the voice, concentrating, throwing everything at it: which isn't much. Things tear within my psyche. A sickening sensation of my thoughts, of me, ripping apart. My muscles clench in sympathy. And for a moment, I catch a glimpse of something. A face. A grinning shadow, a mirror reflection, but so much more varied.

"Such a long drop for you. Such a long fall."

Then the pressure's gone, and I'm rising. A tiny, chubby pale hand is clamped around my index finger. We shoot toward the surface.

Then out of the darkness a great maw opens. Teeth the length of my forearm loom over and under us. Wal looks at me. I shrug.

This is not a good day.

But this I can deal with. The megalodon's rough teeth brush my arm, but here I cannot be hurt and certainly not by something dead.

It's odd, but for a moment I'm curious. A slight objectivity clouds my fear, or burns it away. This is what it is to be an RM: to be endlessly curious, to endlessly count down the hours, to peer at the life around me and not be involved in any of it other than the taking. It's with almost a sense of ennui that I consider the rows of pale teeth flexing in the meat of the megalodon's mouth.

Wal's hand tightens around my finger. His lips are moving but I can't make out the words, just the panic and I remember where I am.

The force that dragged me down has gone. I squeeze Wal's hand with my thumb, concentrate on the boat and then we're there, coughing and spluttering on the deck. I reach around and clutch at my shoulder where fingers had dug so deeply in, and dry heave out my pain.

Mr. D is waiting with towels. He chucks one at me, and then Wal. "What took you so long?"

"I thought I was safe here."

He shrugs. "You're not dead, are you? Not even bleeding."

"It grabbed me, the damn thing grabbed me, and then it spoke." I'm still spluttering.

Mr. D stops still. "What spoke? What did it say?"

"That I would fall. That I would be alone."

Mr. D's eyes widen. "What do they have planned for you?" he whispers.

"Who? Who has what planned for me?"

"Nothing. I'm sure it's nothing. Sounds like the All-Death—the death that exists outside the linear, the now and the then. I wouldn't worry about it too much. It likes to grab and mutter. Most of the time it doesn't make any sense."

"Like an oracle?" I ask, thinking back to high school and Year Ten Ancient History.

Mr. D shakes his head. "It's more like a drunk old uncle at Christmas time, or a senile great-grandfather. Just nod your head sagely and listen, but don't take it too seriously. I've not known it to actually have much of a handle on reality. It may even have you confused with someone else."

"OK," I say, wanting to take some relief from this.

"Yes, but it is a little disturbing." Mr. D doesn't know me all that well if he thinks that's going to offer any comfort.

"So what do I do?"

"Wait and see."

Wait and see; it's always wait and see! I glance at my watch. "I have to get back to work."

Mr. D smiles. "You're Regional Manager, you're one of the Orcus. You never stop working, whether you want to or not."

Which is exactly why I feel like an impostor.

Wait and bloody see? I already know what's coming. I don't need Mr. D or the All-Death to tell me. No matter how hard I try, it's never going to be enough.

14

Home.

The house is silent, but for the last few drops of water dripping from my suit. Boxes are still stacked against one wall. The place smells a bit musty; some windows haven't been opened since we moved in. The air-conditioning's been off for a while and I'm sweating before I take my first step. Everything is lit with hard Brisbane summer light.

Lissa's left a note on the kitchen table: *You know where I'll be. Oh, and one of us has to get milk. Hope you enjoyed the fishing.*

I don't know about "enjoyed." In fact, I feel more confused than ever. How could Rillman bring about an end to death itself? It's impossible. Life is built on death, the passing on of things, the dreams and devourings. Take out Mortmax and all you have is chaos and a Stirrer-led apocalypse. Rillman can't want that. It makes no sense.

Out of the living room and into the bedroom. I drag off my wet clothes; fabric making sucking noises as I tug first pants then shirt and underpants from me. My hair's plastered to my forehead.

This All-Death disturbs me. A dim echo of its voice scratches away in my ears. And I can tell it worried Mr. D as well. He couldn't have got me away any faster if he tried.

A quick shower, a little product for the hair, and a dry suit and I'm looking... well, I'm looking better. I'm head of Mortmax Industries in Australia and I look the part at least. Very funereal, but classy funereal, I reckon.

I look at my watch, Lissa should be at work by now.

I shift. This time I feel like I can hold it together. Maybe it is getting easier. Lissa jolts as I appear behind her in Number Four. Oscar and Travis jump, and I get the feeling that if I'd appeared any closer to Lissa I'd have received a fist to the throat.

I don't care that there are two burly men surrounding her. I wrap Lissa in my arms, and I kiss her hard.

"What was that for?" she asks when she is done kissing me back.

"Sorry to leave you alone this morning," I say, once I catch my breath.

Lissa smiles. "I'll live."

I don't want her to just live. But I can't say it here. I hug her again, tighter. Stopping only when someone behind me clears their throat.

Lundwall from the front desk hands me my messages. "I've emailed the details to you."

There are phone calls from Sydney and Perth. Tim is down in Melbourne, sorting out some issues there, and I don't expect to see him until the Christmas party tonight. People look to me for advice and I'm not sure what I need to give them: certainly more than I'm actually capable of.

I sometimes pity my staff, looking up to me as though I know what I'm doing. Poor bastards.

Lissa follows me into my office. I sit down in the throne and it whispers a greeting that only I can hear.

Her phone plays the "Imperial March," confirming an app update. Ah, the schedule's running through, being reconfirmed now that I am sitting in the throne, and all the multitudes of variables are factored in. She lifts her eyebrows as she takes in her jobs for the day.

"Busy day?"

"You should know."

"We'll do something tonight, I promise."

"Of course we will," Lissa says. "It's the staff Christmas party."

Then she's out of here.

Oscar clears his throat. He's standing at the door. "A word if you please, Mr. de Selby."

"I know, I'm sorry I left you in the lurch."

Oscar shakes his head. There's a sort of sternness in his eyes that I've not seen in anyone since Morrigan died. "This will work much better if you do what we tell you... and you keep us informed of your plans."

"My plans tend to change from moment to moment."

"Just keep us updated. That is all I'm asking."

"Did you see anything last night?"

Oscar shakes his head. "Other than the RM who visited you? Nothing."

They're a little more on the ball than I thought. Well, that's good, right?

Oscar watches this work its way across my face.

I clear my throat. "I'll keep you posted on my... um... movements. I'm sorry, if I forget. Just let me know, though—what exactly is the difference between what you're asking and being a hostage?"

Oscar grins. "Unfortunately very little, other than the very large sums of money you are paying us for the privilege of our protection."

Talking of being a hostage, I wave at the huge amount of paperwork in front of me. "Yeah, I've got stuff to do."

He nods. "I'll be at the door. My replacement will be here in half an hour."

"What? You're telling me you need to rest?"

"Only if you want to live."

Everyone's a comedian.

I sign off on a couple of investment suggestions. Read the latest data from Cerbo on the approaching god, which isn't much, but I know I'm going to have to contact him soon.

The lack of information I have at my fingertips is frustrating, so I flip through Twitter.

Death@MortmaxEuro: *Ah, plague so wearying.*

Death@MortmaxUS: *Train wreck@Festival LA. More B-list stars, but one A. Expect a thousand tedious retrospectives.*

I resist the temptation to read the online news, then check my email again. There's one from the South African RM, Neill Debbier.

Mr. de Selby,
While I am aware that you are no doubt busy with all things
Death Moot—not to mention the attempts on your life—I
would be appreciative if you were to visit my offices. My diary
is flexible today. You are welcome at any time.
*   Regards,*
*   Neill*

It's a change from Suzanne who seems to want everything now, now, *now*.

What the hell. I look at my desk with its teetering piles of paper. No time like the present.

I don't shift directly into his office—well, I try not to at any rate—that would be rude. And in these times, when RMs—OK, only one RM, but we're all a team, aren't we?—are being attacked, it could induce a panic.

I'm not sure what a panicked Neill would do, but I don't really want to find out. I'm only beginning to understand my own abilities and RMs are notoriously closed mouthed. There are more secrets within our organization than I would have believed just a few months ago—secrets, like landmines waiting for me to inadvertently stomp on them. But then again, what's a landmine anyway, but a really, really nasty secret?

The shift is relatively painless this time. "Yeah!" I punch the air a little.

Neill's Ankou, David, types away for a moment or two, pointedly ignoring me.

I cough.

He looks up, feigns surprise. "You're early," he says.

Why does everyone seem to know what I'm doing better than me? "When were you expecting me?"

"Based on your movements, around your lunchtime, so very early morning here."

Based on my movements? I wonder just who it is who is watching me. I don't have anyone spying on the other RMs, maybe I should. Yeah, as if I could afford to lose more staff.

"Are you ready to talk to the boss?"

"Of course I am."

I get what looks to me like a smile of pity. David presses down on a somewhat prehistoric intercom, a big brown box as clunky as all hell. I get the feeling they don't bother with Bluetooth here, but then again, Mr. D used to use sparrows as his main form of communication, and his "data-storage" consisted of scrunched-up balls of paper and Post-it notes.

The intercom buzzes a moment before Neill picks up.

"Yes?" The voice is warm.

"Mr. de Selby's here."

"He's early. Excellent."

Neill's through the door almost at once, his hand out, giving me a professionally firm handshake that lasts one or two seconds too long.

"Come in," he says gesturing at his open door. "We have a lot to talk about, you and I."

The door is heavy, the windows barred. Like my office, he has views of both the living and the Underworld. But the bars obscure it somewhat. All I can see are street lights. It's late here, does Neill ever go home?

"As you can see, we are quite secure here."

I want to say something about how needing such security doesn't suggest security at all. But I bite my tongue.

Neill's throne is almost identical to mine. The wood is a little paler, the carvings a little different, perhaps telling a story of an older continent. After all, the Orcus had its origins, like all human life, in Africa. Although some of the carvings definitely aren't of humans.

Neill sits down and sighs. His skin brightens, flushes a little as he leans back in his chair. I wonder if that's how I look. I know I've grown somewhat dependent on my throne.

Neill pours, then passes me a glass of twenty-year-old scotch. Without even bothering to ask if I want one. The bottle of scotch is the only thing sitting on his desk, other than a couple of sheets of paper, over which he has made notes in an extremely neat hand. I try not to look but I think I can see my name. Neill slides the papers away and into a drawer under his desk. I almost expect him to pull out a gun. See what a paranoid state I'm in?

"There are some things you're better off not reading," Neill says. "Besides, my spelling is atrocious."

I sip my scotch. It's good stuff. I compare this with the beer Mr. D has been foisting on me. My old RM has sunk a long way. "I think you need a mentor, Steven. Hope that doesn't make me sound too much like a wanker. But Mr. D, he was never the best of us, had a habit of making enemies."

"I've already made a deal with Suzanne Whitman." Not that I trust her in the least.

Neill's expression hardly changes. "I wouldn't trust her. Suzanne is many things, but trustworthy is not one of them."

Is this bugger reading my mind? "And why should I trust you?"

Neill smiles. "Mr. de Selby, there really isn't anyone you should trust. Not friends, nor family. Everyone can betray you. Why, you can betray yourself—and that's the worst sort of betrayal, isn't it?"

"You're telling me that trust is pointless. Then why bother making any deals at all?"

"They're no guarantee against betrayal, but they do, with the right amount of paranoia, make it harder. It's as much about information. Sharing."

"What do you want from me? You seem to know every-thing anyway."

"Not at all. I know less than you think. But I do have something for you. Rillman—I have heard that he's caus-ing you trouble." Neill sighs. "You're not the first. Rillman is a pain, and your Mr. D should have stopped him years ago. Do you know that he regularly crosses the boundary between the land of the living and the Underworld?"

"What?" Well, that explains a lot. The bastard's got a passcard to Hell. I'm not sure whether I feel relieved he's back on the table as a suspect or horrified by the implica-tions of what he can do.

Neill's eyes crinkle with the slightest of smiles. "Death holds no dominion over him. You might want to ask just who is letting it happen."

"Do you have any idea?" He can't give me this and not have an idea!

Neill shrugs. "Perhaps your new *mentor* knows. She has promised you much. The Orcus has plans for you. You would do well to ask just what they are."

"Why don't you tell me now?" I want to bang my fist on the table.

Neill grins. "If I could. Yes, but then she would know. This, I can get away with. This, you should have been able to guess yourself. You're new, of course the Orcus would fit you into their strategies. But if I tell you any more I risk . . . Well, it would not be good."

"I'll think about your offer." I finish my scotch and force a smile, wondering if he's being genuine, if I can even trust the information about Rillman that he's given me. I've seen Neill's Negotiation, just as I've seen all the others: one nasty gift I wish I'd never received.

You see someone decapitate their foe, you think differently of them.

"Yes, please consider it carefully."

The phone rings. He glances over to it. "I need to take this call."

He stands up, shakes my hand. "Be very careful, my friend."

I nod and shift out of there.

There is a knock at my office door, almost at the same second I arrive back. I'm a little woozy, but otherwise OK.

"Come in," I say, trying to hide the irritation from my voice.

A giant of a man walks into the room. At first I think it's the New Zealand–South Pacific RM. He's at least this big, but it's not Kiri Baker. I feel guilty—another couple of movements I haven't let the security crew know about.

The big guy blinks. "Just thought I'd let you know there's been a shift change." His lips move a little oddly, as though they're scarred. I know I shouldn't but I stare at them, trying to work out just what is wrong.

He comes toward me, his hand out. "Jacob. I'm Oscar's replacement."

"Thanks," I say, standing up to shake his hand. "I really appreciate what you're doing. And I've promised Oscar that I'll be good."

His hand encloses mine. And I catch the movement of his other hand far too late: it's not open.

Jacob's fist slams into my head. I see stars, literally all sorts of unnerving constellations. *Aquarius—today you will have the shit beaten out of you, dope. Dress for wet weather, and probable death.*

"You're welcome," he says, swinging another fist at my head. I sense him changing. Shrinking somehow, or maybe it's just that the room is spinning. "You're so welcome."

Shift. Got to shift. Close my eyes. Focus on anywhere but here!

But that's the end of me. Five shifts in such close proximity was never going to happen. I'm on the floor, stunned, one nostril sheathed in a bubble of blood that's expanding and contracting with my breath. He lifts me up easily, and the bloody bubble bursts. I'm shaking my head, trying to stop the ringing in my ears. All I can see between long blinks is the carpet, and my blood splattering in Rorschach patterns.

I try to speak, just manage a couple of grunts. And then we shift. It doesn't feel like far, but I've no way of knowing. For a moment my assailant's heartbeat races.

More carpet, a familiar color. A door swings open, and we move into another room. I'm tossed into a chair. The door clicks shut. Darkness. A chance. I've got a chance.

I try to get up, legs hardly like springs, and the Hulk punches me down again. "Not yet, we've a way to go," he says, in the dark. "I've just started with you."

15

My head's clearing. The ringing's gone, replaced with a headache almost the equal of my worst hangover.

I can only hear one heartbeat. Nothing else. A single steady beating that races again for a moment, then slows. Something just happened. I'm not sure what. There is a metallic clunk. The air smells of dust, with a background hint of industrial cleaning products. Where the hell am I?

A match is struck. Some sort of fragrant candle must be burning because I can smell oranges, or the candle-chemical equivalent of them. Or I am having a stroke. My swollen eyelids admit a little of that flickering light: it's as red as the blood that I can taste in my mouth.

I open my eyes, and recognize the room, even with the candlelight. It's the broom cupboard on the third floor of Number Four, the same broom cupboard that Morrigan used to imprison Mr. D when he began his Schism. The door in front of me is solid wood and is bound in some sort of alloy. You can pretty much guarantee that no other cupboard in the world has that sort of door.

And no one is likely to visit this space anytime soon.

This is not good. Morrigan had the whole place sound-proofed before he threw Mr. D into it. I should have had the door knocked out, and a regular one installed. But I never expected to end up here myself. I try to move. My hands are free but rough cord digs into the flesh of my arms: the movement only tightens my bonds. This is seri-ous malevolent-scout knot-work.

"I wouldn't do that if I was you." The voice is unfamil-iar, clipped and rasping, certainly not Jacob's. Cold metal brushes my cheek. "Don't move if you want to keep your eyes."

I freeze. The knife travels down my face, drawing blood here and there. I try and shift. Nothing. Something's damping my abilities here. I guess that's how Mr. D was contained here. Yes, this room has to go.

Time for some bluster. "You're going to have to work harder than that if you want to frighten me with a knife."

"I will, really I will." He sounds amused.

I turn my head as far around to the right as I am able and nod at the candles behind me. "You've certainly picked an intimate setting for a... Well, what is this? A torture session?"

There's a wry exhalation, almost a laugh, and a hand passes in front of my face. It's lined with scars all across the palm. "You RMs. You really think you know it all."

"I tend to find it's the Ankous with the problem, Mr. Rillman."

There is a definite intake of breath. I don't know whether it's an act or not, but he sounds genuinely surprised. "Where did you hear that name? I thought they had forgotten me."

"Oh, around the traps. You're quite a popular bloke here. Mr. D talks of you with a great deal of fondness."

"That shit ground my name out of the company's history. You will not speak of him again." He strikes the back of my head, hard enough that I bite my tongue, and see stars.

"OK, I won't. Just tell me: why are you trying to kill me?"

"Oh, you're something of an experiment, Mr. de Selby. A new RM, first in living memory. Who would have believed it?" Rillman says. "We both know there are deaths, and then there are deaths."

"How did you do it?" I ask, my tongue swollen and bloody in my mouth. "How did you die and come back?"

Rillman snorts. "Does it offend you? After all, you've done it. All you RMs must, death is the only way to win at the Negotiation. It is the single requisite, wouldn't you say?"

Rillman walks around to face me. There's something not quite right about his features. He's hiding them from me. They're waxy, and his hair doesn't look quite real. Now I think of it, Jacob had something of that look about him, too. Rillman smiles tightly and slips back behind me, where I can't turn my head to follow. He's just a blur back there, a blur holding sharp things.

"Look, I know you failed an Orpheus Maneuver. But that—"

Something strikes me hard in the back of the head again. Next, I realize I've come to, I can't tell how much time has passed but it can't be much. Rillman walks in circles around me, agitated. He steps in close, almost enough for me to headbutt him. He slides the knife across my cheek.

"You will not talk about that. I did not fail. I was betrayed. Ask your Mr. D. Here you will not talk about anything."

"What the fuck do you want?"

"All in good time."

He lifts the knife from my cheek. Drives it into the meat just above my knee. And God help me, I scream. Not that it does any good.

"Knives don't need to terrify, they just need a good cutting edge or a point, or in this case, both."

Blood and spittle run down my chin. "Can't we just... What do you want?"

He pulls the knife out of my knee, and slams the pommel into my jaw.

"I want you to shut up."

I spit more blood, and a tooth. My mouth is a mess, I have to keep spitting or I will choke, but it doesn't stop me from straining against the ropes binding me here. It doesn't stop me from growling in his face. "This is my region. You come in here and threaten me."

I'm almost convincing.

I try to shift again, damping field be damned. I'm desperate. I need to get out of here. But there is a cold hand, a pressure sitting in the back of my mind. Not that different to the force that held me in the Tethys.

Rillman lowers his waxen face toward mine, and smiles. "Every emperor, every RM, can be destroyed. You must know that now. You must know that nowhere is safe for you and your kind."

"Then kill me." I lift my neck to him. "Just get it over and done with."

"Oh, if it was that easy, I would."

And he's right. Already my wounds are healing; there is less blood in my mouth. The flesh of my leg is drawing together.

The phone in my pocket starts ringing, I'm amazed that I can get a signal in here, but there you go. "They're going to start looking for me," I say.

Rillman nods, reaches into my pocket and pulls out the phone. After two stomps of his left boot the phone's in pieces on the floor. "Yes, and I am sure that the broom cupboard is the first place they'll look. They're not going to worry about you for several hours. I have time."

He swings a fist into my ribs. Things break. Things tear. I'm choking on my own blood again. For a while I can't see anything. Rillman is right; this could go on for a while. My nature is such that I can take a lot of pain.

"She was mine. And I lost her. Of course, you can't understand that, because you didn't. You cheated. You stumbled and pratfalled and somehow, you called your love back." Another blow to the side of my head. "Fourteen years of marriage. Do you not understand? What do you know of that kind of love?"

More teeth are loosened. Blood chokes my throat.

What do I know of love? I think of Lissa. Wonder if I'll ever see her again. I haven't spent enough time with her, not nearly enough. There is so much we haven't done together. Things we haven't experienced. Christ, I want to marry her.

I don't care if it's unwise for RMs to marry. I don't care if it's the stupidest thing in the world. She's my girl. Mine.

"Why are you grinning?" Rillman demands.

"What do I know of love? I got her back. I got her back, you prick."

There's another couple of punches. More pain. A knife is jammed into my spine and left there.

When the pain dulls, and I can breathe again, I lift my head. "What do you want, Rillman?"

"Agony, isn't it? And with the way you heal I don't need to be delicate."

He pulls out another knife, pale as moonlight, and as narrow as a regular dinner knife. He grabs my left pinkie finger. I struggle against him, but he is stronger than I am, and the ropes that bind me are tight. "This knife isn't steel," he says, "but something I picked up in the Deepest Dark. Let's see how it works."

He pushes the blade over, and then into, my pinkie finger, hard. Skin and bone part in a swift and agonizing jolt. I feel the cracking of that bone through my entire body. I scream. And I scream. And I scream until something tears in my throat.

"Oh, we have so much more fun ahead, believe me." I struggle, my bonds tighten, and Rillman lets me; so confident that I can't escape.

He brings the knife toward my cheek.

But this time I'm ready for him. I swing my head up against his skull. Bone cracks into bone. Rillman goes down hard.

He groans. I rock backward and forward in my chair, and then I'm tipping over, landing on Rillman. I crack my skull into his head, again and again. His knife is next to him on the floor. I slide over toward it, grab it with a hand sticky with blood and cut at my bindings.

The knife's damn sharp. I'm free in a moment and I stagger to my feet. Rillman groans again. And I kick him in the head. Once. Twice. I bend down and rest the knife against his face. There's a rather large part of me taking too much delight in this.

"Oh, we have so much fun ahead, believe me." I try and reach the other knife in my back, but can't.

I find my finger on the floor. The little thing's twitching. I wonder whether, if I left it alone long enough, it would grow a new me. I push it against my wound and finger and hand begin to reconnect. It's agony, but I'll be whole again soon.

I need to get out of this tiny room. The walls are closing in.

I stumble over to the door, swing it open and stagger outside. Rillman is on the floor behind me. He isn't going anywhere.

Laughter and music echo down from the floor above. I stagger to the stairs and climb up to the fourth floor. The nearer I get the more I can make out. Christmas carols? Worse than that—contemporized Christmas carols doof doof doofing.

I kick open the door. And there are my staff having their Christmas party. A big Christmas tree is in one corner, someone is giggling by the photocopying machine. Tim is talking to some bigwigs from the state government. For all this, everything seems so forced; a party going through the motions. The door slams shut behind me.

Everyone, glasses in hand, spins around, and there I am. Me with my blood staining my shirt. Me with a bloody knife in one hand. Me with the torn and gore-stained pants. Me with blood squelching in my shoes with every step.

I walk over to the bar and pour myself a Bundy—a tall glass, neat. My pinkie finger still dangles a little. I down the rum in one gulp. No one has moved, not even Tim.

"Oh, and merry fucking Christmas," I say, waving the glass in the air. If it weren't for the bar I'm leaning on I'd drop to the floor in a heap. I nearly do, and whatever shock my presence created is broken. The whole room seems to move toward me.

"What the hell happened to you?" Tim asks, rushing from where the two government guys stand: both of them looking at me curiously. What are they going to write in their reports tomorrow?

I lift up the mess that is my left hand—though it's not nearly as messy as it was—and point at the door. "Downstairs. Broom cupboard. Francis Rillman. The fucker tried—well, more than tried—to torture me."

Tim's out of there, running back the way I've come. I look around me. Where's Lissa? Then I'm swaying. The rest of my staff aren't sure what they should be doing. I don't blame them. I can hear their elevated heartbeats. And then there's one I recognize.

"Steven! Oh, Steven."

Lissa's there, she's found me, she's holding me up. I've never been so happy to be held up, to be bound up in her arms. There's stuff we need to discuss. Not here, not now, but as soon as we can.

"Where were you?" I ask.

"Your office. Jesus, Steve, I've been trying to call you. I was getting worried, but I thought…Well, you've been all over the place lately." She touches my face. "Oh, my darling."

"Francis Rillman just tortured me." I grin at her. "I've never been tortured before. I think I did I all right."

She walks me to a chair. The staff are all looking on. The poor green bastards, I really should say something, but the breath is out of me.

"Could you get the knife out of my back?" I manage at last.

She pulls, then reconsiders. "Maybe we should wait for Dr. Brooker. It seems to be lodged in your spine."

"Might explain why it hurts so much."

"It's going to be OK," she says, wiping blood from my face. And while I don't seem to be bleeding, there's a lot of it.

"Yeah, absolutely."

No one else seems sure what to do. I get the feeling that I'm letting them all down. I don't want to do that. After all, Rillman's taken care of. My wounds will heal and no one else has been hurt.

I get out of the chair, with a little help from Lissa.

"Sorry," I say to my crew. "You all party on. Really, it's OK. Someone turn up the music."

As inspirational speeches go it really doesn't cut it.

Lissa wipes some more blood from my face. "Steven, most bosses just get drunk and flirt with their staff at Christmas parties."

Tim belts back up the stairs, panting. Oscar's behind him looking very pissed off. Tim passes me my phone. It's whole again. I blink at it. I can see where the glass front is finishing healing itself: the tiniest tracework of cracks. Must be a cracker of a twenty-four month plan.

"Rillman's gone," Tim says. "There's just the chair, and blood." He looks from me to Lissa and back. His eyes are frantic. I can tell he wants to hit something. "You poor bastard."

I don't have time or the energy to comfort him. "The guy was out cold when I left him."

"Well, he's not there now."

I look up at Oscar he's only just getting off his mobile. "What happened? How did he—"

"Rillman, it has to be him, he killed Jacob. Stabbed, in his own house."

"So who was it that I was talking to in my office?"

"I don't know."

"That's reassuring."

"Look, someone died today," Oscar says. "I'm going to find the bastard who did this and there will be payback. No one does this to one of my crew."

I nod, a bit woozy with lack of blood. I know how he feels. I'm mad enough about this as it is, but if Rillman had tortured anyone else I would not be able to express my rage. At least physical damage is only going to be a memory to me.

Poor Jacob is dead and gone and, for all I know, he wasn't even properly pomped. That's too high a price.

"He was working for me, too," I say. "We'll both make the bastard pay."

A thought strikes me. A dark one. "Do you have a photo of Jacob?"

Oscar nods, fiddles with his mobile and passes it to me. The face I'm staring at is the face of the man who hit me. This is not good.

"That's him, the man who attacked me."

Oscar shakes his head. "Couldn't be. He's been dead for twelve hours."

Great, Rillman can change his appearance. The question is, can he change his appearance only to those who are dead? Or are all the living open to him as well?

Just where might Rillman be now?

My gaze shifts from Oscar to Tim and Lissa, then to the crowd of Pomps around me.

Paranoia plus.

16

Didn't I tell you to keep out of trouble?" Dr. Brooker grunts, looking at my hand. The finger has melded nicely. Not bad for a couple of hours. The wound in my leg is scabbed up too. He looks from me to Lissa and Tim. "I did tell him to keep out of trouble."

I'm on a drip, blood filling my veins. I'm on my second bag, and I'm starting to feel great. Brooker had nearly fainted at the sight of me. Anyone else and I would have been dead, or at the very least in a coma, he reckons.

"This is getting irritating," I say.

"It'd be rather more fatal than irritating if you weren't who you are. So it's definitely Rillman?" Tim says.

"Yeah, but I still can't understand why he did it. I mean, I can't have pissed him off. The bastard doesn't know me." Rillman may not be the first person who has wanted to torture me, but he's certainly been the first to try.

"I think Rillman's testing the limits of your abilities. Trying to find out what can kill you."

"Neill said that Rillman's been a thorn in Mortmax's side for a while."

"Not here," Tim says. "There's no record of a Rillman for years in our system." He sighs. "Do you think that perhaps the Orcus are using you to draw Rillman out? I mean, there are links, plenty of them. If Rillman's seeking an end to the status quo you would be attractive to him."

I chew on that for a while. "Yeah, I'm new to my powers. I don't have any allies as such."

"And you managed what he failed to do," Lissa says. "You brought someone back from Hell."

"You pomped him. You said he seemed calm."

Lissa nods. "Maybe resigned is the better term. Most dead people are that. Perhaps he had decided on his plan of action. Maybe he was seeking me out. Death would be an easy way of doing that. He knows how we work, and it seems no real obstacle to him."

"Think about that," I say. "Think about how reckless you might be if death holds no fear, no real consequence, and you want revenge."

"It might make you willing to experiment more. Particularly in unconventional ways of killing an RM," Tim says.

"You're telling me that no one has ever tried to kill an RM before?"

Tim rolled his eyes. "Well, obviously they have, but without success, unless it's part of a Schism, killing off an RM's Pomps, weakening them until they're able to be killed. It's messy, convoluted and can really only happen inhouse. Remember, as you've probably read in my briefing notes," Tim says, giving me a stern look, "RMs give

Pomps the ability to pomp. You turn them into the doorway that gives access to the Underworld and closes out
Stirrers, but they also give you something in return.
Through them you are able to shift, to heal. One of the
reasons the party was so subdued had to do with the
amount of energy all of us were expending to keep you
alive."

"That, and the music, I mean those Christmas carols
were tragic!" I say. Lissa glares at me, reminds me to stay
on track. Tim shakes his head, but continues.

"Rillman is obviously aiming at non-traditional
methods."

I remember Mr. D's words about a paradigm shift back
when Morrigan was around. "He's trying to effect a
change. A real change to the system."

Tim nods. "You'd have to admit that killing an RM
without destroying their Pomps is a much less bloody
transition." He grins. "I hate to say it, Steve, but if it's
going to come down to me getting it and you getting it, or
just you getting it, I know what I'd rather—"

"Hey!"

He raises his hands in the air. "With the proviso that I
can get my revenge. I'm in no hurry to lose any more
of my family."

"So why would Rillman want to get rid of me? I can't
believe it's just because I succeeded in my Orpheus
Maneuver and he didn't." But I can believe that, part of
me at least. If I had failed, and for a while I thought I had,
bitterness would poison me.

"Did Morrigan have any allies? Maybe Rillman was
one of them," Tim says

"No, I don't think so. Morrigan ended all his allegiances

brutally. By the Negotiation I think his allies and enemies were indistinguishable."

Tim nods. "Even the Stirrers were working against him."

"What we need to do is find Rillman before he actually succeeds in killing me. As well as organize a Death Moot, run Mortmax efficiently and—"

"Don't forget about the Christmas party." Tim smiles, nodding to the door outside. "Well, you've already ruined that."

Dr. Brooker grunts, looks at us both quizzically. "Christmas party?"

Oh, shit.

"Didn't you get your invitation?" Tim and I say at the same time.

"Maybe we need to cancel the Death Moot," I continue, changing the subject.

Lissa and Tim shake their heads. "No. That's one thing you cannot do. A Death Moot must never be canceled. It's a sign of weakness, and you don't want to present any weakness to the Orcus."

"But people are trying to kill us."

"Death may well be preferable," Tim says.

Speak for yourself. "How do I look?" I say, getting up, straightening my hair as best I can. My fingers catch on what I suspect are large clumps of dried blood.

Lissa smiles at me. "Like Death warmed up."

At least someone's kept their sense of humor.

I don't feel safe at home.

The rest of the Christmas party was, well, in a word, awkward. Death is something of a party killer at the best of times. Particularly when I spent a good deal of it staring intently at every staff member, or asking difficult questions that in theory only my people should be able to answer. Yes, there's going to be a staff meeting about *that*. Some of the basic pomping facts that these people didn't know shocked me. I was almost relieved when a truck collision called a good half-dozen of them away. Call me mean-spirited, but I am Australia's RM and death is my business.

Lissa had stayed by my side the whole evening, even submitted to my paranoid questions—with curt, often embarrassing, answers. Of course I knew it was her, I'm intimately familiar with her heartbeat. I have to believe that Rillman's mimicry doesn't extend that far.

Lissa's asleep almost the moment her head hits the pillow. I text Suzanne: *Need to talk.*

A few seconds later I have a response: *Yes, you do. Usual place. Let's make it another lesson.*

Yeah, but this time I'll be directing the questions.

I shift there. The Deepest Dark whispers around me. I wince, expecting more pain than I actually get.

Suzanne smiles at me, and she's in my coat. I'd ask for it back but she seems wounded in some way, a little less confident. It was less than twenty-four hours since we were here last, and I had left her to witness to the fate of one of her agents.

For the first time I see something—I hesitate to call it human—inside her. A vulnerability that I had never expected to encounter in an RM. It actually stops me for a moment. Reminds me that I'm not the only one capable of feeling pain.

"Your agent?"

Suzanne shakes her head. "It wasn't good. I don't want to talk about it. He is no longer in any pain."

Above us the great inky mass of the Stirrer god swallows an ever-increasing portion of the sky like some gargantuan and evil lava lamp.

"I was tortured today."

"I am aware of that," Suzanne says. "Don't forget I have ten Pomps on your payroll. They're switched on enough to pick up a phone. I knew you would be in touch soon enough. Your Lissa, she's sleeping?"

"Yeah, what's that got to do with anything?"

"Everything. This is your Lissa. This is all of them." Suzanne crouches down, picks up a handful of dust and does whatever it is that she does. It dances around her hand, shining ever brighter. I can see Lissa's face there, her eyes closed, whispering in her sleep. Then, with a single chopping gesture, the dust drops to the ground. "They all need sleep. Not that it is enough in the end. Gravity changes them all. They shift down, they grow heavy in their bones. They lose swift thought and swift action. They decay. That is all they have, a trudging forward into decrepitude and dust. And yet it is so beautiful. So tragic. And far better than it was before. She sleeps, your girl, but it is not enough to hold back the final sleep."

I don't want a lesson in the obvious. I want answers. "I know this. I've grown up around death," I say. "I was a Pomp, just as the rest of you were Pomps."

Suzanne gives me a patronizing pat on the shoulder. "You only think you do. You don't know death the way we *know* death. That knowledge is coming, but you don't have it yet. You're never going to feel gravity again, Steven. It doesn't apply to you, the death you will find will be fast and violent and centuries hence, if you're on your game. You will have time to see the beauty and ugliness of life for what it is: fleeting and yet, somehow, eternal.

"And how you come to that knowledge won't have anything to do with what I say, or Neill. I can guarantee that." So she's onto me, then. I try to not register any surprise. "It will come to you in its own way, as everything else has come to you, because that's how it works."

"I'm a bloody slow learner."

"There's nothing to learn. This is a bone-deep truth, whether you understand it or not. A hundred years from now you will be the same as you are now, and different in ways you can't even begin to comprehend. You've no choice in the matter."

"But there are choices to be made."

"As much as any of us can make them. We're all fighting the same fight. The enemy hasn't changed. That's a constant, too."

But I feel it has. Morrigan, in his dealings with the Stirrers, has set something in motion. Something I can't quite articulate. Suzanne watches me trying to get it out, and sees that it obviously isn't going to come.

"Rillman, what about him? He wants me dead," I say, finally.

"And yet you are most obviously not."

"Tell me how I can find him."

Suzanne looks away from me, toward the city of Devour. "If I knew a way, believe me, I would have pursued him a long time ago."

An idea strikes me then, an unpleasant one. "Are you using me as bait?"

Suzanne shakes her head. "You've drawn Rillman out.

Before, he was all secrecy—back-door plans and sneaking in and out of Hell. You would make excellent bait, but I fear that the moment we used you as such Rillman would go underground again. I want you on my side," Suzanne says. "Neill's bloc is growing too powerful."

I peer over at her, surprised. "I thought he was your bloc."

"We may help each other from time to time but we are not in agreement on much. We know how to put up a unified front when we need to. But he worries me now."

"What difference does it make?"

"When you have centuries, it makes all the difference in the worlds. Believe me, you will learn that."

"What are your plans for me? The All-Death—"

Suzanne grimaces. "What did that meddlesome thing say?"

"That I will be alone. That I will fall."

Suzanne looks almost relieved, as though I've merely reaffirmed something. "We're all alone," she says. "Rillman. You. Lissa. You will learn this, Steven, if you're half as smart as I think you are. The longer you live, the more alone you are."

I turn from her, and consider the darkness of the Stirrer god above. I remember with utter clarity the immensity of its eye in that vision granted to me by Stirrer rage or my newborn power. I'd stared it down. Of course, I'd been too stupid to do anything different. Me there in that darkness, hurling its worshippers back away from the land of the living. I'd felt the strength of Orcus unity, a strength that had extended all the way down to my hundreds of Avian Pomps.

Absolutely meaningless. I knew that if it came down to

it, I'd be fighting that dark alone and it scared the shit out of me.

"I don't think we have centuries anymore. Maybe my presence is what the Orcus needs, someone to add a little urgency to the proceedings to draw your attention back to that approaching hunger filling the sky."

The look that Suzanne gives me is not nearly as patronizing, though I still feel as though she considers me as little more than a dog that has just learned to fetch.

"We know it's there. Its presence is undeniable and we are doing something about it," Suzanne says. "You have to believe me."

"I really wish I could."

Suzanne nods. "This morning, I will send Faber to you. He will show you our latest work."

"Seven am," I say. "And make sure he isn't late this time."

Suzanne flashes me a vicious smile, and shifts out of there. I stand looking up at the dark. Wal drags free of my arm.

"I really hate how she does that," he sighs. "Keeping me stuck to your arm; it's very rude."

"I don't think she likes you," I say.

"What's not to like, eh? Eh?"

I don't even know where to begin.

The next morning I shift to the office, leaving Lissa to sleep under the protection of my Avian Pomps. Oscar is already there waiting outside my office. He nods at me, lets me pass through the door.

Downstairs someone is dismantling the broom cupboard's door. I can feel it coming undone even from here, and I'm pleased.

It's one place Rillman, or anyone else who might want to lock me away, can't use.

I feel Cerbo's arrival a few minutes later. Oscar knocks on the door.

"Come in," I say.

Oscar swings open the door. "He says you are expecting him."

"Yes, I am."

Cerbo nods at me. Today he's wearing a green bowler that most people could only ever get away with on St. Patrick's Day, and only a certain few of those. He carries it off with a quiet dignity.

He turns to Oscar. "It's quite all right," he says. "I have no intention of killing your boss. Couldn't if I tried."

Oscar lingers at the door a moment longer.

"This isn't Rillman," I say. "He's not going to be able to pull that one on me again."

The door shuts. Cerbo raises an eyebrow at me. "Quite the hired goon."

I let it slide. "Suzanne said you would show me what you know about the Stirrer god?"

Cerbo smiles. "And that is why I am here, Mr. de Selby." He gestures at me. "Now, if you would stand up, and come toward me."

"I was kind of expecting a PowerPoint presentation."

"What I have is much better than any computer-based simulation. Now, up, up! Get your rear out of that chair!" He seems to enjoy shouting at an RM.

I get out of my throne and walk around the desk.

"Hold my hand," Cerbo says reaching out toward me.

I hesitate, and he grimaces. "Oh, for goodness sake. You're not even my type!"

That's not why I'm hesitating, but his words push me hard enough into action.

Cerbo's hand is warm, and he grips mine hard. "This is something new. A technique Suzanne has been developing. It's based on the subset of skills required to shift."

I groan.

Cerbo squeezes my hand. "No, it is not shifting *per se*. For one, it is more…well…cinematic, Mr. de Selby. And two, it demands a little more. You'll see what I mean." He closes his eyes. "Whatever you do, don't let go. This is no pixie-dust journey we're going on, and I'm not Superman."

I'm trying to imagine Superman in a green bowler as Cerbo reaches into his jacket pocket. He pulls out his knife.

I have to fight the reflex to pull away. "What the fuck are you doing with that?"

Cerbo's eyes flick open. He regards me disdainfully. "Don't worry, it's not for you. I've been Ankou for nearly two decades to an RM who is centuries old. You pick up a few things, but I have yet to uncover a really easy way to kill an RM without first killing their Pomps. Even Morrigan couldn't do that. This knife is for me." He takes a deep breath, grits his teeth, and then runs the blade over the back of the hand holding mine. Blood flows quickly. "Remember, don't let go."

Between heartbeats, this happens: we are in the office, and then it is just a space distant beyond my imagining below us. We're vast and tiny at once, and shooting along a tunnel brighter than any glaring sun. I have to cover my eyes. Cerbo squeezes my hand even tighter. For a moment I am reminded of the All-Death's implacable grip.

Then we're in a space I've only seen once before. I

remember it a little differently but at the time I was fighting to save Tim and Lissa's lives. First I am surprised by my weightlessness here. The only force binding me, giving me any sense of up or down, is Cerbo's hand. We're quite close, our hands by our hips, gripping each other as children do. Awkwardly and tight.

"Welcome to the ether. The void beyond the Deepest Dark, where the souls find flight and through which the Stirrer god approaches."

"Cool," I say.

"Indeed."

We're not flying so much as being propelled, and the source of that force is generated by Cerbo's bleeding fist. Around us souls drift, but we are moving faster than them. Occasionally I have to flick my body to one side to avoid striking one.

"Careful," Cerbo says. "You'll lose your grip."

I strike a soul then. Feel it shatter around my head. It burns, then chills on contact like ice. I swing my head back, and see it re-form behind us. After that, I don't bother avoiding them. It's like traveling on the flat bed of a ute in a snowstorm. I almost start to enjoy myself. The speed of it, the freedom. Is this how souls feel, once they are dead?

I ask Cerbo, and he shrugs.

"We cannot go far, just a few steps into the infinite. Blood is no substitute for death. But it is far enough." A great eye gazes down at us, and we race toward it, cold air roaring in my ears.

We're a long time getting close to that eye. But I can't help staring at it, as I've stared at it before, though it was much further distant then, and I was on the ground, not in this weightless place; and granted a vision, not this whistling wind-bound actuality.

"It sees us, doesn't it?" I ask, having to shout above the gale.

"I think so," Cerbo says. "But we are nothing to it. I've done this a dozen times over the past three months, and every time I am much faster getting here."

"Three months?"

"That's when we first noticed it. Well, Suzanne did. A change in the ether, a sudden rise in Stirrer activity."

"Do you think Morrigan knew about this?"

"Well, he was dealing with Stirrers. He may have known about it for some time. Or maybe it was just a coincidence that he started his Schism when he did. Do you believe in coincidence, Mr. de Selby?" Cerbo jabs his free hand toward it. "It's impressive. Very godlike, wouldn't you say?"

Darkness bunches around the mass, part stormcloud, part slug. To one side souls coruscate, and seek to flee its bulk, but even as we watch, a black tentacle extrudes from it, snaps out and drags some of those souls back into its side. A thousand, two thousand, perhaps. Screams ring through my head.

"Already it is wreaking untold damage," Cerbo says. "And the closer it gets, the harder it is for souls to escape. God knows what this is doing to the psychic balance of the universe."

We swing past the great eye. "Remember, here it is just psychic mass. When it strikes the Underworld, and through it, earth, that mass will manifest."

"How?"

"We don't know but—I'm sorry, but I think we better

get out of here." Cerbo's eyes are wide. I swing my head in the direction of his gaze; feel my heart catch.

A tentacle rushes toward us. As it draws nearer I can see fringes of what look like blades. They ripple and flex. That merest filament of that limb would cut us to pieces. The ether has suddenly lost its appeal. What the hell is wrong with PowerPoint?

"Hold on," Cerbo says. "Hold on."

He pulls out his knife, brings it back down against his hand and we're suddenly reversing, flipping back, moving away, faster and faster.

And then my grip loosens. Or Cerbo releases his.

I'm left, spinning. Losing speed. Floating in that dark, Cerbo already a diminishing shape in front of me.

17

Here I am, alone in the darkness, about to be sliced into pieces or snatched into the maw of the enemy. The limb of the Stirrer god belts down toward me through the ether. It's so big I really can't comprehend it. I'm less than an ant to it, but the god will have me none the less. I feel Wal tear free of my arm. He scrambles out from my sleeve, takes one look at where we are, at what's coming, and shoots back under my shirt.

I try and shift. Nothing. Here I don't seem to have any purchase on reality. There's nothing to shift from. This isn't my normal state. It is neither the Underworld nor the land of the living. Desperate, I try again. I've virtually stopped moving. I'm just spinning a slow circle. *Fuck.*

Where's Cerbo? Surely he'll come back for me.

But would I, if that thing was approaching?

I imagine him telling Suzanne, "He was the one who let go, the fool. He deserved it."

Maybe this was their plan after all. If that's the case it's worked. I'm a dead man.

Ah, but I've been dead before. A calm, pricked with some sort of madness, envelops me. I grin, a wide and mocking grin. *Fuck it all.* That rage and joy which fills my dreams flares up and out. I'm not afraid of death, I *am* Death. No matter that this space beyond space is not my realm.

I reach into my jacket, my hand steady, calm as though this was any stir. My fingers close around my knife—the knife every Pomp has, to draw blood to stall a stir. The thing approaching is a Stirrer god. And I know how to deal with Stirrers. I slash my knife down hard, deeper than usual. Blood boils from my skin, arcs around me. The potent blood of an RM. And suddenly I'm bound in light, a ball of it. Purer and brighter than any star.

The tentacle flinches for a moment. Pauses. I see it illuminated in that hard blood-forged light. The blades are motionless, though each seems to pulse, and I realize that for all their sharp edges they are more like flagella than anything else. The flesh beneath is not black so much as gray, the color of ash. Beyond it the eye is watching me, and its wide pupil narrows. I can't help myself. I wink.

The universe draws a breath and then I'm racing backward. Smashing through the cold, dark air heading home. But it may not be enough.

The tentacle's pause is momentary.

Whatever I did only stunned the Stirrer god, or surprised it; less than a flea bite. I can hear the god giving chase, a great whistling roar, louder than the wind, and above that noise the scraping of its knife fringes sounds remarkably like the groaning limbs of the One Tree.

It's gaining. It's gaining.

Its shadow descends over me like a wave, but a

sword-gnashing wave, all cutting edges and hunger. I cringe, fold my hands over my neck.

I drop into my office. Hit the floor hard, knocking the breath from me, and almost slamming into Cerbo, which wouldn't have been such a bad thing, I'm thinking. My breath comes quick and, with it, rage. Cerbo's on his arse pale and panting, he slides away from me, gripping his green bowler absurdly in both hands. The whole building shakes as something strikes us above. Whether it's metaphysical or not, it hits hard. I throw my arms over my head, but the ceiling holds.

"You let go," Cerbo says, looking at me eyes wide with fear or guilt, or both.

"And you couldn't come back and get me?" I'm on my feet in an instant. I grab him and shake. I'm pumped. My heart is pounding, I barely realize that I'm lifting him off the ground.

"I didn't have time," Cerbo squeaks.

"Didn't have time?" I shout.

Oscar swings open the door. Tim's with him.

"What was that?" Tim demands. They both stop, staring at me shaking Cerbo.

I put Cerbo down. I straighten my jacket and run my fingers through my hair. "Stirrer god, I think."

Cerbo nods. "That's never happened before." He looks at Tim, then Oscar. "It's all right. It nearly had us, but it can't. Not here, not yet. A finger tap is not an invasion. Now, if you would excuse us, Tim and Mr. Goon, there are some things I need to discuss with your boss."

"Yeah," I say. "Some things...Tim, I've just discovered something you should be able to do. It will be bloody, of course, and you really wouldn't want to do it. But—" I glance over at Cerbo. "Jesus, what other things should Tim be able to do? I want you to teach him. I need him to know this shit."

Cerbo dips his head. "It would be useful. You are working at a disadvantage."

"You got time to talk to this bloke?" I ask Tim. Cerbo is giving him another pained look.

"Yeah, I'll make time." I peer at Tim, he looks a bit under the weather. Maybe he didn't stop drinking after the party.

"Great, I'll send him through when we're done."

Once Oscar and Tim are gone I gesture to an office chair.

"I really am sorry," Cerbo says, sitting down. "No matter what you may think, it was not my intention to put you in danger. The Stirrer god recognized you. It certainly reacted."

"Wonderful. I've got enough enemies without a bloody god gunning for me."

"Too late for that," Cerbo says, straightening his hat.

"It's very close now, isn't it? How long do we have?"

"Best estimate? Twelve months."

"And worst?"

"Well, it just knocked on the door, didn't it?" he replies, gesturing above us.

I look up at the ceiling, at the space that I suppose I dropped through. There's a tiny black smudge there.

"So how do we stop it?"

Cerbo looks at me. "Believe me, that's what we're working on. I just don't know."

I glance at my bleeding hand. The wound is beginning to close but not as fast or as painlessly as I would like. "But it's going to involve blood, isn't it? And lots of it."

"What doesn't in our line of business, Mr. de Selby? You tell me."

"I want you out there. Teaching Tim what he needs to know. Show him what you did. Show him how to shift. But please, don't do anything that's going to kill him."

And then, with a brief dip of his head, he leaves the room. I'm alone.

I snatch up the black phone.

"We need to talk. And now!"

"The markets," Mr. D says, and is gone before I can protest. All I can do is fume into the silence of the handset.

The markets are crowded and run along the southern bank of the River Styx, its black water flowing languidly toward the rolling sea. The crowds that gather here and buy the produce are silent in the main. It is an eerie thing, that silent shopping. There's not a hint of haggling, no spruiking, no musicians or other street performers, though a flute is playing distantly and atonally. This is a mere shadow of a living market. A memory. The tents shift, the goods within change—kangaroo hide one moment, spinning tops or fruit the next—echoing centuries of commerce. Money is exchanged, and it is various—old coins and paper; plastic, too. I can hear the click-clack of an old credit card machine.

Here, where there are so many dead, the red of the sky mingles with the blue glow of the dead's flesh. And far above us, a single branch of the One Tree reaches out across the river and the city. I can just make out the shapes of tiny figures up there, finding a place to rest, and a final passage to the Deepest Dark.

"What do you think of these oranges? Too soft?" Mr. D asks.

"You're really an extremely frustrating man." I lean in toward him, and it's all I can do to stop myself from jabbing him in the chest.

Mr. D grimaces. For a moment his face is almost as full of motion as the days when he was RM. He may have demanded we meet in the markets of the Underworld but I did not come here to look at oranges, silver jewelry, brewing ash or Troll Doll pencil erasers. Wal's not talking to me after my flight from the Stirrer god. He's fluttering around a nearby stall throwing me dirty looks and eating a dagwood dog. There's tomato sauce bearding his chin.

"How much did you know about the Stirrer god before you died?" I ask Mr. D.

"Very little, believe me. I was out of the loop."

"But you knew it was coming?"

"Only that something was coming, and then Morrigan's little Schism distracted me."

"Well, I've seen it up close, and let me tell you it terrified me."

"There was a guy called Lovecraft. Wrote horror stories."

"Yeah, I know who he was. What about him?" I say, irritated at this turn in the conversation.

"Well, with Lovecraft, sure, he was a horrible racist, but he got something right. Sometimes terror is the only response."

"Terror. OK, so what about Rillman?"

"Rillman really was a surprise to me. I thought him long gone." Mr. D squeezes an orange speculatively. "I do like a good orange. Oh! Now it's gone and changed into a pear!"

"Enough about the—"

Then I catch something out of the corner of my eye. A movement not quite right, a little too energetic, just a little too alive. There's a man, standing by a nearby stall, who isn't dead.

His arms don't glow with the blue light that every soul emits in Hell. Nothing living, not as we define it, should be here. I watch him, and try to act like I'm not watching him. His shoulders are broad, and he's wearing a beaked plague mask and a wide-brimmed black hat. Is this the same guy who cut the window-cleaning assassin's rope? He moves to another stall, beak bobbing up and down like a toy drinking bird, as he inspects with far too much interest what appears to be a collection of old *Archie* comics. I can just make out Jughead's face and crown.

"Do you see that?" I ask Mr. D.

"See what?" He shrugs, putting down the pear.

I'm getting the sort of vibe that if I make any movement toward our *Archie*-perusing beaked mate, he'll leg it. "If you can't see him, don't worry." Though how you can miss a non-glowing man in Hell wearing a plague mask is beyond me—even in the markets. The fellow really is going to look peculiar anywhere outside of Black-Death period dramas or fancy-dress parties.

"Well, you're worrying me now," Mr. D says, and looks ready to turn around. I slap a hand onto his shoulder.

"No need for that," I say. "You're not the target. Besides, how would they kill you? You're already dead."

"There are ways and means, believe me."

Hmm, maybe I need to know some of them.

"Don't you get any ideas," Mr. D snaps. "What's he doing now?"

"Anything but looking in our direction," I say.

Then he's gone. I refuse to let that stop me. There is some muddy sort of swirl where he was, a sort of crazy wake–black hole combo. I look from Mr. D then back to that murky mass. It's shrinking, and fast.

I know I'm going to regret this. I sprint at the swirling, what I guess—hope—to be a gateway and dive into it.

Silence. Icy fingers clutch my heart and squeeze—my left arm throbs. It's a real effort not to yell with the sick, deep pain of it.

Then I come out of the dark, skidding on my belly, feeling oddly refreshed. I spring to my feet, my fists clenched.

I'm still in the Underworld. Mount Coot-tha rears up beyond the river. The One Tree creaks, casting its great shadow over everything. I recognize this place! I can see the old gas stripping tower—the structure that was in part responsible for me becoming what I am. I remember the agony of the summoning ceremony I performed in its living-world clone to enter Hell and call a trapped Mr. D to me. How did I ever endure that? I just did, I guess, I had no time to react or think it through. Maybe I could again, but knowing what to expect, I doubt it. How the hell does Rillman manage it time and time again? Who's helping him?

The masked man stands by the tower, waiting for me, shifting his balance from foot to foot.

I stride toward him. "You!" My hands are balled up at my sides. I'm bigger, meaner, faster. I'm an RM. This is my territory. I loom over him. Finally, I'll get some answers! A grin goes rictal across my face. "No point in running."

"You're right," he says, in a voice I can't quite place, dancing to my left and around me.

And then I'm on my arse, blinking. My nose is bleeding, my head throbs. I have the far-too-fucking-familiar taste of my own blood in my mouth. Whirring wings flash just outside of my line of vision.

"You all right?" Wal shouts, his voice thick as treacle in my ears. I blink; he's blurry and indistinct. And still holding onto the dagwood dog.

"The prick sucker-punched me!" I say.

Wal grins. "Well, you have to be a sucker first."

Thanks. Yeah, another comment from the poster boy of my fan club. "Do you always have to be like this?"

"What are you saying? When was I any different? Grow a sense of humor."

I have to admit that he does look concerned. You don't often see an RM stunned and bleeding in their region. It's not particularly good for my ego, especially as this is the second time in two days. At least no one else has seen me this time. "He seemed to know what he was doing," I say, as Wal flies around me, searching for any other injuries.

"No shit." He lands heavily on my shoulder and I get a spatter of tomato sauce down my shirt front.

"Have you ever seen him before?"

"I don't have X-ray vision."

I sigh. "Just what help are you?"

"I'm here, aren't I? Even with a god driving down on us in the dark of the ether, something I'd rather not experience again, by the way—I'm here. And you know I always will be, you whiny bastard. We're stuck together, and I've got your back."

"Yeah, look, I'm sorry." I struggle to my feet. Wal flies

from one shoulder to the other. The movement makes my head spin. "I've got work to do."

"Be careful," Wal says. "I can't look after you up there."

"I'll do my best."

"That's what I'm worried about."

18

Tim's on the phone shouting at somebody. He hangs up when I slide a chair next to his desk. I look at the dark rings under his red eyes.

"You really look like you had a big night last night," I say.

"And you look like you've just been punched in the nose again," he shoots back.

I touch my hand to my face. Yep, blood. "Just spent the morning chasing someone through the Underworld. Turns out I should have ducked when I caught up with them."

Tim passes me a box of tissues. "Who do you think it was?"

"Not Rillman, at least. It felt too different from him. An Ankou, I think, but I couldn't get a good enough fix on them. At least they didn't stab me. There's something almost honorable about a good old punch to the face." I apply tissues. "Talking of Ankous..."

"Cerbo's lesson was instructive."

"Do you think you could shift?"

"Give me three weeks, and I'll be shifting everywhere. Right now, the thought of doing it again makes me want to throw up. Steve, sorry I ever doubted you."

"This situation with Rillman is out of control, Tim. What the hell are we supposed to do?"

Tim shuffles his papers, lifts his eyes to mine. "We keep going. There's nothing else we can do. We keep going carefully and cautiously, and we do not stop. Whoever Rillman is, and whoever he's working for, they can get to us anytime they want. They've already proven it. And if Rillman can shift then there's nowhere that's safe. We just have to keep going, until either we stop him, or he stops us."

My mind turns to things that we may have some control over. "How are you going with those Closers?"

Tim frowns. "I can't find out anything. People are being very tight-lipped at the Department—and I mean *very*." He sighs. "I can't remember the last time I came to work with a hangover. I got three of them drunk last night, after the Christmas party, and nothing. Not a bloody peep. But this is my best guess." He hands me a small sheaf of papers. "These are based on my suggestions, when I was running that portfolio."

He looks at his watch. "We've a job interview at 11:30. You'll need to be there, since we're using your office and all."

"Really? This morning's been busy enough as it is!"

"Who is it?"

"Clare Ramage. She looks good, on paper anyway. Lissa found her. I'm surprised she didn't mention anything, but, then, the week we've been having, eh? We won't know for sure until we can get her into your office, see how she handles the Underworld."

"What do you think?" The office is just a formality, both Lissa and Tim can usually tell beforehand.

"I think she'll be fine."

"OK I'll see you at 11:30. And I'll read this, right now. That's a promise."

"Make sure you keep it. None of that slipping a book-mark through it bullshit," Tim says, and maybe I shouldn't grin at him. Shit, we're so good at pushing each other's buttons we don't even need to try most of the time. Tim groans. "Now, get out of here. And be careful who you let into your room, unless you don't intend reading that, because if that's the case, buddy, I might just have to torture you myself."

He sits there, glaring at me. I stare back sheepishly.

"I'm on it," I say. "Really."

Tim just harrumphs under his breath. "Close the door on your way out."

I walk back through to my office, stopping at the kitchen to make some coffee and feeling all those eyes watching me. Maybe I *was* a little too hard on everyone last night, or maybe it's that my nose hasn't quite stopped bleeding yet. I drop Tim's notes onto the desk: they land with a satisfying and vaguely threatening thump.

After ten pages I'm glad Tim's working on my side.

The first page outlines possible threats to Australia's population should Mortmax fail. Regional Apocalypse is at the top of it. There's a half-dozen end-of-world scenarios— some of which I wasn't even aware were a possibility— and how Mortmax might be involved in them.

It's a pretty damning, but I must admit, honest appraisal. And I can see why Tim may have been pushing for closer government ties to Mortmax, and just why he might have been so resistant to the family business.

And now, since we came so close to a Regional Apocalypse, and streets were crowded with Stirrers, I know why they might just rush through an organization like the Closers.

I'm twenty pages in when the phone rings.

It's Neill. "I heard you had some trouble yesterday," he says.

"Yeah, I suppose you could call it trouble." I find it hard to keep the suspicion out of my voice.

"Death Moots create a certain . . . well . . . chaotic energy, but this is the first time this has happened. Are you sure there's no one trying to challenge you?"

"No one's killed a Pomp yet," I say. "There's just been attempts on me."

"You sure it's not that cousin of yours?" Neill asks. "It's usually the fookin' Ankous that are the problem."

"Not my cousin, I'm sure of that." I try a different tack. "Do you have a government liaison?" There's silence down the line for a moment.

"Yes, it's only something very new. I never thought we needed it before, but they were quite persuasive."

"Define persuasive. Insistent? Or coercive?"

"Well, it's certainly made stopping Stirrers much easier," Neill says. I'm putting my money on the latter.

"We've a group here called the Closers."

"What are they?"

"Police, but a unit devoted to us. You have anything like that there?"

"Not that I know of. Just a unit that keeps a closer eye on our paperwork, our visits to morgues and funerals, that sort of thing. But liaison or no, our communications with the government are a little limited. You could say that we both have secrets that the other may not like. Why do you have such a unit there?"

"The Regional Apocalypse. I think it worried them. I can't blame them, of course. It worried me."

"Times are changing," Neill says, and there's more than a hint of bitterness in his voice.

"Yeah, they're changing, all right."

I put a few more calls through, speaking as directly as I can to the various RMs. All of them seem to have something of a government presence, several when their territories cover more than one country—some have as many as twenty.

For most of them, this is something new. And for the ones that it isn't they've noticed an increased scrutiny. But that's not the only thing. Their lack of concern about the issue is disturbing. Something doesn't feel right. This is definitely going on the agenda at the Death Moot.

Talk doesn't stick to the government departments, though. Every single one of them is pitching an alliance at me, or at the very least a mutual back-scratching sort of set-up. I'm non-committal.

I haven't hung up from the last call for more than a few heartbeats when the phone rings again.

Alex.

"Steve, I can't talk for long," he says, his voice low. "You're going to get a call soon. From Solstice. They've found the body of the man who tried to shoot you. Well, we think it is."

"Where?"

"Look, when I say they've found the body, I mean *we* did; but they've taken it away."

"Did you get much of a look? Did it fit my description?"

"No, I didn't get a look in. The Closers were already there when I arrived." Alex's voice lowers to a whisper. "I really don't like that crew. There's something…off about them."

"Tim hasn't been able to find out anything about them, either."

"Yeah, no agency is that secret. There's always some-one who knows something, and is willing to talk. Usually, when there isn't, you have to wonder." There's a quiet murmuring in the background. Alex raises his voice. "Look, I've got to go. But I will talk to you soon." He hangs up abruptly.

There's another call. I don't recognize the number.

"Yes?" I say.

"Nothing to worry about, it's just Solstice."

"What can I do for you, Detective?"

"Nothing, really, it's more what I can do for you. I thought I might send some fellas over to keep an eye on your house."

"My house, or me? Am I a suspect in my own shoot-ing, Mr. Solstice?"

Solstice clears his throat. "Of course not, but then again…stranger things, Mr. de Selby, stranger things. It wasn't your body that they picked up at Toowong Ceme-tery with injuries that suggest a great fall."

Toowong Cemetery sits on Mount Coot-tha, or One Tree Hill, as we know it. One of the many points close to the Underworld, it made sense that my attacker would have used it. Why hadn't I thought of that?

"Have you identified the body?"

"Well, that's just it. There's not a lot to identify, but what we have suggests that this person was a Pomp. I'd like you to take a look at him, so there—I suppose there is something you can do for me."

"Where are you?"

He tells me. It's an address, just off Milton Road, in the inner city. That's peculiar. It's not the usual morgue (or as the government likes to call it, Forensic and Scientific Services) out on Kessels Road to the south of Brisbane. This has gone wide of the usual coronial pathways. I didn't even know there was a morgue there. I'll have to check this with Tim. I don't like the idea of dead bodies being stored where we can't get at them. It throws me, to be honest.

But I want to see that body. I shift.

It's like any morgue I've ever seen, though it smells of new paint and disinfectants. It's cold, tiled halfway up the walls. A body obscured in black plastic lies on a stainless steel table, and there's the familiar, thin smell of death that can't quite be removed, no matter how many cleaning agents you use. Could be worse, Dad had some absolute horror stories about morgues in the fifties, little more than corrugated iron sheds—things started smelling pretty high in there come late spring. And the flies...No flies here, at least.

Traffic rumbles somewhere in the distance—Milton Road, I guess—though here it's quiet but for the murmur of refrigeration units, and the chirruping of a computer with what I imagine is some sort of email notification. Someone's getting a lot of emails.

Solstice looks pale beneath his tan. Even the dragon tattoo on his forearm has lost its lustre. I won't go so far as to say that he looks sick, but it's close. I sometimes forget that not everybody deals with death as often as me.

"When did you start using this place?"

Solstice smiles. "That's classified. But it's new. Not even the coroner knows about this one."

"Do any of my people?"

"No, but we only keep 'persons of interest' here. And you know about it, now."

I don't like it. How could we stop a Stirrer from stirring here? "So where is he?"

Solstice walks to the nearby slab, pulls back the plastic sheeting.

There really isn't much to identify. Everything's there, but it's pulped. Features are warped and flat, and insects, or some other sort of creature, have had a go at digesting bits of what's left. The skin is chewed and tunneled, mined as though it was some sort of resource, and I guess it is. All flesh and bone is.

"Someone had gone to a bit of effort to hide the body. If a maintenance fella hadn't decided to work on the northwest corner of the cemetery he might have sat there for even longer."

I know I'm not getting the full story. I know they snatched this away from the cops, but I try to not let that show on my face.

"There's no license or wallet, obviously, and his finger-prints have come up blank. We're waiting on dental, but I'm not feeling that hopeful. But then there's this." He pulls the plastic sheeting down to the waist.

Interesting.

Along both of his arms and his chest are a series of interlinking brace tattoos, and a couple of other symbols that may have some esoteric potency, or be a load of bullshit. It's always hard to tell but they're certainly the sort of tattoos that a Pomp might have. He even possessed a bit of death iconography on a shoulder blade, a cherub like mine, though his is bigger.

"If he was a Pomp, he certainly didn't belong to me. I can feel it when my Pomps die." It was something I haven't had to experience yet, but no doubt will, soon enough. Every RM does. "He's been too long gone for me to tell if he belongs to anyone else." Could he belong to Suzanne? No, that doesn't make sense.

"Do you trust the other RMs?" Solstice asks.

I snort, can't help myself. "Do you know how RMs actually become RMs, Mr. Solstice?"

Solstice shakes his head. "A certain negotiation," he says. "Something about a tree?"

Which is pretty good. He certainly knows more than I did when I was just a Pomp. I think back to the Negotiation, wondering why something so bloody had such a civil name. After all, two mumbling death-lusting stone blades were involved. "Let me just say the process doesn't even begin to encourage trust. I wouldn't trust those bastards as far as I could throw them. Backstabbers, every one of them. After all, it's the only way you become RM. Back, front and side-stabbing, with a little slashing thrown in as well."

"And what about you?"

"I never wanted this job. And you know, I hold that as a badge of pride."

"Can't make it easy for you…lacking that ruthless-ness. And yet, here you are, RM."

"I did what I had to."

"I suppose they'd all say that, wouldn't they? Doesn't everyone, who rises to a position of power?"

I glance at my watch. "Are we done? I've got an appointment."

"Yeah, we're done."

"And about those fellas you want to send over. Don't bother, we've got our own people."

"You trust them?"

"Absolutely."

Solstice smiles. "Just turn a blind eye to any cars parked across from your place."

"This is inhouse," I say between gritted teeth.

Solstice shakes his head. "Not when people die, it isn't."

I grin nastily at him. "That's how death works."

19

W ell, would you look at that?" Tim says. "You're early."

Tim's sitting in his office and that's where I've shifted again. "Right place, wrong time. At least your pants are on," I say.

"You don't have a clue what's going on behind this desk." Tim lights a cigarette. "I thought you were reading those briefing notes."

"Funny you should say that. I was interrupted by a call from Solstice." I open Tim's door, and wave across the room at Oscar. He grimaces at me. "Tim, I don't like how the Feds keep poking their noses into our business."

Tim sighs. "Steve, it's all about accountability."

"It sounds like you agree with their approach."

"No. But I understand it." He ashes into a Coke can. "You read my notes?"

"Most of them. But this group doesn't feel like that. I spoke to Alex, too. He says he can't get anything on them. This is Australia. We don't have any covert groups."

"What about us?"

"That's different. We're not so much covert as unacknowledged. We've been around since life began."

Tim walks with me to my office then heads to reception to wait for our possible new recruit.

Oscar's waiting outside my door. There's a certain percentage of rage beneath his professional demeanor.

"Sorry," I say. "Had an interview with the police."

Oscar grimaces, though I think he's coming to terms with me a little. "How hard is it to phone, eh?"

He opens the door to my office. Lissa's sitting in one of the chairs.

I turn to Oscar. "What's this with the security breaches today?" I ask. He grimaces again and shuts the door in my face.

"And don't you have your own office, Ms. Jones?"

"This was the only time I knew I would be able to see you," Lissa says. "There's not much window in either of our schedules... You look a little pale."

"I've been chasing shadows all day, not much chance to get a tan." I drop into the throne. "How is it that everybody knows about Rillman except me? Did you know he's regularly been crossing into the Underworld? Suzanne—"

"What about Suzanne?" Lissa says sharply.

I try not to look guilty. "Mr. D says she's told him that Rillman has been making trouble for years. Just not here. Seems it took my promotion to bring him back to Australia." It's another thing Morrigan has to answer for.

I sense another heartbeat in the building. "We have a visitor," I say. "Clare Ramage?"

"She's good," Lissa says. "One of the best I've found. Even has a bit of family history in the trade."

Oscar knocks on the door, then swings it open, giving me the thumbs-up, and a woman (Clare, I'm guessing) in her early twenties walks into the room. Tim follows her.

I scan her face to see how she copes with this space. She tilts her head. Good, she can already hear the creaking of the One Tree. My mind's not on the interview, though. I'm back at that odd morgue, trying to piece things together. Who was the assassin working for? And when did bodies stop being processed through the usual channels?

I sit through the interview trying to look interested, but it's Lissa who asks most of the questions. I hope I appear affable and bossish enough, and not that distracted. It's over in under an hour. Once Clare's gone, Tim and Lissa talk it through.

"What do you think?" Lissa asks me. I blink at her.

"About what?"

Lissa snorts. "Clare?"

I wave my hand absently at the door. "Miss Ramage was fine. Eminently employable."

Tim's phone beeps. He grimaces. "I've got to take this one."

"Ankou?"

"Nah, the Caterers. Since the ceremony they've been calling me every bloody second hour, because somebody went and left this to the last minute."

I don't know whether to be offended that they're dealing with Tim instead of me. "Yeah, you better." Tim gives

Lissa a look that I can't read, and she nods. Oh no, this better not mean another lecture for me.

When Tim's out of the room, Lissa frowns. "You're losing focus again."

"No, I'm not," I mumble. How can I explain that, if anything, I'm more focused than ever before, it's just the picture that's changed. "Take my word for it, I'm not. Clare's got the job, I can make her a Pomp tomorrow. Give her one more day to think about it, and to be normal, eh?"

Lissa nods, tries to pull a smile, fails. I can understand why she's worried about me, but she doesn't need to be. Not about this. "You don't want to give her too long."

"Worried she'll change her mind?"

Lissa gets up, pecks me on the cheek, walks to the door. "Who wouldn't?"

"You, me, Tim."

Lissa laughs. Bad examples, every one of them.

I'm left alone. Lissa was the first person I turned into a Pomp: Lissa. She'd been one before, of course, but when she was resurrected back into her body, I'd had to return her powers. In those dark moments, as the Stirrers surrounded us, there had been an intimacy that was terrifying. We'd looked into each other's soul and found an echo and a challenge of, and to, our own.

I lean back in my throne and my eyes close, just for a moment.

Knives. A swinging scythe. Mist the color of blood.

I jolt awake. Fucking hell! A bloke could cut out his eyelids just to stop these visions.

Something catches my attention. A differently beating heart, a slight change in electricity. Someone has shifted into my city unannounced. And not just anywhere...

Now, that, I can't allow.

I squeeze my eyes tight, take a deep breath to prepare for the unpreparable, and shift myself to Mount Coot-tha. Old One Tree Hill.

Someone's on my turf and they shouldn't be.

20

Mount Coot-tha. Heart of the city of Brisbane, and its Underworld twin. I arrive in the middle of a bunch of tourists. None of them seem that impressed with my swearing, or the way I hop around on one foot. This shift felt like a spear being driven into my thigh. That's something new. I thought I was getting better at it. But it passes quickly, even if I'm red-faced with embarrassment.

"If you've finished your little dance," Suzanne says. "We can start today's lesson. Though take your time, I'm finding this all very amusing."

"What are you doing up here?"

"Testing your abilities, and I must say that you surprised me. I didn't really expect that you would sense me. If I had I would have showed up in, say, Tasmania. You get a gold star."

"I don't like this shifting around, unannounced—it sends a bad message," I say.

Suzanne's good humor slips a little. "It does nothing

of the sort. If you can detect me, or any other RM, then they can detect you. They will know that you know they are here."

"No one can sneak up on me?"

"Not quite," Suzanne says. "An electrical storm can shield their presence, but an electrical storm is hard to shift into, and an RM who is in the middle of one tends to be wary."

"And why should an RM be wary of another RM? Aren't we supposed to be all unified?"

Suzanne raises an eyebrow. "Don't be naive. RMs can hurt you more than anyone else, except, perhaps, for this Mr. Rillman. When an RM comes unannounced you be ready. And try and remember if you have crossed anyone."

The Kuta Cafe at the top of Mount Coot-tha is open, and up here, there's a bit of wind, enough to take the edge off the summer heat. The last time I was here I spoke to Morrigan still thinking he was a friend. I know that Suzanne isn't; even "ally" would be too generous a term.

Brisbane stretches itself out around us, a vast carpet of tree-smeared suburbia. The CBD rises up in the east, a tight bunching of skyscrapers around which the Brisbane River wends, leading to Moreton Bay. A series of low, flat mountains marks the western horizon. The air is clear, a typical Brisbane summer's day.

But sometimes I'm seeing and hearing the Underworld simultaneously, a superimposed view of the land of the dead. The ruddy river. The massive root buttresses of the One Tree. The creaking, creaking, creaking as its mighty limbs are moved by the restless winds of Hell. Wal's face shifts on my tattoo. He can almost take form here, and I know he wants to.

"Do you want a coffee?"

Suzanne shakes her head. "Just a quieter place, away from all these tourists." She winces as though she has a headache. "It's too bright here."

"Just about anywhere is quieter in Brisbane than this," I say.

I lead her up to the observation platform. It's just us, now. Maybe our presence has something to do with that. Put two RMs together and there's always a bit of electricity. Though there are some kids running on the lookout below. The air crackles with the buzzing of cicadas, the kids' shouts and the ubiquitous creaking of the One Tree. This is my home.

"Lovely," Suzanne says. "Looking down at it from here I must say what a beautiful and intimate little city you have. But it's not quite the right venue for what I have planned. Are you all right to shift again?"

"Of course I am," I say.

"You're getting better at it at last." There's a glint in Suzanne's eye. "Deepest Dark then," she says.

I follow her there. And I don't throw up.

"So, Faber introduced you to the Stirrer god?"

"Up close and far too personal. It nearly killed me, thank you very much."

"Ours is a dangerous business. And none more so than when facing that god."

"Yeah, particularly when your guide lets go of your hand."

"I assure you that Faber was utterly mortified by what happened. At least you were quick-witted enough to do what had to be done."

"Yes, I was, wasn't I?"

Suzanne laughs. "There's hope for you yet. You needed to see it up close. You needed to feel just what sort of a menace it has become. To understand why this thing terrifies us—all of us—in a way that defies the usual squabbles of the Orcus."

"I had an idea already." When did Suzanne start taking this seriously? Is she playing me? But she's always playing me!

"No, you had no idea. This thing will be beaten, or it will destroy us. Life, and the Orcus. We thirteen have not faced such a threat in lifetimes beyond counting. There is nothing written about such a thing. But there are murmurings. It, or something very much like it, was defeated before. There are things you need to know. You've a rich heritage of which you are barely aware. Starting with the basics. Do you know why pomping hurts?"

"Because it does. It makes sense, there's that whole exchange of energy thing. If we're going to take something out of our universe and put it into another, of course it'll hurt."

Suzanne looks at me, and laughs. "Physics has nothing to do with what we are about, Steven." Suzanne shakes her head. "No. The pain is an additive, something the Orcus constructed through ceremony and hard work, and then entered into the process. Pomping used to be pleasurable, addictive."

"That would have been dangerous."

"You have no idea. Before there were thirteen, pomping was a nightmare. One you perhaps know too well."

My ears prick up at that. Nightmares. She sees it and smiles.

"Yes, we all have them. You've heard of the Hungry Death?"

"Just a few stories, stuff Dad would tell me when I was a kid." But the way Dad had told them, I'd never taken them seriously.

"They're just stories now, but there was a time when they weren't." Her voice slows and grows sonorous and rhythmical. "Long ago, before you and me. Before the world is the shape it is now, or shape it was before, there was only one Death. And it was called the Hungry Death because it was always hungry." She crouches down and trails a finger in the dust of the Deepest Dark. Following her is a dusty wake, now thirteen trails, which then rise and race around her fingers. They coalesce into a form—vaguely human, vaguely Stirrer. She seems to shake her head at the whimsy of it, flicks her hand and the Hungry Death is just falling dust again, but it's broken a little of her rhythm, for a moment she is just the cynical RM again. "If only it was that easy to dismiss. That painting of Mr. D's, the lurid one by the peasant."

" 'The Triumph of Death'?"

"That's the one. Picture that. You got it?" I nod my head. "Now imagine that painting, but there is only Death. And it is everywhere. The Hungry Death was a walking, shifting apocalypse. Random and violent in a...I suppose...more focused way than our world actually is, and I would suggest that you'd agree that ours is a pretty random and violent one."

"What happened to the Hungry Death?"

"You know. Close your eyes, and you know." I do nothing of the sort, just stare at her. She blinks.

"I don't blame you," Suzanne says. "When I tell you

there were thirteen warriors who went to battle with it, do you start to get the idea?"

I stare at her, dumbfounded.

She sighs. "OK. Thirteen warriors. They fought the Hungry Death, and what a battle it was, fire and brimstone, storm and earthquake. All of that, real 'Book of Revelations' stuff. They fought it. And they defeated it. Six times. And each time it came back. They cut it into pieces. And it came back. They ground its marrow to dust and it came back. They even ground its marrow to dust and turned it into some sort of paste, and yet it did no good.

"Finally a seventh, desperate battle. And this time, the earth a wasteland about them, the world a wound and the dying everywhere, they had begun to question why they had even tried fighting it in the first place. They held that Hungry Death down and this time they devoured it. Thirteen warriors, and each of them absorbed one-thirteenth of the Hungry Death's essence. And it has stayed that way through time.

"You see, it was never truly vanquished. Death cannot be. The Hungry Death lives on in each of the Orcus. It is our power, and the thing which each of us fear. That is what you dream about, Steven. Death untrammeled, blood and knives and the scythe. We all dream these dreams. It is why we don't need to sleep—its power sustains us—and why we don't want to."

I blink. "So I somehow ingested a thirteenth of the Hungry Death?"

"Absorbed is perhaps the better term. The Negotiation, why do you think it is so brutal? To become an RM you must appease the Hungry Death, blood must flow, and it is the only way to draw it out of a previous RM. And once it's within you...Surely you have felt it there? Not just in the dreams. Don't you sometimes feel its delight in death and destruction? It's the Hungry Death that makes it easier for you to deal with the things that you must see and do. And through you, it makes it easier on your Pomps."

"So what's the All-Death? It spoke to me, and not just in a dream."

"It's an aspect of the Hungry Death, too. We use it, of course, to generate the schedule, because it exists outside of time. Through it we know who is to die and when. It knows so much, and bereft of the Hungry Death, it is relatively benign."

"It didn't feel benign when it grabbed me."

"I said relatively. It remains a part of the Hungry Death."

"So what was it, this thing in me before it became the Hungry Death?"

"Something like the Stirrer god, perhaps. We don't know. This all happened a very long time ago. Generations before even the oldest RM, before even the invention of writing."

"And all it wants is death?"

"Yes, but not in the way that the Stirrers do. Which makes me believe it really isn't like them. You must be able to feel it, the pure joy it takes in death. Stirrers wish an end to life, this needs life to sustain it. I know you feel it."

Yes, I do. Why wasn't I told about this earlier? Mr. D with his all-in-good-time. My dreams have been such a horrible space, not least because of the pleasure I find in them.

"To think of such a cruel thing in here," I tap my chest.

Suzanne pulls my hand away. "You mustn't think that. It isn't cruel, merely inventive. Couple that with a clever and cruel creature like *Homo sapiens* and you have all sorts of madness, all sorts of ways of killing." Suzanne's eyes gleam. "It is better that it exists inside us, spread across the world, and that it is only fed every few generations in a Schism and a Negotiation. Think of the ruthlessness that we forestall with our existence. Our world, our myriad of societies, exist merely because we have given people time. We have given them the space to live longer, to develop culture and technology. Death remains, as does genocide and madness, but it is not all encompassing."

I remember my Negotiation. The Orcus gathered around Morrigan and me in a circle, the hunger in their eyes. I now know where most of that came from. Come the next Negotiation will I look that way, too?

"So I rule the land and the sea around Australia as Death, because once there were warriors and they killed Death itself."

"No, you cannot kill Death, only shape its form. And no, you do not rule the sea."

"*Why* hasn't Mr. D explained this? Gaps, gaps! I've got so many bloody gaps in my knowledge. What does, then?"

"Water, and the force within it. We've made our agreements with that force to cross the seas. But we have no power there. It does with those souls who die within its substance what it will. I hope that you'll never have to deal with it. Water is a cruel negotiator." Suzanne shivers. "And that is your lesson for today. The Stirrer god is powerful.

But there is a power within us, too. The secret is to use that power without destroying everything those first warriors fought for."

"And how do we do that?"

"I have a plan." Suzanne puts a finger against my lips. "But that is for another time."

I'm still thinking about plans, and Deaths of the sea, when I shift back to my office. Right on target. Tim obviously senses my return because he gives a ragged cheer from his office.

There's a message on my phone. Lissa.

"Call me, babe, when you get the chance."

I dial her number. She answers before the first ring.

"That was quick," I say.

"I was just about to call you again. Where have you been?"

I mumble something about Death Moot prep, feel a pang of guilt. If only she knew. Maybe I should just tell her about the deal with Suzanne now.

"Steven, we may have a problem. Actually there's no may about it."

"What is it?"

"Stirrers. Something new. I suppose you could call it a nest of them. I need you to come here."

"A nest? Why the hell can't we feel them?"

She gives me an address in Woolloongabba. It's a couple of suburbs south of the city. About ten minutes' drive away if the traffic isn't too bad.

I look at the schedule. There's no one spare. Besides Lissa and I should be able to handle them. I hesitate to shift there. If I can sense a shift they may be able to as well.

Oscar's standing outside my office door. I open it and he looks at me. "Going to need your help—and Travis's."

"Not a problem."

"How fast can you drive that Hummer of yours?"

Oscar gives me one of the biggest, maddest grins I have ever seen.

21

I don't expect to see Alex, but he's there with Lissa. Both of them look pretty grim.

There's no small talk. Lissa leads us up onto a flat rooftop above Vulture Street, a major tributary to the M1, the motorway that feeds into and out of the city. The traffic is building rapidly.

The Stirrers below us move with a confidence that only comes from inhabiting a body for weeks. They're sitting on the front verandah of the house, drinking what look like stubbies of beer. The house could be like any other in the suburb, or Brisbane, for that matter. It's a classic Queenslander, verandahs all around, tin roof. Very much like my parents' place. But this one has known better days; the paint's peeling so badly that we can see it from here. There's a pile of rubbish in the backyard, but that's common enough. The only odd thing about it is the roof—it's crammed with aerials, peculiar prickly bunches of them. What the hell do they need those for?

We're across the river from the city center. I can feel Number Four, and just down the road is the Gabba cricket stadium. It offends me that this is happening so close to where we are based, and even more that it's almost next door to one of the greatest cricket pitches in the world. How could Stirrers have grown so brazen? But I guess if I had a god hurtling through the ether toward earth, I'd be brazen, too, and perhaps pressured to perform. To make good, and ensure that my god was pleased.

What worries me more is that I can't taste them in the air. There's nothing. If anything, the space they occupy is too neutral. It's neither living nor dead. Are those aerials responsible for that?

The air is still and humid. Sweat sheens Lissa's forehead. Oscar and Travis are feeling it, too.

"What is this?" I ask. "The aerials. The house being so near the heart of the city. Why?"

"Yeah, I've never seen anything like it," Lissa says. "And we still wouldn't have, except for Alex."

"Alex?" I look over at him. "You found this?"

"Yeah," he says. "I tried to get in touch with you. When I couldn't, I called Lissa. Should have known she'd be able to get onto you."

"I've been a little busy today. Sorry," I say, guilt pangy and all.

Alex nods; looks like we've all been busy. "I've been looking into the Closers and this address came up several times. Something about a safe house, or being locked into the grid. I came and had a look, didn't get too close. You can tell why."

"How'd you come by the information?"

"Slightly illegally," Alex mumbles, not quite able to

meet my eye. It's not the way he likes to work at all. "Been digging around emails in the Closers' server."

"Seems he has quite a knack for the cyber-espionage," Lissa says approvingly.

"Yes, well." He blushes. "That's just between you and me. I really shouldn't be here, but I want to see this done properly." Alex is about as straitlaced as they come. For him to do any digging would have been painful indeed.

"You did good." I paint a brace symbol on Oscar's wrist, Travis is already done: the paint is simply red acrylic mixed with my blood. The brace symbol is a potent guard against our "problem." It used to be, at any rate. "You have to wonder how long this has been going on." I nod at Stirrer House down below. The implications are somewhat frightening to consider. How many other Stirrer houses are there out in the 'burbs and country towns? Places where we don't keep as much of a presence?

Lissa grimaces. "A while, at best guess. I'd say three weeks, maybe four."

Solstice knew about this and he didn't tell us. Just what game is he playing? I'm going to have to give that bastard a call. Looks like the war may be building up again.

"That Stirrer god of yours is getting closer, isn't it?" Alex says.

"It's always drawing closer, but distance is a weird thing, in the Deepest Dark." If only he could see it as up close as I have.

I look around at the assembled group. "Oscar, Travis: you two call this through if we have a problem. I don't expect one, but then again, I didn't expect to come across a Stirrer safe house in the middle of Brisbane. Alex—do you want to come down with us?" I tap the brace paint. Alex nods grimly and submits to being painted.

Oscar and Travis don't look happy, but they're not going to be any good to us down there. In fact they could be a liability, even with the brace paint.

"So, how are we going to do this?" Lissa asks.

"Frontal assault will work best," I say.

"Do you want to wait for some backup?"

"Don't be silly, we've handled worse. And besides, this needs a subtle touch, I think."

"You think you can manage that?" Alex snorts, trying to tough it out. He's seen me battle hundreds of Stirrers on George Street, even saved my life with a few well-placed shots himself. But this is different.

"Do you think *you* can? We were having this sort of fun when we were five," I say, giving Lissa a bit of a hug.

Alex grimaces. "You weren't the only ones with Pomp parents. I know what I'm doing."

There are two dozen sparrows gathered around me, pecking and hopping, looking innocent as all hell. You wouldn't know that they've all pecked my hand and supped a bit on my blood. Two blocks away wait eight crows. The heavy guns don't require my blood; they're less traditional than the sparrows on that front.

When I'd first become RM I'd managed to stall several hundred Stirrers in one go, but that had just been a flare-up of my new powers—apparently that's the way it works. Since then, in the few times I'd done this, I'd returned to the original method, blood and touch. Keeps me honest, I suppose.

A sparrow jumps on my finger and chirps at me

impatiently. I feel like I should be singing some sort of Disneyesque musical number.

Lissa runs her blade down her hand. It's a swift, sharp movement, and then she kisses me on the cheek.

"Be careful," I say.

"You too."

"Let's go."

We split up: approach the house from opposite sides. Half my sparrows shoot around the back, the rest follow me, a mad battering of tiny wings. Alex isn't far behind them, his gun out. I signal for him to approach the back door. He nods. He'll be safer out there, I hope.

I'm almost at the house when the first Stirrer sees me. He drops his beer. I leap over the fence, catch my foot, nearly fall flat on my face. Lissa is already past me. She swings a hand at the Stirrer. He catches it. The bastard's wearing gloves. Lissa swings around with her other hand, slaps a bloody handprint against his head.

I'm on top of the other one now. Its being scrambles and scrapes through me, and into the Deepest Dark. The body's just a body again.

The front door's unlocked. I go in first, cautious but quick.

Lissa's behind me. Every time I blink, I catch a glimpse of what my sparrows can see. Nothing has tried to use the back door yet. Alex is waiting there, gun at the ready, not that it would do much good. My crows are tearing through the air toward the building, their cries and caws growing louder with every wing beat.

I'm through to the living room, and gagging with the stench of rotten flesh. It's the first time in a while that it isn't alcohol or shift induced. And I can't quite believe what I see: two twitching bodies, tied to the ceiling, flies coating their flesh. Maggots carpet the floor beneath, a squelching, writhing mass. The spaces of the Stirrers' skin not fly-coated or maggot-bubbling are marked with symbols I don't recognize, but which none the less drive icy nails of dread through me. It doesn't stop there, though, there's something not right with the geometry of these ceilings, the way their corners meet—or don't—something that baffles my vision like the seeds of a migraine. I can smell stale smoke, too. The ceiling above, near the edges of its warped geometry, is black with scorch marks.

The bodies jerk and spasm. Eyes flick open. Lips curl with the most cunning of smiles. "You'll all be screaming by the end," their mouths, bearded with flies, whisper simultaneously. "It's coming."

The air is charged with a wild electricity. All over my body, hairs lift. My mobile phone crackles in my pocket. In the far corner of the room, a webwork of electricity sighs and hisses in the air. A living, shivering net. It slides toward me; maggots pop and bubble on the floor beneath it. My first instinct is to run. Instead, I slap the nearest body hard. The Stirrer's soul passes through me like a ball of barbed wire. And the electricity fizzles out, as though I've broken the circuit.

The second Stirrer snaps at my hand, ducks my strike, and somehow manages to scuttle across the ceiling. The length of the ropes that bind it limits the creature's move-ment. It blows me a kiss. "She'll be dead, they all will, and you'll know what's coming. And you won't care," it hisses. It starts to chew on the ropes. But we both know it doesn't stand a chance.

I swing a bloody fist at its face, and it's just a body

again. It's another rough stall, though. I drop to a crouch with the pain of it. They have been in these bodies for weeks. Their souls have grown thorns and tangles. My sparrows are hard at work, too. Their pomps are quick on the tail of mine.

Lissa stumbles into the living room. She looks exhausted. "Now, I stayed in some dives back in my uni days, but none as bad as this. Even when I ignored the cleaning roster." She nods at the bodies. "There's a Stirrer in every room."

"You got them all?"

"The ones that your sparrows didn't get to before me."

"What the fuck is going on here?" I do my best to ignore the flashes of my Avian Pomps devouring the corpses, tugging out beakfuls of flesh.

"Something ceremonial," Lissa says, distracting me from their feast. "Maybe the Stirrers were trying to create a life–unlife interface."

"Ah, one of those." I can almost hide the sarcasm in my voice and the annoyance at another gap in my knowledge.

Lissa shakes her head, as she binds her palm. "You haven't got a clue what I'm talking about."

I kiss her forehead. I'm just happy that she's all right. "Not really. Hey, at least I'm being honest."

She submits to the kiss. There's a line of blood across her cheek. I brush it away as best as I can, but really just turn it into a smudge.

"I know. Look, Steve," she says, "I've been doing some research. If we weren't so distracted, so damn busy, I'd have told you by now. A life–unlife interface would draw the living to Hell, and the unliving here. Sort of like a door, more like a carousel, and the more Stirrers there are the faster it'd spin."

"So this would let someone enter Hell?"

"Yeah, if they were crazy, and protected somehow." I think of those arcane tattoos on my failed assassin's chest and arms. "They'd have to be a Pomp though. It's a neat way of avoiding the use of one of the Recognized Entities. I mean, you couldn't imagine Aunt Neti or Charon allowing this sort of thing."

Maybe this explains just how Rillman came back from the dead. It would certainly explain how my shooter managed to be hanging outside my office with a squeegee and a pistol.

"Well, that's one interface destroyed at least," says Lissa.

"Yeah, but they're great at hiding them. Could you feel it before you walked inside?"

"Not at all."

"What's Solstice playing at keeping this secret?"

"Maybe he doesn't trust us. Maybe he was curious to see what we'd do about it," Lissa says.

"We're going to have to be particularly rigorous then."

We walk through the house, checking that each Stirrer is still. Then I start opening cupboards, Lissa behind me. There's nothing in the kitchen, just ancient pizza boxes, and more maggots. I'll have to hose down my boots. The bedrooms are empty too, but for the corpses above us.

"Do we call and have this cleared?" Lissa asks. Each city has a team set up for removing Stirrers caught out of morgues.

"No," I say. "Solstice and his team were aware of the house. Let them clean up the mess."

In the hallway ceiling there's a trapdoor to the roof. I drag a chair over to it, push it open and peer into the ceiling recess. Something crashes at my head. I throw up my hands. And then it is gone, whatever it is, and the ceiling's all wooden beams, dust and heat.

"Are you all right?" Lissa asks.

"Yeah, just jumpy. Must have been a trapped bird." I look into the ceiling recess again. Here I can see the rough welds that hold the aerials to the roof. There's no wiring. They're attached to nothing but corrugated iron. And yet, I'd seen lightning dance toward me across the living room floor. I climb back down, scratch my head.

"What I want to know is how they managed to get into the living world without us feeling them," Lissa says.

"Thunderstorms," I say. "We've been having a lot of thunderstorms. The electrical activity can shield almost anything. And look where they set up house." I point out a window at the transformer station nearby. "That and the aerials have gotta pump out a lot of distortion. What did Alex say they called it? A grid? Suggests to me there are more of them."

Lissa leans over and pecks my cheek.

"What's that for?"

"You seem to be learning things at last." Then Lissa's eyes widen. "Where is Alex?"

A dog's barking somewhere, and then it stops. A shot rings out from the backyard.

We both spring to the back door. It's bolted shut.

I try and fix on my Avian Pomps, but they're gone. The three crows and dozen sparrows I had out there aren't watching Alex anymore. I realize, then, that they're dead. I try and catch their memories, but there's nothing. In the confusion of battle I'd not noticed I'd lost track of them.

The door might be dead bolted but it doesn't look too

sturdy. I kick it hard. On the third leg-jarring belt with my boot the door bangs open.

Two Stirrers have cornered Alex in the backyard. My Avian Pomps are bloody lumps of feathers around him. A Stirrer has Alex by the wrist with one hand and it's swinging out at him with a knife. Alex is doing his best to keep his distance, but the Stirrer's pulling him in. The other Stirrer reaches out a hand to grab him. This one must be newer; its movements are clumsy, its hair and neck draped in spiderwebs.

Lissa and I race down the stairs from the back door toward Alex. I take the one with the knife, slap a bloody hand around its neck, another around its waist, and jerk it backward in some mad parody of a dance.

The other Stirrer gets a moment's notice and it swings its head toward Lissa. Alex punches out with his now free hand, and as it stumbles, Lissa stalls it. The Stirrer falls.

Mine shudders in my grip. I hold on as its rough soul scrapes through me. It's a dreadful sensation; this Stirrer's been around for a long time. Once it's hurled back to the Deepest Dark, I drop to my knees.

"You OK?" I demand, looking at Alex.

"You took your bloody time." Alex is shaking, but he manages an unsteady smile.

"I'm sorry," I say. "I didn't expect the strongest Stirrer to be out here. There's been more than a few surprises today."

"The bastard just dropped from the roof and took out your birds. They tried to protect me, but it was too fast. And then the other one appeared, stumbling out from under the house. Shit, I thought I was dead."

There's no point in brooding, in being too scared. Alex is a mate, I have to kill this fear right away. I wish I was better at this.

"So, Alex. You doing anything on Christmas Day?"

"No." Well, that's surprised him. "Mom's whooping it up on a cruise ship in the Pacific, and—"

Yeah, his dad's dead, I don't want him going there. "Well, you are now. Our place. Ten-thirty."

Alex's grin broadens. "You bloody Pomps. Just like my dad. Nothing unsettles you."

I only wish that was true.

22

If someone is opening and closing the doorway to Hell then I need to know just how that might be done. I'm sick and tired of being in the dark about this stuff. I try calling Charon, but he's out of the office. So instead I decided to visit Aunt Neti.

Tim stops me at the opening to her hallway. "I heard you had some trouble in the field today."

"If you call Stirrers generating lightning, and nearly stabbing Alex to death, then yes." I give him a rundown on the house, and what we found there. "Lissa thinks they were building a gateway between the lands of the living and the dead, and I figure that gateway may have been open for a while. And who has been using one lately? Rillman, and whoever the hell it is who's been tailing me."

"You think they're connected?"

"They have to be, don't they?"

Tim shuffles me a little deeper into the hallway and lights up. There are no smoke detectors here.

"If Alex hadn't found out about the house it would still be there. And it would still be doing whatever the hell it was doing." I jerk a thumb down the hallway. "If anyone can tell me about that it will be her."

Tim takes it in. "You want me to come with you?"

"Only if you don't have a Death Moot to help me plan."

He nods, relieved. "The Caterers are coming tomorrow. That should be interesting."

Tim walks back the way he came, and I take a deep breath and head toward Aunt Neti's residence. Wal starts to stir on my biceps. Wings flutter. With every step he takes a more 3D form.

Even down this end of the hall I can smell the cooking. It's a delightful and homely sort of smell—scones again, at a guess.

I close a fist to knock on the door, and the door swings open. I don't know why I bother.

"Is that you smoking, Mr. de Selby?" Aunt Neti's broad, many-eyed face peers down. She squints past my shoulder, checks up the hallway.

"No, I quit smoking a while back. It never stuck with me."

"Well, it stinks on you." She jabs a thumb at Wal. "Smoking cherubs, you're all class."

Wal shakes his head furiously. "Whoa, it wasn't me. I don't even smoke cigars, well, hardly . . ."

"I'm sorry," I say. "My cousin Tim—my Ankou—gets a bit nervous in this hallway. You know how it is."

"Well, he should be if he keeps up with the cigarettes. I was waiting for you," Aunt Neti says, and smiles, revealing teeth as dark as the space between the stars, and gums far too bright a red. There's a flash of an even redder tongue behind them.

I clear my throat. "I expected as much."

Aunt Neti titters. "Now, you come inside, young man. And we'll have ourselves a little chat."

I close the door behind me and enter the cloying warmth of her small parlor, hoping to avoid her embrace. No luck, though.

Aunt Neti's eight arms enfold me. She all but pulls me off my feet. I peck her on the cheek. Mr. D had insisted I do that, and she beams at me again. I get another glimpse of all those teeth.

I've heard rumors that she eats human fingers. Her room leads onto a garden of immense proportions and I peer through the door that leads out to it. Part of it must be connected to the living world because it is so verdant. "Fed on blood and bone," she says, watching me, clapping her eight hands together. "Plenty of it around here." She says that far too enthusiastically.

There are other doors—leading to the other regional headquarters—but all of them are shut. Shadows move behind one of them. There is a scraping and a scratching behind another. How many people have come into this drawing room and not come out? How many live between the walls, between the realms of life and death?

Well, I'm not a person in that sense. So I'm safe here. At least I tell myself that I'm safe here. And I can sort of believe that.

The tiny spider in the corner has grown considerably. It casts a large black shadow onto the wall, and it watches me with the same intensity it did last time.

Neti passes me a plate of scones after cutting them into

halves and slathering first butter, then jam, then cream all over them. "Just out of the oven," she says. "And I've just opened a new jar of blackberry jam."

Mom used to make blackberry jam. Dad would make the scones. And as Mom used to say, "Steven would make a mess."

Wal pokes me in the ribs.

"Thank you," I say quickly. I pick up a scone; take a nibble at its edges. Then a decent bite. "It's delicious."

Aunt Neti beams. "Of course it is, dear. I always make scones when people come with questions. I find it loosens the tongue."

"I need to know who has been crossing over lately," I say.

Neti frowns. "There's been nothing peculiar, as far as I can tell. The last really odd crossing, well, it was you, dear. Since then, we've had nothing but the occasional blip, you know, of a soul not that happy about moving on. And when I say not happy, I mean raving, barking, madly unhappy. Has to be, to make a blip. But that's all. Now, eat up. I spent a considerable time on those scones. Do you know how hard it is to make the flour of Hell palatable?"

I don't ask how, just nod my head. "This really is delicious."

Aunt Neti beams at me. Eyes as predatory as a hawk, waiting, waiting for the right moment. The right moment for what, I'm not sure, but it's making my skin crawl, at least as much as when she put her arms around me.

I clear my throat. "What do you know of Francis Rillman?"

"*The* Francis Rillman?"

"I suppose so."

"He was highly ambitious. He came to see me once. About something...Oh, it was a long while ago. Let me think..."

"It's really quite important."

"Oh, I know that, dear."

"He died recently."

Aunt Neti raises an eyebrow. "Really, I don't think so." She stands up and walks over to one of the closed doors. She's in and out in a heartbeat. I don't get much of a chance to see what lies beyond, but think of a scream made manifest, and you'd be partway there. She drops a book on the tiny table before her, and flips through the pages.

I try to get a look inside it.

"No, no. There is nothing as far as I can see." She passes it to me, and I can see my name there, the last entry, written in neat printing, the letters OM next to it. "This is my list of those who crossed over and back. It's a tiny book because it doesn't need to be that long. He's only here once, like you."

And there he is, a line before me, *Francis Rillman OM(F)*. Orpheus Maneuver Failed, I guess.

"Really? Lissa says she pomped him."

"She must be mistaken, dear. He's been to Hell and back but once. Have another scone, you're far too thin."

Wal reaches down to grab a scone, and she slaps him away. "You, on the other hand, could stand to lose a few pounds."

"Hey, I resent the implication. I'm a bloody cherub."

"Resent away, you look like a cherub who's eaten a smaller cherub, after frying them in batter—and not just one." She winks at me. "Now, let's just say that, hypothetically, Lissa *did* pomp Rillman and that he has come back somehow. Well, I'd not be surprised. You did something similar, after all."

I shrug. "Similar, I guess, though I never really died. But Lissa did, and I brought her back."

"Not without help you didn't." Aunt Neti's laughter peals from her like a bell ringing. She slaps both my knees. "You're an RM. You've died a dozen deaths, a hundred, a thousand, it's all you ever do."

I hate that line of reasoning. I'm really not all that different from my previous life as a Pomp. I certainly feel as confused as I ever have.

"How would Rillman have made it back?"

"Let's see…Rage and lack of compromise. You should know they are potent enough. You had your share of those, I've heard. Don't underestimate the efficacy of either."

23

When Lissa gets back into Number Four, looking exhausted, I drag her into my office. She vents, and I listen. Her day was long, another two stirs, and that after our assault on the Stirrers' house. And surely it couldn't get any hotter than this? Sure, her home city of Melbourne was hot, but it was a dry heat. People are dying, cooking and expiring, then cooking some more in the heat and the storms. And that's not even mentioning the Stirrers crowding around them. I feel guilty, that as I'm her boss and her partner I'm responsible for most of her problems.

Then it's my turn to vent. I talk about Aunt Neti. "She couldn't give me much. None of them seem capable of that."

"It's the way of upper management, and Recognized Entities," Lissa says. "They'll never give you much. It's not in their interest. I swear they love watching us feeling blindly about. They get off on it."

"I don't."

"Give it time," Lissa says, her words remind me of Suzanne's.

"Neti's certain Rillman is alive. She even showed me her book, the diary she keeps. If Rillman has died and come back, then he's doing something new."

"Well, they say he was an innovator."

"Don't sound so impressed when you say that."

"Believe me, you impress me more." She grabs her black bag. "Steve, I've had enough of work today. Can we … ?"

"I don't want to go home yet," I say. It's been a long day, but I'm not ready to face a sleepless night in my parents' place.

Lissa arches an eyebrow. "Well, where do you want to go?"

"I think you'll like it."

The Corolla's down in the car park. We pass people working the night shift. They smile at Lissa as we head toward the lift, and avoid eye contact with me. I don't mind, as long as they're working.

"You've done well with this lot," I say as we wait for the lift.

Lissa sighs. "It sometimes makes me wonder if this isn't the way we should have been working at Mortmax all the time. When it was just families you get people working the job who don't really want to."

That could have summed up both Lissa and me at one point. I'd like to think that we've come to some acceptance of our respective career arcs by now.

"You're happy being a Pomp aren't you?" I ask.

Lissa rubs her chin, an unconscious gesture that I always find charming. "I don't know if happy is the word.

For one I have a lousy boss…But, seriously, I've had to grow up a lot these last couple of months. I've realized that sometimes you don't get what you want or, as the case may be, what you want isn't really what you want. What about you?"

The lift pings. We get in, and I don't answer. Just squeeze her hand, and when the lift stops at the basement car park I lead her to the Corolla.

I drive, Lissa lounges in the passenger seat, not bothering to hide her yawns. "Is this going to take long?"

"No, you rest. I'll wake you when we get there."

She's already out when we pull onto George Street. What an amazing ability to sleep she has. The city is bright around us. We pass the great green Christmas tree in the square and navigate our way through people staggering home from Christmas parties, dressed for air-conditioning and dining, not the soup that is a December evening in Brisbane.

There's a red light at George and Ann. I remember standing on the corner there, with the ghosts of my parents, wondering just how long I was going to live, and how the hell I was going to do it without them. Everyone faces that point in their life. Maybe you spend the rest of your days trying to answer it.

I don't know if my parents would be proud. They certainly wouldn't have approved of all the drinking. But I've done the best by them I could.

The lights change and someone beeps at me from behind. I put the car into gear, and head out of the city… or toward the city's heart. Depends on how you look at it.

Ten minutes later, the Corolla lurches up the last section

of winding road that leads to Mount Coot-tha's summit. Lissa's curled in the seat beside me. I brush the hair from her face and she smiles. It's a beautiful smile, but every time I see someone sleeping a slither of jealousy burns within me. I shove it down. This isn't Lissa's fault, I have to get used to it. Besides, the guilt concerning just who I last spent time with up here takes the edge off.

I pull into a park at the top of the mountain, let the car idle. The lights of the lookout are burning. The air is cooler up here, but it's still warm. There's a storm building in the west, following a pattern that has extended over these last few weeks. Heavy clouds trail fingers of electricity across the horizon. Even with that nearing disturbance I can still feel the One Tree, though its presence is somewhat muted.

In the Underworld it would rise above me at this point, clambered over by the dead, those ready or those forced to take the next step into the Deepest Dark. Here, of course, there are just the living forests, scrubby eucalypts that sing and sigh with the approaching storm.

I've been working so hard and getting nowhere. Everything, despite my best efforts, seems to be slipping out of control. Can you really learn to be an RM on the job? Maybe this is just what being an RM is really like, and Suzanne and Co. merely put on a mask of calm efficiency as they scramble about trying to keep Mortmax running smoothly. That worries me far more than any lack that I might possess. A lot more.

The city below is luminous. Airplanes, their lights blinking, race toward the airport in the east, or rise from it, all of them veering away from the cloud front. Lissa wakes as I turn off the engine.

"Are we there yet?"

"Yeah."

She smiles at me. Her face is too pale. And though I never think of her this way, in that moment she seems so frail. And I have to kiss her. I just have to.

I hold her head in my hands, feeling like a teenager again. The car park's a popular make-out point, the city a carpet gridded with light beneath us. I kiss her and she's kissing me. My hands trace the outline of her body. As the storm nears us, the ever-present veil of heartbeats falls away, and all I can feel is her racing heart beneath my palm. I stroke her breasts, awkwardly at first. It's too open here, but then again, our first sexual experience was an embarrassing masturbation-based binding ritual in a car park.

Lissa pushes against me. Clothes can't come off fast enough. Lightning streaks the sky as if in sympathy.

"Now," she moans.

And it's fast and difficult, in that tiny car, the gearstick getting in the way, not to mention the steering wheel and a seat that almost collapses beneath our weight. But we manage it. There are moments of clumsiness, moments of rhythm. We laugh at each other, forget where we are.

The storm is already heading out to sea. The darkness seems washed of impurities, the city's lights burn brighter. I breathe in the smell of her.

"That was different," she says.

"But good?"

"Insecurity isn't very attractive, you know."

With the storm gone, Lissa's heartbeat is just one of the millions I can feel again, racing, slowing, stalling, failing. But hers is right here, by my heart; her lips so close to mine that I kiss her again.

Oscar's Hummer pulls up next to us, followed by Travis in a little red convertible.

"We might be in trouble," I say.

Lissa smirks. "We're always in trouble."

Oscar gets out of the car, taps on my window. I wind it down and look up at him as apologetically as anyone feeling as smug as I am can.

"Look," Oscar says, "if you want to die, then that's your prerogative, Steven. But if you are killed, who is going to pay me? And this business is very much word of mouth. Are you trying to ruin my business?"

"I'm sorry."

"It's my fault," Lissa says. "I wanted to come up here and watch the storm."

"Did you enjoy it?"

Lissa and I exchange a look that lasts a little too long, and then a little longer.

Oscar is blushing when I look back at him. "Yes, we did."

"You're coming home, now," he says. "Please."

Oscar's driving behind us. I have Okkervil River on the mp3, Will Sheff's voice, shouting out the lyrics to "For Real," filling the Corolla. It's all menace and yearning but right now it sounds as romantic a thing as you could ever imagine. Another storm is building. It's going to pour again soon. The Brisbane River is beside us, shining with the reflected glow of the city. The skyscrapers rise up to our left. Southbank's massive ferris wheel is a circle of fire to our right across the river. The water calls to me a little. I've been an RM for such a short time, but I'm already aware of just how many things are connected to

death, how many places act as interfaces or linkages
between the Underworld and the living world.

The rear-view mirror shows me Oscar hunched over
the wheel of his Hummer. His face is hard; then a lightning burst in the sky above conceals it. Travis is driving a
little way ahead. I don't know what they think they're
going to achieve if something actually happens on the
freeway.

I take our exit from the M3.

And then I sense it. Something wrong. A force or a
presence that didn't exist a heartbeat ago. And it's coming
from beneath us. I rest my left hand on the dashboard.
There's an odd beat, a rhythm, running counterbalance to
the song.

"Bomb! Out!" I'm already slowing the car. I can feel it
building, racing toward a crescendo of shrapnel. There's a
little piece of me, the Hungry Death, I guess, that's loving it.

Lissa looks at me. She opens her door: the road is
streaking by. There's no time. Up ahead, there's nothing
coming, the road is clear. I yank my seatbelt free. The car's
slowing, but not enough. The vibration shifts, increasing
in pitch. The explosion, all that potential energy, is about
to be exhaled in fire.

Lissa leaps and I do something I didn't believe was possible. I visualize it, as Suzanne must have with me, capture
the movement in my skull, and then I shift beneath her.
Fold her in my arms. She doesn't struggle against me,
merely accepts that I can take this punishment. I hold her,
bind her in me. She's warm and still against my cold flesh.

We're out, and rolling. The ground is hard and toothed.
My clothes tear. The road bites, it digs its dirty teeth in
deep. And ahead of us, the Corolla, slowed almost to a

halt, explodes in a series of sharp detonations. Bits of our little car are tumbling from the sky.

I lie on the road, panting. Lissa gets to her feet; there are cuts all over her arms but I've taken the worst of it, thank Christ. She grabs me by the wrist and drags me from the oncoming traffic. When we're at the edge of the road she drops next to me. And then the storm unleashes all that rain, that blinding rushing rain.

Oscar's already pulling in behind us, windscreen wipers racing, hazard lights flashing. Cars are slowing, but Travis is out directing traffic. I've never seen anyone do it with such panache. When a man's that big, people pay attention.

"You all right?" I shout at Lissa. Things are leaking within me, even as I feel flesh and bone knitting. The rain's soaking me. Lissa crouches down, kisses me hard and squints; our communication is more lip-reading than anything else.

"Did you leave the fuel cap off or something?" she mouths at me.

Bones shift. Ribs slide back into place, organs repair themselves: I'm getting better at this. It itches like hell, though.

"Yeah, and I also left a bomb in the glove box. Sorry."

We look over at the Corolla. It's a flaming wreck billowing black smoke. I feel that it saved our lives.

"Jesus!" Oscar says. "Are you all right?"

"Fine. We're both fine," Lissa says. As though none of this is new to us. And it goddamn isn't.

Solstice is down among the wreckage almost before the ambulances and fire engines get there, his face set in a grimace. The storm has come and gone; the air's so thick you could serve it with a ladle.

Traffic creeps past. Gawkers mostly, peering at the wreck, and the various hues of flashing lights.

"Jesus, de Selby. It just goes from bad to worse with you, doesn't it?" He kicks at the wreckage with one steel-capped boot. "I'd understand it if you had a car worth blowing up, but this piece of shit..."

That offends me more than it ought. But at least with Solstice on the scene, I don't have to answer too many stupid questions: just put up with his gibes. Alex is here, too, keeping in the background, looking worried. He's talking to Lissa. Taking notes, and studiously avoiding Solstice.

"Are you getting anywhere with Rillman? Isn't that your fucking job?" I demand.

"The guy's a ghost. The records just stop. No surprises, I suppose. But you know all about ghosts. Do you think this Rillman could be a Stirrer?"

"No. Stirrers don't operate this way. They're not nearly as subtle."

Solstice taps a blackened hub cap with one foot. "Do you call this subtle?" He sighs. "Look, you've had a long night. Maybe you should go home. Rest up, get ready for all the questions I'm going to be asking you when I get my head around this."

He thumps my back, and stares over at Alex. "And tell that hack cop we don't need him here."

"He's here as a friend."

"He's a fucking nuisance, that's what he is."

I walk over to Alex. He's glaring at Solstice.

"What did the prick say?"

"He'd like you to leave his crime scene."

"*His* crime scene?"

"Alex, he has a point. Besides, the less he's thinking about you the better. Have you found out anything new?"

"Just how much I hate bureaucracies. Getting anything on these Closers is next to impossible. Look, the less I find the more worried it makes me," Alex says. "And then the harder I look. I'll find something."

"Good," I say. "That's what I like to hear."

Oscar gets us home quickly. I can't help thinking that, in a way, we're lucky. If that bomb had gone off in the garage, Oscar, Travis and Lissa would all be dead. If it had gone off at the lookout there's no telling how many casualties there would have been. And all because some ex-employee who predates my time with the company has a vendetta against me. Because I succeeded where he failed.

When we pull into the driveway, something else grabs my attention. This day just isn't going to end!

"Are you feeling that?" I ask Lissa.

"Yes, it's not what it should be, but after today, I recognize it."

We both look at the brace symbol above the front door. It should be glowing. It's not.

"What are you two talking about?" Oscar says.

"You're going to have to stay in the car," I say to him. "This is something you can't handle."

Lissa and I slide out of the Hummer and hurry up the front steps and onto the verandah. I have the door open in a moment, and we slip inside my parents' house. Now, I used to sneak in here a lot, when I was dating. I know every single creaking floorboard, every single shadowed alcove. Lissa follows my steps. We reach the living room with barely a sound above Lissa's racing heart and the whisper of our breathing.

Here the sensation, the taste, is stronger. But not as strong as I'd expect.

I signal to Lissa and she nods, pulling out her knife.

I creep through the living room, then into the kitchen. Lissa is behind me, the only person I would ever trust with a knife in that position.

It's sitting there, in one of the kitchen chairs.

"Get out of here," I snarl.

The Stirrer smiles. Blood has settled along its cheekbones. Its eyes are dead: blank. It turns toward us clumsily. Every movement must be difficult for this creature. It can't have inhabited the body for very long, no more than a couple of hours, maybe much less. "You don't recognize me, do you?"

"Am I supposed to?"

The Stirrer nods toward Lissa. "I took over her... remains."

How could I forget? When Morrigan murdered Lissa, this Stirrer used her body. It had even come to me and tried to make a deal.

"You bitch!" Lissa almost leaps over the table. I'm normally the one doing something stupid. I grab her arm, and it's a strain to keep her here with me.

"Not yet," I say.

The Stirrer's grin is a challenge to us both. "You need to listen to me," it says. "Things are accelerating, but we are not as unified as you might think."

"Is that what you told Morrigan?" Lissa demands.

I can feel the Stirrer now. Its absence. I can feel the

things it is drawing away from the world; it's like a cloud that has passed over the sun.

"Morrigan was a mistake. It got out of our control."

I notice the brace symbol tattooed on its thumb. This Stirrer shouldn't exist. And it shouldn't have passed through all the safeguards that I have set up throughout the house.

But here it is staring at me, in a body I do not recognize, for all its Pomp tattoos. Who did he work for? The relief I feel that it's not one of my Pomps is followed quickly by guilt.

"I found him outside your home." It lifts its head and I see the red line slashed across its throat. "I just took what was convenient. You really should clean up more frequently. My host has been dead for some time."

"What do you have to say?" I ask, still holding Lissa back. She's shaking with rage.

"Not all of us are happy to see our god approaching. Some of us are scared. Some of us may be willing to change sides."

"What for?"

"To see the sun again. To live among you, godless. After all, this place was ours long before it was yours. You who live owe us that much—"

"That's it!" Lissa snarls, and shakes free of my hand. "We don't trust Stirrers around here."

She slides her knife over her palm and slams it against the Stirrer's face. There's a soft detonation, the air gathers something about itself, and takes the motion from the corpse. The body drops, all smug smiles and jerky movement taken from its limbs. I look down at it. There's no hint that a Stirrer ever inhabited the body.

Then it smashes into me. The Stirrer's soul. It's as

though I've curled myself around a ball of razor wire. I drop, and howl.

I close my hands around the scythe.
It feels so good, doesn't it?
And it does.
Now let us kill.

Something shakes my shoulder, jolts me awake. My head rests on a cushion and Lissa is holding my hand, whispering soothing nonsense.

"You had me worried there."

"It'll take more than a stall to kill me, no matter how rough. Why'd you wake me from the first decent rest I've had in ages?" I murmur.

"You were screaming. And then you started to chuckle." Lissa doesn't laugh. I blink at her. "When did that start happening?"

"Just then. A stall has never hurt like that before."

Lissa smiles grimly. "I'm glad you spared me from it."

"You're welcome. The Stirrers are definitely getting stronger. And I don't like what that suggests. But next time, maybe we should let the Stirrer speak."

"I don't trust 'em," Lissa says. "Especially ones that take over my body and talk about what we owe it."

"I understand, but—"

"No buts. That Stirrer was in our house. It should never have been here."

Christ, I wish I could see things in such black and white ways. It can only mean that the Stirrer god is nearing. I have to sort this mess out with Rillman and fast; the sideshow is obscuring the main event.

Lissa frowns and crouches down by the corpse. One of its palms is marked in black ink with a bisected half circle.

"Do you recognize that?" I ask.

"Yeah, it's the same symbol our electrical friends in their safe house had on them."

"I think the Stirrers have found themselves something that counteracts the brace symbol."

"Something *that* simple? It's hard to believe it has any efficacy," Lissa says.

"The brace symbol is simple too. It has to be. Mr. D told me that the universe rails against complexity, it likes to break the curlicues and the squiggles down."

"He's a poet," Lissa says, with a wry grin. "Maybe he has something to say about all of this. Maybe you should go and find out."

"Are you going to be all right here?"

Lissa raises her bloody palm. "As long as this works I will."

If you lose your trust in blood, what do you have left? Up until the last couple of days I would have found it impossible to believe anything could trip up the old ways of stalling. Yet here we are.

"Be safe," we say simultaneously.

"I was expecting you. I could feel it, don't ask me how. Maybe we're developing some sort of link. After all, you are the closest thing I have to a living relative," Mr. D says, with two cups of steaming tea on a table by his chair. I don't bother asking where the new furniture came from. The One Tree creaks around us. He's just put down a copy of Fritz Leiber's novel *Our Lady of Darkness*. He's halfway through the book, I see. I slide a chair over to the table. There's no point rushing Mr. D. Even if I'm in a hurry, he isn't.

On the uppermost branch above us is where my Negotiation took place. A Negotiation involving more pain than I'd ever thought possible. I keep finding new limits to that. My capacity to contain it has increased and the universe seems intent on filling it.

On the branches beneath us people clamber and climb, finding places where the tree is happy to absorb them and pass them on to the Deepest Dark. Every soul has a different spot, a different length of time to be spent in the Underworld. But Pomps, once they pass, don't spend much time here. Maybe the One Tree is frightened that we'll mess it up.

"Sometimes I can feel the tree calling me," Mr. D says. "It would dearly love to have my soul. I've been here for so long and the tree is something of a stickler for the natural order of things."

"You're not tempted to go?"

He nods toward the Leiber novel, and the pile of paperbacks behind it replenished by visits to the markets below. "I've a lot of reading to catch up on. Besides, you need my help."

It's as good a reason as any I suppose. If only he was giving me more than the barest slivers of help. I bite my tongue, though.

"What do you think of your little world?" Mr. D asks gesturing out at the Underworld.

"It doesn't feel like mine."

"I was surprised by that myself. You went into this with no expectations. I envied you that."

"What do you mean?"

"There were no expectations to be disappointed. You're the regional Death. This land bows to you, but it also has a very strong sense of what it wants to be. You can either fight it, and it will struggle, even as it bends to your will, or reach some sort of agreement. During my, er, tenure, I preferred the latter. I'd already had my fill of fighting. Nature will win out. I will, one day, let the tree take me."

"But nature doesn't always win out. A Stirrer visited me today. Walked through my braces, and it had this on its wrist." I draw the symbol in the air.

Mr. D slaps my hand. "You don't want to be drawing that symbol here!"

"What is it?"

"Nothing good, that's for sure."

"I thought this was my region."

"It is, but regions are always imperiled, and that symbol's a siege engine of a most terrible sort. I haven't seen it since—"

"Would the name Francis Rillman be tied up with it by any chance?" I get out of my chair and round on Mr. D. "What the fuck is it that you're hiding from me?"

Mr. D smiles. It's an expression that I suspect he thinks is calming but it's actually the most irritating thing I've seen all day, particularly as it is wrapped in his various faces. "I assure you, Steven, that I'm not trying to hide anything from you. I don't work that way, and if anyone should know that it's you." He sees his approach isn't exactly working and sighs. "Yes, Rillman is involved. He was one of the best Ankous I ever had. Better than Morrigan, and more trustworthy—or so I thought. Francis failed the Orpheus Maneuver, but before that he had started a Schism. And like Morrigan he made deals with the Stirrers, but unlike Morrigan he'd designed a new symbol. I can't tell you what sort of genius that must take, but there hadn't been a new symbol in pomping since the Renaissance.

"He used his in a most peculiar way. He stole my powers—well, learned to mimic them. But he wasn't smart enough—or was perhaps too smart. He killed his beloved, Maddie. You see, she was a Pomp. I liked her, too. Steven, always know your staff. Know them as deeply as you can, watch their careers, and watch your back. She was against his Schism, she refused to become a Black Sheep, even tried to stop him. And when that happened everything fell apart for him. He tried to get her back and when I stopped him, well, he wasn't happy. His Schism gambit had failed and he had lost his love. And theirs was a grand love, in spite of his ambitions. It sometimes works out that way. You know, I think he would have succeeded but for me. He certainly had Neti's support."

"Aunt Neti?"

"Yes, she could see the romance in it. But I think, too, she was pleased that he came to her, that he followed the traditions."

"She certainly thinks poorly of me."

"You're an RM. It doesn't matter what she thinks." He sips on his tea. "I really believe, now, that he may have been the inspiration for Morrigan's Schism—only Morrigan was more thorough, and heartless. But that old bastard never got his hands on the new symbol. That, I kept hidden."

"You could have told me about it."

Mr. D nods. "Yes, I could have, de Selby, but I never expected to see it again."

"So after Rillman lost the love of his life?"

"Not just once," Mr. D says, "twice. He found her in Hell, as you found Lissa. Only I was waiting on the border. She returned to the One Tree."

"What did that do to him?" I don't really need to ask the question, and Mr. D sees that, but he plays along.

"He turned to the Stirrers, got in with them even more deeply. I guess he figured that they would know what he didn't. How to get his wife back."

"Did they?"

"No, their skills don't work that way. The bastard has no sympathy from me—you don't deal with the enemy. I actually banished him from my region, would you believe? Thought that would be enough, but then I didn't expect another Schism so close to his. If he's back in the region it's only because I'm dead."

"Could I banish him?"

"I don't think so. You're too new to your powers. It'd probably kill you. No, you're going to have to face him the old way."

"With knives and death?"

"I was going to say with lawyers, law men, the full force of jurisprudence. But sure, knives and death...That could work, too." Mr. D looks mildly annoyed now, which is a fair sign that he is mightily pissed off. He's not even drinking his tea, but continues on.

"Rillman opened the door for Morrigan, gave him ideas. And more, like I said, the little bastard stole some of my powers." He indicates his face. "This. Showy as it is, was mine. He stole that from me, made it somewhat less unique, less artistic." Mr. D squints into his tea, then pushes it aside as though disgusted by what the tea leaves have told him. "I've got some beer up here if you would like."

I shake my head, remembering the ashy rubbish we'd consumed on his boat.

"He stole your ability to change your face?"

Mr. D twists the top of his beer. "Yes, only his approach is a little more utilitarian."

"He can change his form!"

"Only into the dead. Which is very useful if you don't mind murdering people. Also, it makes it extremely difficult to be found." Mr. D sighs. "I'm sorry I have left you such a mess."

"I'll deal with it," I say grimly.

"I hope so, but this may well be beyond you. Rillman's tenacity is more than a match for yours, and he is one of the smartest people I have ever met. And you, dare I say it…"

"Thank you very much," I say. "Now get me one of those beers after all. And tell me every fucking thing you know."

24

By the time I shift home, Lissa is asleep. I check her schedule. She's not starting until late. It's nearly 5:00 a.m. Christmas Eve, though it doesn't feel like it. My eyelids are heavy, but I fear what sleep offers more than anything Rillman can throw at me personally. I pull down the blinds and scrawl Lissa a note.

Oscar arranges for another crew to look after her. The body the Stirrer inhabited has already been collected. I can almost pretend that it was never here, but it's opened wounds again. Looking at the kitchen, where it had sat, and where my parents had been killed, and their bodies stolen. Too many Stirrers have been here. They've poisoned my memories of this place.

I think about its offer. No, Lissa and Mr. D are right. You don't deal with Stirrers. No matter what.

I shift to my office, and work on my presentation for the Death Moot. I check on Lissa from time to time, but she doesn't wake, poor darling.

Tim comes for me around ten. It's meet-the-Caterers

day. He's already been briefed on last night's problem with an exploding car and he's employed more staff to investigate, and to search all the other vehicles for bombs. Nothing's come up yet.

My eyes feel square from staring at my computer for so long. I read Tim my Moot preamble, feeling very good about it, even statesmanlike. There's all manner of stirring stuff, demanding unity, and that the Orcus must act as one to fight this threat. And that it is not impossible. He nods his head at the end.

"I'll rewrite it for you," he says.

"Really?"

"Trust me. You'll even believe you've written it when I'm done."

He's nervous, twitchy. "Is it time?" I ask.

"Yeah, they'll be there soon," he says. "Oscar will walk us over."

Kurilpa Bridge is like a huge game of cat's cradle drawn out in steel and wire. There's a metal canopy above us, providing a little shade. I look back at the way we came, down the walkway that leads to Tank Street with its lawyer-crowded coffee shops and glass-fronted restaurants.

"Maybe we should have gotten a coffee first," I say.

Tim crushes a cigarette beneath the toe of his boot. "No time."

"Why did you choose the bridge?" Oscar asks. He studies first one bank of the river then the other, then pushes his face into his broad hands. There's clearly not enough escape routes—unless you want to dive into the river. There's plenty that way.

"Technically it won't really be the bridge, not as

Brisbanites see it," Tim says. "The marquees will be set up in the space between the Underworld and the living. You'll have quite a view of the city, and the Underworld equivalent, without really touching on either."

"There'll be two marquees?" Oscar asks, and I can tell he's even less happy.

"One for the Ankous, to bitch about the RMs, and the other, the big top if you will, for the main show. Both will be air-conditioned, of course." Tim mops at his brow with a handkerchief. "Maybe the next Death Moot could be in Antarctica."

I grin. "No, they did that in 1963. It wasn't a hit. Too many bloody penguins." I remember Mr. D's stories about that one. Said it was so cold his knees ached for the whole Moot and then a week afterward.

Oscar shakes his head. We're not much help.

"Water beneath bridges is a traditional interface between the lands of the living and the dead. And Mortmax Industries is all about tradition, but I didn't make the decision," I say. "I just bled over it." I pat Tim on the back. "Both of us did, didn't we, buddy?"

Tim shudders. "Don't remind me."

"And there's still a little more blood needed," I say. "We're going to disappear for a while Oscar, but don't worry. We will be back."

Oscar shrugs. "We do what we can, boss. I'm aware there are some places that we can't follow you."

After a couple of joggers have passed us by, Tim and I pull our knives from beneath our jackets. Tim counts down silently to three and we cut our palms, heart line to thumb. I walk to the western rail of the bridge, Tim to the eastern and as one we plant our bloody palms on the bare steel.

Metal thrums. And there is a sound like someone scratching a record, a painful scritch! that runs across the heavens.

Oscar throws up his hands, and then he's gone. But it's really us who have gone.

The sky darkens, then brightens. The whole city contracts, expands and contracts again, as though reality has grown rubbery. And suddenly it is only Tim and I on the bridge. There is no traffic on the expressway, and no people here or on the streets below. The city is quiet. Oddly enough there are birds in the air and the river is teeming with fish. Its surface bubbles, the water itself a murky reddish brown, the same color as my palm print on the rail. The bridge itself is luminous, silver and white, and a bright sun burns in the sky.

"Well, I never," Tim says. "How's that for magic and stuff?"

"Now, where are these Caterers?"

A bell tolls, loud and clear. It echoes and vibrates through the bridge so that it's almost a bell itself.

"There, I think," Tim says.

A right hand, pale, long-fingered and neatly manicured, materializes in the air between Tim and me. Then another. And another until a dozen hands are present. Then left hands being to appear. And twelve men, or women— they're as androgynous as Ziggy Stardust—stand before us, all slightly shorter than me, all carefully dressed in white suits. A pair of them scurry to the center of the bridge and start taking measurements, pulling tape between them, scrawling notes down onto clipboards.

The Caterer nearest to me dips its head. He seems to be the boss.

"Mr. de Selby. A pleasure." He claps his hands. "And what a glorious venue. Shiny, new. Nothing of the gothic about it, and you would simply *not* believe how tiresome all the gothic is." He spits out the word as though it were a bitter poison, revealing neat but very sharp teeth.

The rest of the day is spent walking over nearly every inch of the bridge, marking sections with our blood, anchoring, as the Head Caterer calls it, this reality with our own. With too much blood, the bridge may sink into the living world and the Death Moot will become a crowded affair, and Mortmax will not only be paying the Caterers but also Brisbane City Council for illegally building marquees on this public thoroughfare. With too little, this reality might just drift away and the Moot with it.

Oscar calls me a couple of times, but there is no hurry in the Head Caterer, just a methodical preparation of the bridge. I can respect that, but there are several more pressing situations I should be applying myself to.

By early evening, Tim and I are feeling a little anaemic. And Tim is sick of Caterers bumming cigarettes off him. But the Head Caterer is clapping his hands with joy, and already one marquee is constructed.

"This will be the best Moot in our ten thousand years of catering," he says. "The location!" He points to Mount Coot-tha in the northwest, the shadowy hint of the One Tree. "The air, so vibrant, and yet so suggestive of death. You have done well with this city. I promise you, people will not forget this Moot."

"Ten thousand years?" I say. "You've been doing this for ten thousand years?"

"Yes, and thank goodness for climate control these

days. You would not believe just how feral it used to be. Cold in winter, boiling in summer. Terrible, terrible."

We shake hands, sealing the deal with a little more blood. Then the Head Caterer goes off to direct the positioning of a freezer in the kitchen set-up.

There's a door made of pine, in the middle of the bridge, nothing more really than a frame. One of the Caterers leads us to it.

"Access point," the Caterer says. "You come and go through here. Got pizza and beer coming if you boys would like to stay."

We beg off, it's Christmas Eve after all, and walk through the door. We're back into our reality. There's no Narnia-esque time transition, it's night in the real world as well, just an ear-popping step into a jogger-crowded bridge. We both leap out of the way of an oncoming cyclist. The door that we walked through is gone. Oscar's waiting patiently with Travis and Tim's burly bodyguards.

Lissa's not due home for another couple of hours. Oscar insists that we walk back to Number Four. Tim has a hair appointment in the Valley so we part company on the bridge, Tim heading to the nearest taxi rank with his security.

There's a shortcut from the bridge to George Street via a tunnel. It's well lit, though empty at this time of night. We head through it, Travis walking ahead, Oscar behind me.

Halfway in, the lights flicker and dim, and I realize that this was a mistake. Each end of the tunnel is gated, and both gates slam shut in unison.

I slap my head with my palm. Not again. When am I going to learn?

25

The lights that have dimmed suddenly flare and shatter. A ripple of glass fragments rains down and darkness engulfs us. Oscar is shielding me with his body. I hear Travis run toward us, can picture the gun already in his hand. "Down!" he hisses. "Stay down."

And I'm on the concrete still under Oscar, then he rolls to one side, ending up in a crouch.

I try desperately to make sense of things in the dark. I can hear Rillman's heartbeat. Steady and familiar. My eyes are adjusting now. There, a slight movement down the other end of the walkway. And as if on cue, a light flickers on. Rillman glares at it in irritation.

He walks toward us. He hasn't changed since the photo that Lissa showed me was taken, though that must be several decades old. He's unprepossessing, even in the suit he's wearing, and about a head shorter than me. He could be a bad parody of a chartered accountant, if only he were wearing a bowler hat.

Here he is, I'm seeing him clearly for the first time (no

waxen obscuring of his features, and my eyes not swollen with blood) and he's not so bad. Not so scary. Except his eyes. They gleam with a force, a rage utterly at odds with his demeanor.

"I'd call off your goons," Rillman says. "I really don't want to hurt anyone, except you."

Travis is at my side. "Just keep out of the way," he says to me. He has his pistol aimed at Rillman's head.

"Guns don't frighten me," Rillman says. That makes one of us.

"It's not the gun you need to worry about, mate." Oscar runs at him. It's like watching a steam engine hurtle at a minnow.

Rillman moves out of the way, smooth as oil, but Oscar is turning, too. He swings a punch at Rillman's head, only it isn't there anymore, he's down, hunched at an insane angle. Then he's slipping around and punching Oscar twice in the sternum. The fight's confusing. Darkness and light. Shadows melding. Rillman is in several places at once. I can sense what he is doing, the bastard's shifting in tiny bursts. How the fuck's he doing that? Oscar doesn't stand a chance.

Travis is trying to get a clear shot, cursing under his breath.

Bone cracks and Rillman pushes Oscar away from him as though he's nothing but an irritation. The big man teeters, his arms flailing, then falls flat on his back, coughing up ropes of blood.

I turn from Oscar to Travis. His face has tightened with dismay or anger, I'm not sure. He's stopped swearing. "Stay where you are," he growls at Rillman.

Rillman laughs. He hasn't even got a sweat up and one of my guards is already down. "Stay where I am, or what?"

Travis shoots just above his head. The bullet ricochets down the tunnel. We both cringe. Oscar is on the ground, moaning.

Rillman takes a step forward. And then with no transition he's in Travis's face. A perfect shift. There's a flash of silver. "Oh, dear," Rillman exclaims.

I get to my feet, my arms reaching out toward Travis. But it's too late.

Travis takes a few steps forward, one hand clamped over his neck. Blood bubbles from between his fingers, and he falls hard on his knees. Then he gestures once, weakly—with whatever strength he has left—with his free hand, for me to run. That's all he has in him. He topples forward. One less heartbeat, one less guard.

His ghost looks at me. Blinks and shakes his head. "I'm so sorry," he says.

"You have nothing to be sorry about, Travis. Nothing," I say.

A moment later his soul flashes through me.

Rillman laughs. "Always the professional, eh? Even when it comes to pomping your own staff. You better get used to that."

I peer at Rillman. His hands are empty. What is he cutting with? His nails are short, neat. But I guess a man capable of changing his form, of shifting from space to space, is capable of just about anything in a fight.

My legs are like jelly, but I'm an RM, damn it! "I've been looking for you," I say, and my voice isn't as stern or as strong as I would like it to be.

"Yes, but not nearly hard enough," he says. "You're really rather awful at all this aren't you?"

I shrug.

Rillman pauses, takes a step back. "I thought you would be more impressive. All these weeks of watching you, watching those around you . . . For someone with such loyal friends, you're rather disappointing."

"You couldn't kill me with your bomb. And these insults are nothing to me"

Rillman smiles. "That bomb wasn't meant for you."

"You keep away from her."

"She'll be mine when I have time for her. And you know there is nothing you can do." He flicks his wrists in the manner of a magician. There is a thin line of gray light in his hands. It takes me a moment to realize what it is.

"Surely you're kidding."

He's holding an old-fashioned barber's razor. But the blade is unlike any razor I've ever seen: it's made of stone and it's mumbling. This isn't good; all my encounters with mumbling blades have not been good.

"I'm afraid not, Mr. de Selby." He waves the razor around his head. "This took me some time to fashion. You won't believe the lengths I went to to source the materials. Indeed, I only finished it this evening. I don't really expect it to do the job, but I need to try it on someone, need it blooded with good corporate blood. And why not yours? I rather expect it to hurt."

He comes at me fast.

I try to shift, but can't. Somehow Rillman is holding me to this place, and the time I've wasted in trying to get out of here, means he's almost upon me. I duck backward, but not nearly swiftly enough. He's come in close and he swings up and under. Then down. Almost so fast that I don't see it. Oh, but how I feel it!

The first stroke slides under my ribs, the second opens

up my wrist. Both wounds blaze with agony. I kick out, and my boot makes contact, but he hops away. A dozen contradictory emotions wash across his face: hate, humor, compassion and rage among them. I can't believe I ever tried to hunt this guy. I should have been running.

"Why are you doing this?"

"It must be done. You need to learn, and I need to cut."

Blood flowers around the incision in my shirt. I slide my fingers over the wound, quick. This shouldn't be happening. But I have survived worse injuries. He jabs toward me, and this time I am ready. I swing up with my knee. Ten years of soccer as a kid taught me something about playing nasty. There's a meaty thud on contact, a winded gasp. The bastard stumbles back and I swing a fist toward his face. My knuckles strike his nose. That's gotta hurt; it certainly hurts my fist.

Rillman blinks, steps back. His eyes narrow.

"I'm not the only one who bleeds," I say.

Rillman takes a step toward me but then my winged Pomps arrive—shooting through the gates. Crows. The first one strikes him hard, just beneath the eye. Another takes a nip at his ear. Rillman slashes at the bird and the poor thing is sliced in two. But there's another one, and another.

In the distance comes the thwack, thwack, thwack of crows' wings beating. There are a lot of crows in Brisbane. And they are filled with my anger, cruel with my pain.

"C'mon, mate!" I growl, sweat dripping from my face, blood pouring from my wounds. I take an unsteady step toward him, pulling my hands from my belly and clenching them into fists, bloodier than they have ever been before. It's hardly threatening to an ex-Ankou, but it's all I have. I even manage a grin. "You better finish it now or I will find you."

"I invite you to try, Mr. de Selby. You'll only be making my job easier. I think the lesson's done for today," Rillman says, batting at the stabbing birds around him.

Suddenly, there's the sound of flesh slamming into bone. Rillman lets out a great whoomph of breath, stands there blinking.

"That's for my fucking ribs," a newly conscious Oscar growls. "And this is for what you did to Travis."

He swings again and Rillman scrambles backward, his arms flailing.

The world shivers a little, and Oscar's fist strikes air. Unbalanced, he falls. It's painful watching him get to his feet. I'd help, but I'm worried my bowels are likely to spill out the moment I move my hand.

Rillman's gone. There's just the two of us and about a hundred crows looping around in that confined space, cawing and clawing at the air where Rillman had been just a moment ago, a cacophonous cloud of wings and claws and beaks. I'm getting their view, as well as my glued-to-ground vision. I have to struggle to stop them pecking at Travis.

The gates swing open.

Oscar looks at me. "We've got to get you out of here…" Every word comes at a cost. The big man's tan has faded to a ghostly white.

Neither of us look good, and both of us are bleeding heavily. He glances over at Travis, starts toward him.

"Too late," I say, "Travis is dead. Believe me, I pomped him, there's nothing we can do."

"Ah, Jesus." It's the first time I see anything that looks like real emotion pass across his face.

The amount of blood flowing through my fingers suggests that Rillman may not need to come back to finish the job. As a Pomp I would be dead—there's no way I could have handled this sort of injury—but my body burns with energies, long tendrils of power slowly repairing flesh and bone. Every Pomp in my employ will be feeling this as I draw strength from them. I might have a couple of resignations tomorrow. Wouldn't blame anyone.

All that crackle and pop is making me dizzy. I laugh with the head rush of it all—and it hurts. Rillman wasn't joking. I hunch into my wounds, look around me.

"Can you walk?" Oscar asks me, looking almost ready to fall on his arse himself.

"Can you?"

Oscar grins the pained grimace of a wounded bear. Not dead yet. "See if you can shift out of here. Go and get some help," he says.

The wounds are already knitting. I try to shift and all I get for my trouble is a bad headache. I gulp a few deep breaths and straighten my suit, then we stumble out of the tunnel and onto the street. I call Tim; it goes to voicemail.

Then I call Lissa. She doesn't answer her phone, and I realize why. I feel the stall that is distracting her. She's forty kilometers south of the city, too far away.

I key in Suzanne's number. "I need your help. Now."

And she's there in an instant. "Oh, dear," she says. "What has Rillman done to you?"

She looks up and down the street. "Where—? Never mind. This shouldn't have happened."

"Brooker," I say.

She nods. "This is going to hurt," she says, and holds both Oscar's and my hand.

In his surgery, Dr. Brooker almost falls out of his chair, when he sees us. "What the hell happened here?"

"I've been cut up by a bloody barber's razor made out of stone, is what," I hiss. "Oscar's the one you have to see to."

"I know my job." Dr. Brooker looks at me, then Suzanne. "Take him to his throne. I'll take care of Oscar."

"One more time," Suzanne says, and we shift again.

She leads me gently to my throne. And the moment I sit down I can feel things healing faster. It hurts though, and she wipes my brow with a handkerchief that she's pulled from a pocket.

"You'll be OK," she says.

"How can I be? No one's safe. He said he wanted to hurt me."

"He can't, not really."

"Lissa—"

"She's safe. I have her watched. Now, tell me what happened."

I run through the ambush, the fight. The injuries that Rillman sustained.

Suzanne considers this. "He'll go and lick his wounds. Rillman isn't an RM. He will need some rest after doing the things that he did in that fight, to heal his injuries. Throw in the couple of savage punches to the head that Oscar delivered and Rillman will be quiet, he has to be. He may have wanted to hurt you, but it has cost him, too."

"What do you mean you have Lissa watched?"

Suzanne laughs. "She's too important a person in your life not to be watched. You have your Avian Pomps. Well,

I have my own means. She is safe." She tilts her head. "As a matter of fact she's almost here." She jabs a finger in my chest. "Don't think that this gets you out of a lesson. I'll see you in the Deepest Dark later tonight."

She shifts just as Lissa opens the door.

Lissa looks at me. "Was somebody in here?"

"Suzanne. I needed her to shift me here," I say. "I'd get up, but—"

"Jesus, if she—"

"No, Rillman. He killed Travis."

"What?"

"The bastard was fast. He got us just after we walked off the bridge. We hurt him, but Travis died. Oscar looked pretty bad when I left him with Brooker."

Lissa rushes toward me and grabs my face. "And you?"

"I'm fine. I'm fine. Though I've got my twinges. How was your day, my love?"

"Far, far better than yours. Why Suzanne?"

"Tim can't shift yet, certainly not well enough to get me back here. What would you have me do, catch a bus?"

Lissa scrunches up her face. "You know how I feel about her."

"Yes, but she saved Oscar's life. I did call you first."

"OK, enough. Now tell me everything."

I sit in the throne, the heartbeats of my country playing around me. Thirty more people die in the space of my healing, though I'm angry over only one of them. Travis shouldn't have died for me. I've already looked into the schedule; his name is flagged as too early. He had another thirty-eight years.

My wounds have knitted well, though they're quite red and inflamed. Not bad for a couple of hours. I stretch in my chair, look over at Lissa. She's let me grump for a while now. She's rubbing at her brow like she has a headache and looks ready to collapse.

"Are you all right?" I ask.

"Yeah, the new staff are great. So that's one thing. And the other states, especially Sydney and Perth, are doing well, oddly enough." She sighs. "I know accepting Suzanne's Pomps would reduce the stress on us, but I don't want you to do it."

Guilt buzzes inside me. I should feel better about it, somehow justified that me taking up Suzanne's offer was really necessary. How much longer can I keep up this lying? "Well, looks like we're going this alone. Travis is gone and Oscar isn't getting out of a hospital bed for a while," I say.

"Yeah. But we're used to that. Weren't you kind of expecting it?"

"No, I wasn't. Call me optimistic, but I really wasn't."

It's so easy to have these things taken from me, RM or not, no matter how hard I work—or don't. Ah, fatalist much, Mr. de Selby?

Lissa strokes my face. There's an ache deep in the back of my throat and it becomes a burning when I look into her eyes.

I rise from the throne, slowly; every movement has its quotient of pain. I kiss her briefly, pull back and stare at her. Lissa's lips tremble and her face is lit with something that I can only hope I am the cause of.

"It always comes down to us," I say, trying to inject more hope into my words than I feel. Then I kiss her again, a longer lingering contact this time. "What the hell are we going to do?"

Lissa sighs. "What we always do. Keep going. We can't hide from Rillman. He can chase us anywhere. Besides, neither of us is the hiding type—it didn't work with Morrigan and it won't work with Rillman. Tomorrow's Christmas, then it's three days until the Moot. We live our lives and we fight," she says.

Hiding certainly didn't work with Morrigan. But he never wanted me to die—until the end, when he was ready and my running was done. Rillman's motives are so much darker and murkier.

There's loss on the horizon, and we're bolting toward it, faster and faster. Rillman, the Stirrer god, the Hungry Death, the bloody Death Moot. All of it's terrifying me. Lissa must see it there in my face, because she rests a hand against my cheek, bears a little of the weight of my head for a moment.

"It's Christmas tomorrow," I say. "I can't believe it. To be honest, I'd forgotten."

"What? You're telling me you haven't got me a present?"

"Of course I have!"

She smiles, eyes flaring. Gorgeous, utterly gorgeous.

"Just kiss me again," she says.

And I do.

26

The Deepest Dark is a soothing chill against my newly healed flesh. I've showered and pulled a T-shirt and jeans over my scars. It feels odd to be here, out of a suit. Sure, I'd worn a tracksuit down here once, but that feels like it was an age ago.

"You're looking good for a man who nearly died tonight."

"Thank you again for your quick assistance."

"I have a lot riding on you, Mr. de Selby."

"Things are coming to a head," I say. "I can feel it. I need to know how you know so much. And I need to know just what is important."

"These sessions aren't about how I know things, but what I know. I assure you that you will have access to an incredible network of information. Not just Twitter, not just Facebook, or Mortepedia. Give yourself time."

"What network? And what the hell is Mortepedia?"

But Suzanne puts a finger to my lips. "You know about the Hungry Death now." I push her hand away.

"Yeah, let's call it HD, for short."

Suzanne sighs. "And you know that, once, pomping was a pleasurable thing. But do you understand why we use blood?"

"It has to be blood, and your own, and it has to hurt," I say. These are things I learned from my parents, as every Pomp does. And it feels good to say them. "The drawing of lines in the sand must always have consequences. It costs to fight battles. It's not just HD that drives this. You told me as much, when you told me how it was defeated. It's the will to make a difference despite the cost, and the realization that you might fail. If failure costs nothing, perhaps we would be too reckless. If it didn't hurt to stall a Stirrer, perhaps we would just rush in with no plan, our guns blazing and find ourselves surrounded, cut off, defeated."

The grin Suzanne gives me is huge. "Blood isn't just life, it represents how delicate life is. Now, symbols are very important in this business, as you already know. The brace symbol, for one. But something as simple as a gesture can be powerful. If you give yourself to it." She raises her hand, and dust lifts from the ground and follows her, fanning out, then condensing into a tight tube that spirals around her arm. "Try it."

I do, and nothing happens. No surprise there.

Suzanne touches my head. "You were thinking about it far too much. Just lift your arm."

"Right, right, just lift my arm!" I say, flapping my arms like I'm doing some crazy impersonation of a chicken. "Nothing, see—"

Dust swings around me, up and down.

But the moment I realize what I'm doing, the dust drifts

away. A good bit of it gets sucked into my lungs. Suzanne watches me cough, her eyes crinkle.

"Good work," she says. "So much of what you need to do must be done without thought. Without reflection. That's the power and the danger of this job. It must be effortless. If it's too much one way, everything becomes mechanical, without soul, without rhythm. Too much the other, and it is all chaos. Even too much balance is wrong."

"Why?"

"Death isn't effort. It's consequence. It's as natural as breathing, and all the skills that we possess—to shift, to hear the heartbeats of our region, all of them—come from that. Give yourself over to it, and in the giving you will find that there is so much more time to explore the consequences of your actions. If you are always struggling, you can never ask yourself why, or what might be. Now, lift your arm again."

I lift, extending a finger. The dust lifts too. I draw my fingers into the bed of my palm then flick them out. Dust shoots away from me, five trails of it. I lower my hand and it drops. I can feel it around me, waiting for my motion, my guidance.

Suzanne winks at me. "Well done, Steven. I expect to see you tomorrow. But not here. Tomorrow we can meet in my office."

And she is gone.

Wal pulls from my arm. The last thing I expect to see him in is a little Santa hat.

"What the hell's Mortepedia?" I ask, lifting a finger, and watching a slender thread of dust rise up to touch it.

Wal spirals around it. "Some sort of treatment for dead feet? No, that's Mortepodiatry."

I glare at him. "Rillman nearly killed me tonight."

"But he didn't," Wal says.

"He managed to kill one of my bodyguards, though."

"Well, that's the problem. You don't need bodyguards. You're an RM, you should be able to look after yourself. You don't sleep, you can shift through space, and even make dust do…things. What do you need bodyguards for?"

"Lissa—"

"Lissa's stronger than you give her credit for. Think about what you two had to go through just to be together. You think Lissa was being all helpless in that? Lissa's only a weakness if you let her be one. If you let her be a strength…"

"When did you get so wise?"

Wal beams at me. "Always have been, mate, you just never listened."

PART TWO

THE MOOT

27

The barbecue's sizzling, and I'm there behind it, nursing a beer. Dad used to do this. No turkey, no ham on Christmas Day. Just meat cooked to within millimeters of inedibility and salad. Beer, too, of course. We have a couple of dozen stubbies of Fourex and Tooheys Old swimming in ice in the laundry sink.

It's a pretty grim Christmas. Last year there were so many more people. There doesn't seem to be much of a chance of backyard cricket. I look down at the lawn, which is in need of a mow—I'm not going to have time to do it in the next few days. But the kids don't seem to mind. Alex is down there with Tim and Sally. I'm glad I invited him. Christmas is a busy time for us, but for a moment we can pretend it isn't.

A hand slides around my waist. "Look at him down there, bailed up by your cousin. Do you think they're bitching about you?"

Alex is listening intently to something Tim is saying.

"Of course not, they respect me too much," I say,

kissing Lissa on the cheek. I like the feel of her next to me, though she's a bit too bony at the moment, her cheeks too wan. After the Moot in two days I expect our stress levels to improve. Our staff intake is rising, not to mention my own involvement in the business. It's amazing what more than twelve hours without someone trying to kill you can do. But it doesn't feel like it's enough.

Lissa and Tim were right. I was letting things slip out of control. Well, I'm back now. And I know I'm getting better at the job. I've learned so much in the past week.

The more people in this house, the less space there is for ghosts to fill it. And I'm doing my best to ensure that there are no more ghosts in the near future. I miss Oscar's and Travis's presence. But Wal is right, I can handle this. I have my own eyes and ears around the house, some of which are eating beetles. I wince and take a deep swallow of my beer. They're not the greatest taste, even second hand.

"Christmas always makes me feel a little sad," Lissa says.

"You missing your parents?"

Lissa nods her head. "It's been more than a year for me. I've already had a Christmas without them." She squeezes my hand. "I know how hard it must be for you."

"Yeah, but having you here makes it easier."

"Is that smoke I smell coming from the barbie?" Tim yells, and I realize that everyone is looking at us. The barbecue is definitely smoking.

"Must mean the sausages are ready," I say, stacking them onto a plate. Sure they're a little charred, but you've got to keep up tradition.

We sit around a dinner table laden with beer, soft

drink, blackened sausages and bowls of salad. The kids groan when Tim kisses Sally. And everyone ignores my quick pash with Lissa.

Here is what I'm fighting for. This family. These connections old and new. We eat together, we laugh together. And seventy people around the country die. It's not too bad. And there are Pomps for every single one of them.

Perhaps, despite my doubts, the system's working.

Our guests are gone by early evening. The sky is smudged with the last tints of sunset. The city's quiet, the suburbs marked by the distant rumble of an engine, or the bark of a dog. Crows caw in nearby trees and noisy mynas live up to their name, chirping, chirping, chirping, as they hunt cicadas or try and push another bird out of their territory. They avoid my Avians, though, and shoot from the yard every time they hear the whoosh of black wings, the thrashing beat of a crow taking flight.

I sit on the back porch thinking, Lissa curled up next to me. Finally, some time to talk.

"So you're telling me the Hungry Death is real," Lissa says.

"Yes, very much so." I smile at her. "I call it HD."

Lissa groans. "But I thought the Hungry . . . I mean, HD was destroyed," she says.

"No. More like redistributed." I tap my chest. "The Orcus, we're all the Hungry Death now. And the other thing—Christ, I really couldn't believe it. Did you know pomping was once addictive?"

Lissa lifts to one elbow. "Where are you getting all this information?"

"Mr. D. He's been quite forthcoming of late."

Lissa smiles. "I'm glad you two are finally connecting."

"All it took was a fishing trip and a run-in with a giant shark, among other things."

"They say giant sharks are very much part of the male bonding process," Lissa says. She yawns, lays her head down on my lap. "Let's continue this conversation later. Say, once I've had a nap."

I watch her fall asleep, stroking her face, pulling her hair away from her eyes. Having Lissa here this Christmas has made it just about bearable, but my parents' absence is palpable and agonizing. I finish my beer. My head dips, my eyes close and I'm in a dream at once.

The Hungry Death laughs, and dances around the corpses of Lissa and my family. This new family. The one I haven't lost yet.

But you will. *The shadow that is the Hungry Death dips into a bow.* Merry Christmas, Mr. de Selby.

In one swift movement it wrenches Lissa's head from her shoulders, and hurls it at my face. Her dead eyes open, unseeing, never to behold me again.

I wake with a jolt. Only a moment's passed since my eyes closed, scarcely more than an eye blink. Lissa's still next to me, her heartbeat is strong. She's a thousand times more alive than when I first saw her, and I will not see her dead again. Never. I refuse to.

And it's so lovely to know that *that* is inside me, and is part of me in such a fundamental way. So very lovely indeed.

"You know," I whisper to it. "All I really wanted for Christmas was a pair of socks."

I slide away from Lissa. There's an ibis on a nearby

roof, looking like a weathervane. It turns its long beaked face toward me.

"Lissa's sleeping," I say. "Keep an eye on her."

It dips its head, and scrambles across the roof for a better view. A crow shoots above me, landing on our roof with a scrape of claws. I get a confusion of perspectives looking in toward Lissa and away. The suburb is quiet, but for kids riding their new bikes, or people getting ready for a late Christmas dinner. Aircons are sighing, beetles are whirring. There's a clatter and a snap from up on the roof, and for a moment I can taste the crow's gecko dinner. *Ugh*.

I walk back to Lissa, kiss her on the brow. She startles me by actually opening her eyes.

"Where are you going?"

"Somewhere you can't come. Don't worry, I'll be safe—well, safeish. I've got work to do."

"It doesn't stop for you, does it?"

I smile. "You know, there was a while there when I thought it did. That I deserved a break. But when I stop, people die, people who I care about. And when they die, I die a bit, too."

Lissa touches my face, with a hand so perfect, so clear in my mind that I could hold it forever. "Merry Christmas," she says.

And I think about HD, and its last words to me. I can't let it spoil this. I'll be damned if I'm going to give it even a minor victory.

"Yeah, merry Christmas."

Then I shift, leaving her and my Avian Pomps behind.

28

Even this early in the morning Suzanne's Boston offices are a picture of efficiency. People work behind terminals, tapping away furiously, calculating the best routes to a pomp or a stir. A stocking taped beside a noticeboard is the only concession I can see to Christmas here.

Suzanne used to base herself in New York, but found it too noisy; "too clamorous," as she put it. I can understand that—such a big city, so many beating hearts hard up against each other. Washington, she'd never cared for, just as I could never imagine basing myself in Canberra. Capital cities are modern constructs. Our regions were built on different models.

The blinds are up, and it's snowing outside. Suzanne and Cerbo are both waiting for me.

"Merry Christmas, Mr. de Selby," Suzanne says, and pecks me on the cheek before I even realize what she's doing.

"You, too, Ms. Whitman."

Suzanne leads Cerbo and me into her office. "I can't tell you how much I am looking forward to spending a few days in Australia," she says, once she's shut her door and sat in her throne. "I've actually booked a room at the Marriott, a couple of blocks away from the bridge. Beautiful view."

I'm not here for small talk. "Things are getting worse," I say. "Stirrers are growing in numbers and I can't detect them."

"We've had problems here, too," Suzanne says. "The god's presence is making them almost reckless. You've seen it, you can understand why."

"Rillman isn't helping, either." I describe the symbol Rillman designed, and its powers. I'd emailed the details out to every RM, but it doesn't hurt to go over it again.

"No, he is proving to be something of a trial," Suzanne says.

"That may be the biggest understatement I have heard in my life. Are you practicing for a political career? A trial? Christ! And I need to know as much as I can about this god. Is there even any hope of stopping it?"

Suzanne nods at Cerbo.

"All I can tell you is this, and it goes back a ways," Cerbo says, pouring me a coffee, which I didn't ask for but accept none the less. "Six hundred million years ago something happened. Call it Snowball Earth, call it whatever you want, but after that, life grew more complicated, and the Stirrers' grip on this world ended." His voice speeds up: words tumble into each other with his excitement. I've never seen Cerbo so wound up. He's a nerd of the apocalypse. "You can see it more clearly in the Underworld. Look at the base of the One Tree; you'll see stromatolites crowding in like slimy green warts. We even have intelligence—" Cerbo looks at Suzanne, and she nods. "—we've even had intelligence that the Stirrers keep some in the heart of their city. Get out on the Tethys, go more than a few miles out, and what do you find? Nothing, no echoes of anything. Life hugs the shore. There's probably patches or places that correspond roughly to life and death on the earth but the sea of Hell is vast and I haven't found them. Believe me, I've looked."

"So what are you telling me?"

"What you probably already know, and what you will know as time goes by, ever quicker for you—that life is precarious. I think the Stirrer god existed before the Stirrers; a long time before. Maybe it's as old as the birth of the universe and Underverse itself."

"Old doesn't mean smart," I say.

"But it does mean tenacious and robust. That Stirrer god may be the most ancient consciousness in existence."

"So that's what we're up against?"

Cerbo nods.

I think about it for a moment. Try and find the most positive outcome. "Well, life won before, obviously. We're all still here. Things are alive. Life can win again."

Cerbo shakes his head. "But you see, I think that was an accidental victory, a consequence of forces that just slipped in life's favor. That is, if you can even call it a victory. Life exploded after those events, but the desolation beforehand... And this time..."

"And if the world shifted that way again?"

"It may well be worse than the Stirrer god itself. You don't know how bad the earth would be if we returned to those minus-fifty-degree Celsius temperatures."

I shrug. "I've seen *The Empire Strikes Back*."

Cerbo's smile is thinner than his mustache. "Humor is an inadequate defense. And it would be nothing like that. The planet Hoth would be a walk in the park on a summer's day compared to that."

"What do we do?"

"I don't know if there's anything we can do."

Suzanne grabs my hand. "See? See how difficult this is? This is what we are up against. I ask that you not judge any of us for the choices we may have to make in the days ahead. You, least of all."

I open my mouth to speak. Suzanne's phone rings, and mine follows a few moments later. We look at each other. When an RM's phone rings it's never a good thing.

It's Tim on mine. I answer it, trying to work out just who is calling Suzanne.

"Steve?" Tim asks. He sounds a little frightened. He'd been laughing at my table only a few hours ago. I immediately think the worst.

"Yeah." *Just give me the bad news.*

"Neill's dead."

I look at Suzanne and Cerbo. They're both pale as sheets, both getting the same message.

"Dead?"

"Yeah, it seems that Rillman has had better luck in South Africa."

An RM? Someone has managed to do what I thought impossible. "Is it a Schism?"

"No. David, Neill's Ankou, called me. Let me tell you, the guy was in a state. Someone came at Neill with knives, cut him up badly. Cut him into little pieces, is how David put it."

Then Tim's voice falls away. He's still talking, but I

can't hear him. Something is clawing its way into my chest. A force, a strength that's part dark chuckle, part dread fear, part chest imploder. I recognize it at once. With Neill dead, a twelfth of his share of the Hungry Death is drawn into me.

I drop to the floor, maybe black out, because the next thing I see is Cerbo hesitating between Suzanne and me. We're *both* on the carpet.

"Well, can you help me get up?" Suzanne says, the first to recover. Her eyes are bright.

And yet, Cerbo hesitates. "That hasn't happened yet," Suzanne growls. "Here, now. Focus on me."

Cerbo runs to Suzanne's side, pulling her to her feet.

What the hell was that about? I wonder. I'm shaky, but standing now. Suzanne glances at me.

"This is not good," she says.

"But Neill has been dead for a while."

"The transfer isn't instantaneous. The Hungry Death has to find us. It's drawn to our flesh, but it takes time." Suzanne shakes her head. "Poor Neill."

"I thought you said the transition needed blood," I say.

"Well, there was plenty of it—Neill's blood," Suzanne says grimly.

"This changes things," Cerbo says. "Surely you can—"

"It changes nothing." Suzanne smiles so viciously at Cerbo that he quails.

She looks at me. "Tend to your region, Steven. I must tend to mine."

"What about Neill's region? Who's tending to it?"

"Charlie Top. At least, until we can organize some sort of transition. A Schism and Negotiation is messy, but this is far worse. It will have to do. We've two days until the Moot. We can organize something then."

I try and imagine something messier than a Schism. I can't, but then I'm not really the most knowledgeable RM. What I really don't like is the stronger HD inside me. The mere thought of all that carnage pulls at my lips. *He* pulls at my lips, from the inside. It's an effort not to smile, but I won't give HD that satisfaction. This is my body.

Suzanne waves me away with one hand. And I go.

I shift to my office, my head pounding with this new fragment of the Hungry Death. I tumble into my throne and the comfort it provides. The throne is slightly bigger, its edges harder, and yet I find it more comfortable to sit in. I decide I don't like that and I get to my feet, walk about my office, pull open the door.

The office is busy, but that's what you expect at this time of year, and in this trade. Holidays mean nothing— other than a serious inflation of the payroll, according to Tim.

Word has spread fast about Neill. Lissa's left a message on my phone, she's coming in straightaway. I look at my watch. It's getting late. People glance hurriedly away as I catch their eye. This is an office that is spooked. I don't blame them.

I make a show of going to the photocopier, try to look like everything is normal. It seems to have the opposite effect, particularly when I jam the bloody machine. Right, then, a more direct approach is needed. These people haven't deserted me, and I damn well won't desert them. I walk to the center of the office, and clear my throat. I've heard my share of inspirational speeches.

"As you have probably heard, the South African RM has died." The office is silent, listening. "Well, we have a Death Moot to run. In just three days, the remaining RMs will be here. Things are going to get hectic, but I am not going anywhere. Rillman has tried to kill me numerous times, and failed. I will not desert you."

I don't notice Tim until he's standing beside me. Lissa's here, too, now. She smiles hesitantly at me.

"We'll see this out," Tim says.

"We've faced worse." Lissa's voice is hard and strong. She holds my hand. "But it won't mean anything if we don't keep pomping or if we stop stalling Stirrers. We can't let Neill's death distract us. Everything dies, we all know that."

"And we have to make sure that that keeps happening. We have to be strong. I won't let you down." I don't know if that's enough, but it's all I have.

"Where were you?" Lissa asks me, once everyone returns to work—inspired, or terrified, or hunting for the job pages.

"Checking out the bridge," I lie.

Tim looks like he's about to say something, and then seems to think the better of it.

I guide them both into my office, and then the black phone, Mr. D's phone, rings.

29

There's a first time for everything.

I snatch it up.

"Neti's rooms," Mr. D says in a tone I've never heard before. "Now."

Mr. D can be direct when he needs to be.

"What the hell is going on?" Lissa demands.

"I need you to stay here," I say. "Both of you. It's something to do with Neti. Mr. D sounds frightened."

I head out the door, then across the office floor. I'm running by the time I hit the hall. Wal shudders on my arm and begins to slide free, his ink turning to muscle and bone. He tears from my flesh with the hummingbird whirr of a cherub's flight.

"Where are we going in such a hurry?"

"Neti's rooms. Mr. D—"

"Bugger."

I don't bother knocking this time. I open Neti's door, almost hitting Mr. D in the head in the process.

"Watch yourself," Mr. D says.

"Neti?"

"Oh, she's dead. Well and truly, more than I could have ever believed."

But that much is obvious already. There's not much of her left. Her little parlor is splattered with blood. It's everywhere. Strings of it dangle from light fittings, puddles gleam red and slick all across the floor. Is this what Rillman had wanted to do to me?

"I've never seen anything like this," Mr. D says. But I have. HD is having a grand old time, I can feel him tugging at the corner of my lips.

I try and imagine the fight. There are burn marks everywhere, just like the Stirrer safe house. And the smell of cooking flesh, not the usual wholesome odors of scones or cake—though there is some of that in the background. The spider in the corner hangs limp and dead.

Wal flits around us, looking slightly green. "What does this mean?" he says.

"Rillman took a great deal of pleasure in doing this," I say.

"Obviously," Mr. D says.

"Who's going to replace her?" Wal asks, puffing out his chest, and riffling through her collection of china plates. I wave him away from there.

"Something will replace her, but it will be different. And it will come in its own time. That's the way these things work," says Mr. D.

Neti looks so small, but that's because she is in so many different pieces. I'm Death, so it's beneath me to gag, but it's hard not to. Her limbs are spread around the room. Her eyes are sightless. The television chatters; an inane game show. And it looks like she is watching it. Her strength and her menace are gone. Aunt Neti is dead, and murdered with such cruel joy. HD cheers a little.

"Where are the Knives of Negotiation?" I say suddenly remembering them. "Please tell me they're safe."

Mr. D pales. He rushes to the black cabinet, does something intricate with its scrollwork and one of its doors slides to one side. The knives' usual resting place. "Nothing," he says.

My brain ticks over. Rillman must have started with his stony razor, covered with my blood, perhaps to give it greater efficacy. And then, when he had incapacitated Neti, he snatched the knives and put them to quick snicker-snack use, finishing off the job. Then he probably shifted directly to Neill's office. Aunt Neti's been dead a while. Rillman had been anxious to leave in the tunnel, and not just because my Avian Pomps had arrived. He'd never expected to take so long with me.

There is a plate of scones on the table, untouched. Neti was expecting Rillman, or someone. Like she said, she only makes scones when people are coming to her with questions. Her prescience had failed as to Rillman's real intentions.

I wonder if she wasn't working with him in some way. Maybe the Stirrer safe houses, their grid, is being used for something else. Maybe Rillman was using both sides.

I have never seen Mr. D look so rattled. "So what do we do from here?" I ask.

"We talk strategy. Rillman is killing RMs, and suddenly the focus has turned away from the real threat, the coming Stirrer god."

"Well, that's got them scared as well." I sigh. I really don't know who I can trust at all. But one thing is certain; Mr. D doesn't have the answers.

But there's someone who does, and I might just catch her.

"I'm going to have to leave you here to clean up," I say to Mr. D.

"Of course," Mr. D says, though he is obviously affronted. "I of all people know how busy you are."

I give him a quick salute and shift.

Eight long arms snap out at me, but only one connects. It's enough to put me on my arse. The One Tree creaks around us in sympathy with her or me, I'm not sure.

"Oh, it's you." Several hands help me up.

"I didn't expect Rillman would visit you here."

"How did you know, dear?" Aunt Neti asks. She doesn't look happy, but I wouldn't be either if someone I'd considered an ally had just chopped me into little pieces.

"You made him scones. You were expecting his visit." I grimace. "I kind of guessed it."

Aunt Neti scowls. "When you broke the rules, and didn't even choose me to allow your Orpheus Maneuver, well, that was too much."

"Charon was just there," I say. "I didn't realize that there was any other way."

"Exactly. At least Rillman understood how it was meant to be done. I was the one who helped his Orpheus Maneuver. I felt so guilty that it failed, not because of anything I did, but that blasted Mr. D."

"I thought Mr. D was your friend."

Aunt Neti nods. "Keep your friends close, and your enemies closer. You would do well to remember that, Mr. de Selby, when it all comes falling down around you. Rillman failed, and I felt that I owed him. Besides, once you had clearly disdained me, well, what allegiance did I owe to you?

"I was happy to cover for him, to let him return to the land of the living. We REs perform Orpheus Maneuvers all the time; we let the curtains slip between life and death. It's not such a big deal for us, because we're not really alive. But I never meant to create a monster, and certainly not one so dangerous. My indulgence never went as far as the stone knives."

I glare at her. "It should never have gone as far as your lies. You owed your loyalty to me."

Aunt Neti snorts. Her eight arms wave around her, a halo of limbs, and then she's jabbing them in my face. "And what do you owe yours to? Not much, as far as I can see. With your rule-breaking, your moaning. And when did you ever really come to me for advice? There are things you could have learned if you trusted me. But no, you avoided your Aunt Neti, unless it was absolutely necessary. My Francis never did that. And you skimped on your duties, drinking, not showing up for work. People talk, Mr. de Selby, and your Aunt Neti listens."

"And look where that's gotten you," I snap. "A place on the One Tree, and no power at all."

The air seems knocked out of her. She folds her hands neatly around her waist, and dips her head.

"Yes...Well, it's a fabulous view," Aunt Neti sighs. I can see she's already growing listless with death. Soon the One Tree will have her and all that will remain will be a fading memory. "You're right, of course, but it's too late for me now. There are some lessons that you take to the grave."

30

Evening after a long and confusing day. HD is making me jittery. The Moot's looming and I'm home. I want to be with Lissa, but that's not who I've got. The kitchen buzzes with the energy of two RMs. I wonder what Dad would think. I wonder if he would be proud. I doubt it. Maybe, if I'd let Lissa in on my secret. It's been a long day.

I don't like having the meeting here, at home. But Suzanne insisted. Lissa isn't due back for another couple of hours. There is a stir expected at the Princess Alexandra Hospital.

"I never thought I'd see the day," Suzanne said. "But here we are, a Recognized Entity is dead. Killed not by one of us, nor by our enemy, but by that stupid, vengeance-craving man."

"And with those knives. He can wreak bloody havoc with them," I say. "Maybe we should consider canceling the Death Moot."

"No," Suzanne growls. "The Death Moot goes ahead.

To cancel it would set an alarming precedent. We're better off together, stronger. Unless, that is, if he manages to kill us all... Well, that thing that we contain, it won't be contained anymore."

"Where would it go?"

Suzanne's smile is wide. "Imagine your dreams, imagine that made reality. That shadowy, lurching Hungry Death; that relentless slaughter. De Selby, it's in us all, it's in everything living. But in us...us twelve, now...it's magnified, personified. Death is part of life, but without anyone to control it... all that power is not a legacy I want to leave for the world. Still—"

"Still, if it's going to happen, it's better to be dead than deal with it," I say.

Suzanne shakes her head. "If that sort of thing occurs then we've a major biblical sort of problem—actually, nastier than anything in the Bible. Death won't save you. Maybe I'm wrong, Steven, but it terrifies me, and it should terrify you, too."

"I don't think I know enough to be terrified."

Suzanne frowns. "Ultimately that's what it's all about, our business. Managing Death, keeping the Hungry Death under control and following laws more conducive to life. Whenever we fail, whenever we let it slip out of control, bad things happen. That's just the way it works. Our governments may want to impose their own system of management on this, no matter that they don't have nearly the unified approach that we possess. We're older than any system of legislature or governance. If we fail at our business, they have no chance of filling the void.

"You may not trust the Orcus, but believe me when I say that there is a certain purity in what we do, in what we had to give up to become this. You just lost your innocence in a different way. It was torn from you. For the rest of us, we tore it from ourselves.

"We chose this path with our eyes open. We knew the cost of what we did, of those that we killed. I loved my family, I loved my friends, but I knew I could be a better RM than my predecessor. Did I ever tell you that he was my lover?

"I killed him to become this, because he was weak, because I could see battles far ahead that I knew he wouldn't be able to fight. He confided in me, bared his shortcomings, and the only way I could see to deal with his weakness was to take the job from him, and the only way that I could do that was via a Schism and the Negotiation. Do you know what it is like to not just lose the ones that you love, but to deliberately take them away? It eats you out like a cancer. But what choice did I have?

"Ask yourself what Morrigan might have seen coming, what fears drove his decisions. I dare say it was more complicated than just a lust for power. You know us, we're not all bad, we went into this knowingly and passionately and with a desire to change the world." Suzanne lowers her gaze. "You know history, the violence that made each of us Death. But don't you ever fool yourself into thinking you can understand us."

"You're murderers, one and all," I say.

Suzanne nods. "Oh, yes, we are. And all of us suffer for it. This job is our punishment as much as it is our prize. This business and the Hungry Death inside us, it's horrible isn't it? I pity you, sometimes, Steven, that you don't even have the comfort of your passion to protect you. Oh, how that must hurt, and there is no one to share it with.

This job isn't about giving up everything for your love, it's about giving up your love, for everything."

"And where does that leave you?"

"I didn't say it was the right choice, but it was the choice we made. I'm not expecting sympathy, or even understanding. Just acceptance. This is what we have done. All of us suffer, that is the only thing that truly links humanity. We exist, and I truly believe this, to reduce the quantity of suffering in the world even if it means we must bleed ourselves."

I can't look at her. Love and family, even in the face of suffering, are the most important things to me. The only things I have left to believe in. And maybe that is being selfish. I know it's selfish. How can I be an RM if I can't give them up?

She grips my hand. "Oh, Steven. There's so much you still don't understand. I pity you. The lessons of your time are far crueler than anyone could expect."

"Don't pity me," I say, and I've never seen her look so amused.

She grabs my face, jerks my head toward hers, and kisses me hungrily. Her lips are as cold as mine, her heart as silent and stealthy as the one in my chest. For a moment I am intoxicated.

Yes, it would be easier. She would understand me in ways that Lissa can't hope to. We could have this forever.

But the thought lasts only for a moment. I pull away, wipe my mouth with my sleeve. *Bloody hell, what was I thinking?*

"No," I say.

Then I hear the intake of breath. Recognize the new heartbeat in the room.

"What are you doing here?" Lissa's eyes are wide with hurt, but they're ready to ignite into anger. All it needs is someone as unsubtle—or cruel—as Suzanne to set it off. Or someone as stupid as me.

My cheeks are burning. It's not as if I did anything wrong... Other than lie to her. Just how did that happen again?

"I'm surprised he didn't tell you," Suzanne says. "I made him an offer he couldn't refuse, and well..." She looks at me slyly, "He didn't refuse it."

"You bitch!" Lissa snarls. "You can't keep out of my family's business, can you?"

"Business is business, Lissa. Nothing more. What happened between your father and me... I understand why you might blame me. But—"

"I don't blame you." Lissa's right hand clenches into a fist. "Oh, hang on a minute, yes, I do."

"That's enough." I raise my hands in the air, step between the two of them. "It's all just a—" And Lissa's fist connects with my jaw. She looks from me to Suzanne and back again. I'm not sure who she meant to hit. I don't think she is, either.

"You bastard," she says—that's definitely aimed at me. "You had to go and do this."

And she's out of that room before I can open my mouth.

I rub my jaw, spin on Suzanne. "You set me up! You arranged for her to come home!"

Suzanne's face hardens. "You didn't see this coming?"

"No, I didn't."

"Why the hell did you flirt with me?"

My face is burning. "I never—"

"You did. The coat, the lingering looks."

"I thought I was just playing your game." And then rage explodes inside me. "Piss off, now. *GO!*"

"I'll let you get away with that, but only because I feel a certain element of sympathy. Particularly with what lies ahead. But you will never talk to me like that again." Suzanne shifts away.

I'm left in the empty room. I run to the hallway. Lissa's nowhere to be seen. Out onto the verandah, and then onto the street. Heat slaps me in the face nearly as hard as Lissa's right hook.

I don't mind the pain. I deserve it.

Where the hell is Lissa? I close my eyes, feel her heartbeat. She's back in the kitchen. I run to her.

"You lie to me about not meeting her, about not accepting her offer, and then you're kissing." She wipes at her eyes. "If you want to be with one of them, I can understand that. They're your people now. But to try and keep us going, while—oh, Jesus, Steven. I never thought you'd be such a prick."

"Yeah, I'm a prick. I won't argue with you. I'm an absolute arsehole."

"Agreeing with me isn't helping your case."

"But I love you."

"Did you take up her offer?"

"Yes, but I had no choice."

"You could have chosen to tell me about it," Lissa says. "You could have told me everything. I'm a grown-up. You could have trusted me with this."

"There's no lies between us," I say, which is technically a lie. Why do I keep digging myself deeper and deeper holes?

"Just half-truths." Lissa shakes her head. "So, Steven, you got your ten extra Pomps. But you lost one as well. I'm not going to take this. Not now. I'm leaving."

"OK," I say, because I don't know what else to say. I'm sick with shock. "But I love you."

"Maybe you think you do. But this isn't love. These lies aren't love." She steps toward me. Her heart is racing at 130 bpm, and then it slows, shifts down to eighty. "Now, you know what you need to do?"

"No."

"Do I have to spell it out for you? I'm resigning."

"But—"

"If you don't do this I'll hate you forever."

"We need you. Mortmax needs you."

"Don't you dare play that card. You'll do all right. You have her help, after all."

"I don't want her help."

"It didn't look like it when I walked in."

"Lissa—"

"Just do it!"

I look into her eyes, and she holds my gaze. I reach over and she grabs my hands. It was such an easy gesture once, but now so awkward. My hands shake. She's closed to me, but then she opens up, and I can feel her anger as a visceral thing, a burning agony. It shocks me, even though I was expecting it.

I don't want to do this. It's too painful. I'd let go but she's holding my hands so tightly that my fingers hurt.

I draw the energy back from her, the bit of me that makes pomping possible. I unpick it from her essence. I've never had to do this before, and maybe I couldn't if Suzanne hadn't taught me. It's as easy as opening a door.

But what it reveals…Here, I can see how I have wounded her. How stupid I was. We're both crying by the time it's done. My lip quivers. "I'm so sorry."

"So am I," Lissa says. She pushes past me, heading into the bedroom. "Don't follow me!"

A few minutes later, she's back in the kitchen with a bag bulging with her clothes. She drops it, and a black skirt and blouse tumble free. She glowers, kicks her bag away in frustration. She's no longer a Pomp. She's no longer my girl.

I crouch down to help her pick up her things. She pushes my hands away.

"I can manage," she says.

"You don't need to leave, I'll—you can stay here."

"You'll leave me in your parents' house? Where everything will just remind me of you?" She bends down, grabs the clothes and shoves them back into her bag.

"We can work this out. I can do better. No more lies."

Lissa scowls, her lips move as though to frame some sarcastic response and then she seems to think better of it. "I need time to think."

"But I—"

"And you have a Death Moot to run. Don't let me get in the way of that."

Why didn't I tell her about Suzanne? What stopped me from mentioning it? I have no excuse, or I have far too many.

"Lissa, I was set up. I'm sure of it. She wanted you to walk in." Even to my ears that sounds far too desperate.

"So I could see you kissing her?"

"Yes! This won't happen again…Christ, it didn't happen the first time."

"Really?" Lissa throws up her hands. "Yeah, I've seen how it didn't happen. Don't you see? I've watched all this play out before." Lissa picks up her bag. "I can't be this person. Not with you. Mom and Dad, they had their problems, and I swore I would never be like that. And I won't."

"But—" I reach out toward her.

She steps away from me, throws her bag over her shoulder. "I'll come back for the rest later."

"Where are you going?"

"Somewhere. Anywhere but here. And don't send any of your bloody Avians after me." She walks back down the hall, and I follow her to the front door.

"This could have been so good," she says.

"It still—" Lissa shuts the door in my face. I flinch backward, then grab the handle, fling the door open. Lissa is hunched down on the stairs, sobbing.

"I thought you were going away."

She clambers to her feet. "Oh, fuck you."

"Stay with me, I can protect you."

Lissa's eyes flare. "You can't even protect yourself! The prick blew up our car, Steven. If he hadn't, I wouldn't be waiting for a fucking taxi right now! He killed Travis and Jacob, he nearly killed Oscar."

"But he'll track you down."

"I'm not a Pomp now. You know that's going to make it harder. I've pulled out of the game. If he comes after me, and if you do, too, you better be prepared for the consequences."

"You can't—"

"Don't tell me what I can and can't do. You stay away until I'm ready. To forgive you, or not to forgive you. You lied to me. And you lied to me about her."

"I wanted to spare your feelings."

"No, you didn't want it to be *difficult*. And that worked out so well. Love isn't easy, Steven. It's hard."

I want to ask her why she's leaving, then. Why she's taking the easy option. But I'm the one who has wounded her. I have no right.

She slams her bag onto her shoulder again, and swings around toward the road. "Don't come near me."

I stand there, my mouth hanging open. I deserve it. I'm a fool. I can no more touch her now than when she was a ghost.

A taxi pulls into the street. Lissa looks back at me as it stops beside her. Her eyes are hard. Then she jumps into the cab. I watch it go.

There'll be time to make it right. But not now. Now she's safer away from me. I have to believe that. The day after tomorrow, the Death Moot begins.

A sparrow looks at me. I nod at it. And send the little Avian Pomp after the taxi.

31

I'm still in shock on the morning of the Moot. A day of prep has done little to dull the pain. Lissa's taken up residence in a hotel. The blinds are shut, and my Avians have no view of what is going on beyond them. Only her heartbeat reassures me that she is alive.

It took me three years to get over Robyn. I'm not going to lose Lissa.

Tim was more sympathetic than I thought I deserved. Maybe he's terrified I'm going to lose it. By 8:00 a.m. he has rewritten my opening address, and left me to link my speech with some animations I've sourced from Cerbo. I've never used PowerPoint before, but have found some amazing transitions. I'm feeling almost professional.

It must be the calm before the storm. Rillman's been quiet, there have been no attacks, which worries me. What is he planning? Not a single RM has called me. Perhaps they are steeling themselves for the two days ahead, perhaps they are too busy hiding from Rillman. I'd have at least expected Suzanne to ring to gloat, or to apologize.

Only Solstice gets in contact. Reckons he might have something on Rillman, but he wants to follow it up first. I talk to him about Lissa. He offers me some security, two guards. I think about it. Suzanne said she had someone watching Lissa. But do I trust her? Not really. Not after what she pulled in my kitchen. I give him Lissa's address. The Death Moot is going to keep me busy for the next forty-eight hours, and my Avians certainly aren't going to be able to get inside the hotel she's staying in.

Then I check on Oscar. He's doing OK, but Brooker doesn't expect him to be out of bed for another week. I talk to Oscar about Lissa, and he listens, but offers no comment. I tell him I think I'm ready to look after myself, and he smiles. "Yeah, I think you are, too."

I receive one call from the Caterers, everything is prepared, that the bridge is waiting.

I walk over to Tim's office, knock on the door.

He opens it, and smiles at me nervously. "Ready?"

"Yeah."

He comes over to me, straightens my tie. "You are now. How'd you go with that PowerPoint presentation? Hope you didn't put in too many fancy transitions."

"Of course not."

I grasp his hand and we shift onto the Kurilpa Bridge.

And here it is. Everything has been set up for this moment. This Moot. The bridge is just wide enough for our marquees. It certainly wouldn't be in the mortal realm, not if you needed to accommodate all the pedestrian traffic as well. The marquees are worth the rather large amount of money we paid for them. As is the lighting, and the aircon, which is keeping the space to a comfortable twenty-five degrees.

The Orcus sits around the table, each in their throne. Li An smiles at me. Kiri nods. Anna Kranski gives me a little salute. Devesh Singh is mumbling into his coffee. Charlie Top, now Middle and South Africa's RM, is tweeting like mad on his phone. Suzanne is sitting at the other end of the long table, a coffee by her side.

Here we talk as equals. And we're all looking a bit ridiculous. I've bought them all Akubras to wear—it seems the thing at these international conferences. I want to laugh but the Hungry Death bubbles beneath my skin, whispering to its eleven selves, calling them, and they call back. Its presence has never manifested itself so strongly before. I find it quite terrifying, and a relief that it's not just focused in one person.

How could you handle all that hunger and not go insane?

En masse there is a density and a gravity about the RMs that is impressive. I can't quite believe that I share it. Neill's absence is a void that can't be ignored, though no one is talking about it. That will come later, I guess.

I begin my speech welcoming them all here. They laugh in the right places, though I can't say my delivery is that good. Lissa helped me come up with most of the jokes. I'm still not sure what happened. How could I break her heart so easily? Maybe I thought I'd earned it.

The Moot progresses. The first topic on the agenda is something small, a matter of profits in the last quarter. Suzanne brings that one to the table. I'm actually surprised that she uses a PowerPoint presentation; I was kind of expecting something with animated dust or lightning. The topic is dry, but people seem interested. Maybe it's a break from all the events of the last week. The morning session moves surprisingly swiftly, though I don't hear too much of it.

I'm thinking about my core presentation this afternoon. I have so much to discuss, and, even with Tim's rewrites, I'm not sure that I can pull it off.

Lunch is called at around twelve-thirty.

With all of us together the air is charged with the sort of electricity you'd expect just before a massive storm. In fact, there's one forming in the western suburbs. Thick, rain-heavy cloud is growing darker and darker, and it's heading our way. I'm outside, taking a breather from all the food and the talk. Li An has joined me on the bridge. I don't know why, though. He hasn't said anything yet, and we've been out here for ten minutes.

From the bridge we can see both the Underworld and the living one. On one side is the cultural precinct starting with the sharp lines and angles of the Gallery of Modern Art, and on the other rise the skyscrapers that make up the CBD. The storm is building on Mount Coot-tha. I watch as the Caterers run from line to line on the marquees, double-checking that everything is as it should be, and will stand up to the tempest.

Li An nods at the Caterers and finally speaks. "Happens all the time, these storms," he says. "You get used to it." He spits out an olive pit and frowns. "Never get used to the miserable catering, though. After ten thousand years you'd think they'd know how to use a bain-marie."

My face burns. He doesn't stop eating the nibblies, nor swigging down on a glass of white, though, all of which cost me more money than I want to think about right now.

He pats my shoulder gently. "Of course, you won't need

to worry about that, soon." He sighs. "Got any of those little sandwiches? I do like those little sandwiches."

What the hell is he talking about? I open my mouth to thank him for the vote of support when the air is split with a tremendous thunderclap.

Two black flags, marked with the brace symbol, snap in the wind above the Ankous' marquee. The RMs call it the whinge tent. As far as I can see it's justified, the title and the whingeing. We make them work hard and then some. Tim knows he doesn't have to put up with my shit, but the rest of them don't have the advantage of a family connection. This must be their only chance to vent.

Tim stands by their marquee with the other Ankous, apparently holding court. He looks far more comfortable than me, though I've noticed that he's drawing on a cigarette faster than I thought was humanly possible.

He nods at me. Yeah, something's going on there, and he's not happy. He gestures at his phone; I yank mine out of my pocket a moment before it signals that I've received a text.

Be careful, Tim's written. *They're up to something.*

A few more specifics would be helpful.

A hand, a big hand, slaps down on my shoulder and I somehow manage not to yelp.

"Good spot, this," Kiri Baker says. He's about as broad across as I am tall. He smiles a wide, bright smile. "Nice."

I nod my head. "Yeah."

"So, you still seeing Mr. D for advice?"

"Yeah."

"He still doing that face thing?"

I nod, and Kiri shivers. "Fuck, that used to scare the

bejesus out of me. Dramatic bloke, isn't he? Gotta have a hobby, I suppose." He slaps me on the shoulder again and squeezes. "We southerners have to stick together, eh?"

Hm, that didn't count for much when we had a Schism a couple of months ago.

Kiri sighs. "It's a shame we'll never have a chance to know what might have come of that." I turn sharply and look at him. He's grinning. "Desperate times. Now, I've got to get some of those little sandwiches." He walks back into the marquee.

What do these people know that I don't?

It's my turn at the podium again. I pull out my Power-Point; relate all that I know about the Stirrer god. The things that Cerbo has told me, my own experiences. I even mention the visit from the Stirrer that inhabited Lissa, suggesting that Stirrers may not be as unified as we once thought.

I cannot feel any heartbeats, which is a blessed relief. Must be the storm. I look at the eleven RMs before me. They may be my people now, but I can't show any weakness. My only strength, Mr. D reckons, is that none of them is likely to remember what it was like to be new to the job. They expect a higher level of knowledge than I have.

Huff and bluff, I think to myself. If there's anything I'm good at it's bullshit.

"We have to do something," I say.

"But what?" Charlie Top asks. "My resources are stretched as they are, particularly now that I'm shackled to South Africa, too. Do you not know how many wars my poor Pomps are working? Will you give me more crew to work them?" He looks over at Suzanne. "Not that it matters," he says under his breath, and makes a show of looking at his watch.

"I don't have any to give," I say. Everyone laughs at that, and I fail to see the joke.

"Exactly," Charlie says. "You developed world RMs never have anything to give. We're all part of Mortmax and yet what do you all do? Cut back our supplies or provide them with so many conditions that—"

"It's not the time to discuss this," Kiri breaks in. "We have deeper issues at stake. Rillman has killed an RM. Mortmax's thorn has grown thornier. We all felt it, we've all borne that new burden."

"Which is why de Selby must know these things," Charlie says. "Why he must understand the issues of our regions before it's too late."

"It's what I'm after," I say. "A unified approach to dealing with this problem."

"Yes, but what you don't understand, Mr. de Selby, is that the threat Rillman offers is more immediate," Anna Kranski says.

"How can it be more immediate than *this*?" I slam my hand on the projector and the inky black illustration of the Stirrer god that covers the far wall shakes. "It's coming. And it's getting faster and hungrier and more powerful."

"We have months, if not years, to resolve that issue. Well, you will," Charlie says. "Perhaps you might want to work out how to use PowerPoint, too. All those transitions!"

My jaw drops. "I thought the transitions worked very well."

Charlie Top snorts. "In my experience things aren't ever as neat."

"And what exactly is your experience?" I demand.

"I was old before you were born."

"Ha! What's a few centuries?" I say.

"Actually, Mr. de Selby, a few millennia."

"Well, I've yet to see the wisdom of them." I close the PowerPoint presentation. "We know so little, because we share so little. We have to be united. We have to be because there is no one else but us."

Charlie looks over at Suzanne, and smiles sombrely. "He may just be ready."

What the fuck is he talking about? And what the fuck have all those veiled comments been about? I get the feeling I'm about to find out.

Kiri whistles and jabs a thumb toward the doorway. "There's one motherfucker of a storm coming."

Wind shakes the marquee like some curious, angry giant. Then the tent is gone, hurled into the air, and I'm having some sort of Dorothy Gale moment. Lightning dances across the river, spanning the water at some points so that it looks like a bridge of flame. And at its heart is a figure, grinding two knives together. Around him stand half a dozen Stirrers, their arms tattooed with a familiar pattern, their hair writhing with esoteric energies.

Sensing the threat, my sparrows and crows swarm, but they can't draw close. The moment they do, lightning blasts them out of existence.

Suzanne grabs my hand. "This is it, Steven. I'm sorry it's all going to rest on your shoulders."

"What the hell are you talking about?"

"You never were the brightest one, were you? Just look after Faber for me. He has always been such a loyal Ankou." She grabs my face, kisses me once on the cheek, and then the lips, the latter a lingering thing that possesses a surprising tenderness. "Pity, I think I would have enjoyed getting to know you better."

They can't be serious. They can't leave all this to me! I didn't even want to be RM, and I certainly don't want to run all of Mortmax Industries. I can't.

The other RMs surround us. I remember them circling me while I fought Morrigan in the Negotiation, with all that hunger in their eyes. There's none of that rapacity now, just a grim fear. These Deaths are going to face their own mortality. They've forgotten what that is like, and now it's time to die. But for me, it's all too familiar.

It's one thing to serve it out, to be the creeping replication of cancer cells, the rupturing or blockages that halt a heart, or the shriek of metal against metal and the burn of petrol waiting to ignite on a highway. But it's an altogether different thing to be on the receiving end.

"We've been working hard to bring Rillman out into the open. The man has been actively lobbying against us in various parliaments for a long time. And he can be extremely persuasive, as you would expect from a man who came back from the dead. We never thought he'd get his hands on the knives so swiftly. Steven, you have proven a remarkable accelerant."

"Yeah, people say that about me."

Suzanne ignores me. "You were the perfect bait though; imagine, an RM who had also completed a successful Orpheus Maneuver. How could Rillman ever resist that? I'm sorry about what he did to you."

"And Lissa? Walking in on you—me...?"

"We needed Lissa out of the way. She was in too much danger, and if anything happened to her, we know how that might affect someone at the stage you are in of your career. The last thing we wanted was a rogue RM. I must apologize for that. It was my idea. I sent one of my own Pomps to the Princess Alexandra so that she'd come home. You were set up again."

"Again?"

"Well, Morrigan did it so successfully. We thought we could as well."

"Successfully? Look how that ended up."

"Hm, well, there's a theory that bait is best when it doesn't realize just what it is. Even Mr. D agreed on this. Why do you think we allowed you to have him as a mentor? You are the first RM in the history of the Orcus to have such a guide!"

Mr. D was in on this, too? I thought we'd reached a nice balance of trust and untrust, and now . . .

"Who else knew about it? Tim?"

"Tim's canny, but no. He does now. All the Ankous do. He loves you too much to keep something like that quiet. Steven, people love you, despite you making it so hard for them. They really do."

"So you baited the hook with me? Thank you very much."

"You were being watched. We wouldn't have let Rillman hurt you very much. And as for your relationship with Lissa, you did a good enough job of messing that up yourself, despite my help."

"But did your spies have to punch me in the face?"

"Let me tell you, he was disciplined for that."

"For punching me?"

"No, for being caught and needing to."

The lightning cages and crackles around us, a net of

fire that sets the hair on my flesh on end. The other RMs look at each other, and then at Suzanne.

The Ankous' marquee follows its twin into the air. Twelve Caterers rush toward the kitchen, place their hands on it and are gone. Can't guess how much this is going to cost.

I can hardly hear Suzanne's voice. "You have to get away from here," she's saying. "The Ankous are already gone, including Tim. They're safe for the moment. And find your Lissa. Things may not end as badly as we fear, and if that's the case we'll find you. If they do end badly, well . . . you'll know."

But I know it will end badly. I know they're all preparing to die. This is the path they have chosen, the plan they laid out when I became RM.

Suzanne is shaking her head. "Steven, you may be a bit slow on the uptake, but really, your heart is in the right place. You're the only one of us who might stand a chance with the Hungry Death inside of them. You're the only one who might hold out against the coming darkness."

I want to hit something, anything. "So all that shit about you having a plan, about doing something. The plan was to leave it all up to me."

"Not just you. You will have our Pomps, our Ankous, and your precious Mr. D. Let me tell you, he won't give in to the One Tree for anything now with the kind of influence he'll have."

Like I'm ever going to talk to Mr. D again. Fuck him. Fuck all of them.

"You have to realize that the Hungry Death has been manipulating us all these years, driving our Negotiations to greater and greater violence. We started playing its game, and that's not how you control something like the Hungry Death. You made me realize that. So, Steven, you're not as stupid as you think.

"You'll succeed at this in a way that none of us can. Surely you can perceive what an important moment this is? Just what we're giving up? This is *you*. This is all *your* doing. You've made us all a little bit human again with your presence, your...flaws. Don't forget that."

She leans toward me, fast, and kisses my lips hard, one more time. My face burns. "There has to be another way. It's not too late. Please—"

"No. You're going to need all of the Hungry Death inside you to defeat what's coming. We're giving up our disunity in favor of your sense of purpose. Madness, isn't it?"

"Neill didn't want this, did he?"

Suzanne winks at me. "Why do you think he's dead?"

"You organized that somehow. Made it easy for Rillman to get to him!"

"I'm a ruthless RM when I have to be. Don't hold it against me, de Selby. It's all I know, it's the reason I can't do what you have to."

Lightning sparks against the bridge, a flashing beat of fire that webs its steel masts. Everything seems caught in the flame. I feel like I'm in an out-take of *Highlander*.

"There can be only one," I mumble. My legs are weak. This is too much. Here I am, sick with fear in the eye of the storm.

Suzanne smiles. "Now you're getting it. But there will actually be two. You, and the Hungry Death inside you. It will test you, oh, how it will test you. But then what doesn't? You'll be Death, Mr. de Selby. Death of a whole world. What a glorious thing."

The bridge shudders, jolts. And then Rillman shifts onto Kurilpa, followed by his Stirrers. Lightning flashes everywhere, arcing around us. Suzanne and I look at each other, almost embarrassed by the melodrama of the moment.

"He's nearly tiresome enough to make death pleasurable," Suzanne says.

Rillman shifts to the rail of the bridge. He smacks the knives together. Lightning shivers from the blades, dancing between him and his Stirrers. They're generating it between themselves somehow, just as they've been generating the storms in Brisbane, I realize. The lightning curls around Rillman in a way that no lightning should.

I can feel something building. Electricity crackles in my ears. There's a moment of silence, an indrawn breath.

"Death is coming!" Rillman roars, and lightning drives into the assembled Orcus. They don't even flinch, though behind them I'm throwing my hands up over my face.

"Just get on with it!" Li An yells, ripping off his Akubra, and batting out the flames.

More sparks. Rillman has really invested in the show. With each burst the Orcus loses more of its civility. Clothes sear and burn, but flesh remains unharmed.

This isn't going to hurt them. It's what will come next: the edge of stony knives.

Kiri turns to me. He pats my back, reaches out a hand. "No hard feelings, eh?"

"None," I say, biting down a harsher response. This is not the time or the place.

Kiri grins, then bows. "Let's get started, eh?"

He's surprisingly light-footed as he sprints toward Rillman. The knives flash out. Kiri drops beneath the first blade, swings a fist toward Rillman's face. He connects, but barely. The second knife juts from his chest, eight inches of blade. Kiri looks at me, and then at the rest of the Orcus.

"Well, c'mon!" he roars, spittles of blood trailing his exclamation.

Whatever seal of indecision there was, breaks. The rest of the Orcus run toward Rillman, Suzanne pulling back. "You really can't stay here," she says.

"I want to stay."

"There's nothing you can do here. Just be ready for what comes. Promise me you will go."

"Why do I get the feeling I'm still being played?"

Suzanne shrugs. "Steven, I think it will always seem like that. But the truth is that you're always bigger than the game. That's one of the main reasons why we chose you."

Rillman pulls the blade from Kiri's chest and blood fountains from the wound. Kiri stumbles back. But he doesn't fall. He swings another fist at Rillman's head, but there's a gray blade arcing, dancing in front of him. Kiri's fist goes one way, and his arm the other in a spout of blood.

Now Kiri falls.

Suzanne shoves my shoulder, pushes me back. "Just go!"

"And what if I don't?"

"Then we've made the biggest mistake of our lives. Christ, Steven, man up. Don't fail us."

I try to shift. Nothing. "I can't," I say.

"Of course, there's too much electrical disturbance, far beyond any normal storm. You're going to have to jump off the bridge."

"Really? But that's water beneath. What if—"

"He will not interfere. We have treaties, it's not like you're snatching souls from him. Go, or I'll throw you over the fucking edge myself."

"I could—"

Suzanne grimaces. "Get the hell out of here."

I run to the nearest rail, clamber to the top. Electricity races up my arms and I smell hair burning. It's a long way down. I glance back at Suzanne, but she's already striding toward the melee with a sense of purpose that I can only envy.

Right then. I take a deep breath and step off into the air.

When I hit, the water's warm and murky, the current strong. I'm down deep, and thrashing in the dark. Something brushes my arm. I kick out and up, no breath in me, my clothes heavy.

When I break the surface, coughing and spluttering, my lungs burning, snot running down my cheeks, the bridge is already forty meters away, the air still crackling. Someone's screaming, but I can't tell if it's Rillman or an RM.

There's a gentle tugging on my foot. A dim, stream-lined shape beneath me.

Please, no more sharks. I've had enough of sharks.

I close my eyes. And shift.

32

My head throbs, feels like it's about to pop. What the hell have they asked me to do? What were they thinking? All Suzanne's talk of disunity, but then to be so unified in marching toward their destruction. Surely that belies their argument!

I can't do this.

But I have no choice.

They've chosen me. Does it make them brave or cowards? After all, they're leaving me with one god-awful mess.

I can't do this alone. But then I realize that I'm not. That I've never truly been alone. Lissa, Tim, Alex—they've got my back. They've never failed me.

Lissa! I need to find Lissa.

Suzanne's logic seems right on this one. Rillman will hunt her down if he can't find me, and I doubt Solstice's protection will be up to the job. But they're the least of my reasons. I would die for Lissa.

I shift to a point in the center of the city. To the

immediate west, the lightning storm is a webbed incandescence. My senses have expanded, but they are still dulled by Rillman's electrical web. I search her out. There is nothing. She is not in the city. I try her hotel room. It's empty. No, not quite. I can sense something, a recent death nearby. I shift to the room next door. There's a body there. A Pomp, one of Suzanne's. The poor guy's throat is slashed. This is not good.

I grab my phone. It's dripping wet, but it seems to be working. A no-signal message flashes at me. Maybe that's from the dunking. Maybe it's Rillman's electrical attack. I shift to Number Four.

Chaos! All the Ankous are here, their heartbeats clamoring. I stand in the middle of them, saturated with river water. I can't help scowling at them all.

"How many of you knew about this?" I demand. None of them look me in the eye. They're all frightened.

"Tim?"

He shrugs. "I didn't know anything. You think I could keep this a secret?"

"Is there anything I can do?"

"Not unless you can shift back onto that bridge," Li An's Ankou says. I don't know her name. I'm going to have to learn all their names. No time for that now.

"No, not with the amount of electricity being generated," I say. "There's no way."

"And while we quake, our masters die on that bridge," she says.

I grimace. "Well, if there's nothing we can do about Rillman, I need you to return to your offices. Keep everything running. We can't let the Stirrers take advantage. The Death Moot is a bust, but we have work to do. Your people need you. *I* need you, all of you, to keep doing what you do best. They're not dead yet." Though I can't help thinking of Kiri, the blade jutting from his chest; the ease with which Rillman took out Travis. "Go! See to your schedules."

One by one the Ankous leave.

Now it's just Tim and my staff. They're all looking at me. "And that goes for you, too. We have souls to pomp. Stirrers to hunt down."

They scatter quickly to their workstations. I motion to Tim. "Meeting, now."

"I swear," Tim says. "I knew nothing about this. Not until they shifted us here, together."

"That's OK," I say. "I've got to find Lissa. I can't feel her, she's not in the country anymore. Rillman's likely to go after her."

"And just how are you going to find her? She's not a Pomp anymore."

"I have my means."

Tim raises his eyebrows. "And I have her email password. It was an accident," he says quickly. "I didn't mean to uncover it, but—"

There's a commotion at the lift. Alex. He's paler than I've ever seen him. Someone tries to stop him but he just pushes past them, and stalks over to us.

"I've been trying to call," Alex says. "But the phones are out, all over the city. Did you have anything to do with that?"

"Rillman," I say. "He's killing the RMs, and I'm stuck here. Maybe Solstice—"

"That's just it. That's why I've been trying to call. There is no Solstice," Alex says. "There are no Closers. It's a front. I don't know how he managed it, who he bribed, but Internal Affairs are raiding his offices now.

The staff—half of them are Stirrers. We're going to need your help, or more people are going to die."

Lissa! Solstice had people following Lissa! If they're Stirrers...

Tim's already running through the office, directing staff to call every Pomp they can. I look at Alex.

"You and Tim are going to have to deal with this. I need to find Lissa, she's in danger."

He nods. "We can handle it."

I shift home and rifle through what is left of Lissa's things there as I boot up my Notebook. No clues. My phone chirps; a text from Tim: Lissa's email password.

I get online, open her email and there it is. A ticket booked to Wellington. She has an aunt living on the North Island. Flights to New Zealand are so cheap these days it makes sense she'd visit her. By my laptop is the photo album of Lissa's. She must have been flicking through it before our fight. There's an old Polaroid from a Death Moot marked "1974." Lissa's parents are pressed into a small group with Suzanne—she's looking as fresh as ever. I recognize that forced grin.

Lissa's mom's face is fixed. She must have known by then. Christ, any business is a small world. I know how I would feel if I thought Lissa was seeing someone behind my back. How did I ever let this happen? I should have been up front about the deal from the beginning.

Then I see Rillman, his tight smile, his arm around Don, Alex's dad, at the side of the group.

It's him all right. But that's not what catches my eye, makes me suck in a sharp breath. There's a tattoo running down his forearm. A tattoo I've seen before.

Smauget. The dragon.

Solstice is Rillman.

Or Rillman became Solstice.

What might Stirrers do on a plane?

I focus my mind on Lissa, reaching out across the distance, reaching out beyond the edge of the shore. And *there*. I sense her! I've never shifted into a moving vehicle before, let alone a plane, but she is my center, my heart. I could shift to her anywhere.

A moment later I am thirty thousand feet in the air, standing next to Lissa.

I exhale, a sigh that really wants to become a scream, but I stop it before that. Shit, how did things get so bad, so quickly? Lissa looks at me and scowls, but that doesn't disguise how tightly she is holding onto her seat. It seems the plane's hit some nasty turbulence.

The flight's crowded. If anyone is surprised by my sudden appearance they don't show it. I look down the aisle. No one seems to have noticed me, but that may well be because of the bad weather.

The seat next to Lissa is empty, and I drop into it.

"That seat's taken," Lissa says. She looks tired, but resolute. There's maybe one too many Disney pins on her blouse, as though she's overcompensating.

"We need to talk," I say.

"I told you not to follow me." She doesn't let go of her seat. The seatbelt sign is flashing. She sniffs the air. "I can smell smoke. You've been smoking?"

I shake my head. "Of course not. I only smoke when I'm drunk."

"And when aren't you drunk these days?"

I brush the insult aside. "There's something you need to know."

"You've left it a bit late, wouldn't you say?"

"I don't think it's ever too late for us. I have to believe that." I lower my voice to a whisper. "It's Solstice. He's Rillman."

"What?"

"I don't have time to explain, but he's got two guys tailing you. Don't ask me how I know. I think they're Stirrers."

Lissa's face hardens. "The prick!" Then her eyes narrow. "You got him to tail me. You're the reason they're here in the first place."

"Look, no matter how much it might look like that, he wants you dead. He knows I'm hopeless without you." I don't mention Suzanne's guard or the fact that he's dead.

Lissa doesn't look too satisfied with the answer I've given her, but she's already thinking the problem through. "Right. If they're Stirrers you're going to need a Pomp by your side."

"You'd do that?"

"Bloody hell, de Selby, I love you."

Yeah, she does. No matter how things turn out, no matter how stupid I've been, she loves me!

"Then you have to know I would never cheat on you. That I couldn't."

"But why did you lie to me?"

"Because you were so against the whole idea of Suzanne's offer. Lissa, I didn't want to hurt you."

"How about a little trust?" she says.

"Exactly!"

And now we're glaring at each other again.

"This isn't over," Lissa sighs. "Just do what you have to do."

She reaches up and touches my lips with her fingers. There's serious voltage in that gesture, more electricity than anything Rillman generated on the bridge. It silences me and, oddly enough, focuses me on the job at hand.

I hold her head and transfer my power into her: feel that familiar link. It's such an intense intimacy. For a moment, we are closer than ever. Bound in each other. Feeling what the other is feeling. It's like gazing in a mirror with another's eyes. The familiar becomes unfamiliar. Our eyes widen. Our breaths quicken. What wounds me most of all is the hurt I sense within her. This is my fault. I caused this pain, and anger.

I shudder with the strength of it, and then my fingers drop from her brow. Lissa is a Pomp again. She blinks at me, and I catch myself blinking, too.

"I should never have hurt you," I whisper.

"Steven, this is about us. Not just you. We got into this quickly; it was always going to be difficult. I—I'm not used to long-term relationships. I thought it would be easy, and—but I wouldn't have it any other way. Trust me next time. Trust me to be strong enough, because I am."

Yeah, she's stronger than me.

"And what about you? Why don't you trust me to do the right thing? I made a mistake, but I would never cheat on you. I'm not your father, and—"

The plane shudders. The storm outside is building. We have to find those Stirrers.

I look around. There's no one I'd consider suspicious. Then I glance at the front of the plane. The toilet light is on, and it's flickering, flaring from dim to bright. And always just before the lightning bursts outside.

"In there," I say, slipping Lissa my knife once I've surreptitiously slit my own palm.

I walk down the aisle to the toilet door. One of the attendants shuffles toward me, gripping the seats tightly, but my glare is enough to stop them.

At the front of the plane I can hear the pilots' muted talk in the cabin. They don't sound too happy. Having a Stirrer so close wouldn't be helping either. Reflex times would be slowing. Everybody on the plane including the pilots probably has a headache. Not good when you're trying to fly through a storm. And looking through the nearest window I can tell this is a whopper.

I knock on the toilet door, and the moment I touch it, I recognize the presence of the Stirrer. Right then. I lean back, put my shoulders against the door behind me, and kick as hard as I can.

The door crumples. The Stirrer's sitting on the toilet lid. Its eyes widen, almost comically so.

"You."

"Yeah, me."

Someone crashes down the aisle toward me. Another Stirrer. I turn my head in time to see Lissa leap out of her chair and stall it. And then my Stirrer is swinging a fist at my skull. I duck back, and it grabs me by the lapels and swings its head against mine.

Hey, that's my move.

I almost drop to the floor with the force of it. I slam my bloody palm in its face and it staggers back, its eyes flickering. Outside, lightning crashes and crackles. The plane swings violently to the left, a drunken sort of lurch.

I slap my palm against its face again, and this time it collapses on the floor. Then both souls lance rough-edged and furious through me. I drop to my knees as shocked attendants rush in my direction.

I look over at Lissa, and she's OK.

Then it hits me, a psychic fist clenched around my heart. Hard nails of pain rip through my flesh. It's another fragment of the Hungry Death. I'm floored by it. My back bends, my limbs stiffen. It lasts only a moment, then I can move again.

I get to my feet; giddy with power.

I push the attendants out of the way, which is easy. They scramble toward their seats. The seatbelt lights are still flashing and there's a rough noise coming from one of the engines. The plane drops, people scream. All the lights above Lissa's head go off, then flare back on in a way that no lights should.

I realize I shouldn't be here. How could I have been so stupid? I'm barely containing all this death pouring into me. My flesh creaks, my eyes feel like they might burst with the strain of this. Another fragment. I grit my teeth and stagger down the aisle. I can taste blood. It's filling my lungs, lubricating or facilitating the arrival of the Hungry Death.

Maybe that will be the last one. Maybe Rillman has been stopped. I think of the battle raging on the bridge, all those RMs dying, cramming me with this manic, lustful energy.

I try and shift. I can't. It's like the Sea of Hell again. Something is holding me to this place—or someone.

"You need to be in your seat." A flight attendant, perhaps a little braver than the rest, is at my side. Every passenger on the plane is staring at me. A couple of the bigger ones are considering doing something. What? What could they do against me?

I swear that, for a moment, the attendant recognizes me on some deeper level: what it is that I am. Or maybe she just sees a crazy person. She nods her head, swallows a deep breath. "OK, sir."

She scrambles away, moving like a crab; I've never seen a flight attendant so spooked before. Someone else is already asking for assistance. I can tell she really wants to go to her own seat, that she's as scared as the others, but it doesn't stop her. She helps them with their seatbelt.

A dreadful hush descends upon the plane. HD is rapturous, positively bloody gleeful. I push it down.

I'm back with Lissa; stepping over the Stirrer corpse. "I have to get out of here," I say.

"What's wrong?"

"Rillman. He's killing RMs. I'm absorbing more of the Hungry Death. I could destroy this plane."

"Shift then. The Stirrers are dealt with," Lissa says.

"I'm trying." I close my eyes, concentrate. It's no good.

Another wave of the Hungry Death strikes me. The lights around me explode. The plane can't handle what's going to happen. HD swells. I try to shift again. Still nothing. I look around wildly for an exit hatch.

There, not too far away. I take a step toward it.

Lightning strikes the plane, a dozen incendiary bursts. And some of them are coming from me. Outside, the storm is raging, with a darkness deeper than anything the Stirrers are capable of. The plane judders, swings, drops. I slam into the ceiling. The attendant has hit her head. Blood flows. A trolley hurtles past me, crashes into the attendant. Her death pulses through my flesh. People scream. HD howls out its pleasure.

I try to shift again. Still no good. I'm fixed here by the transformation occurring within me, the new and horrible thing I'm becoming.

Lissa looks at me. She has her seatbelt on tight.

Shift, damn it! Shift! They're all going to die if I don't. But I can't. It *wants* them to die.

And all I have is the thin fabric of you, the Hungry Death whispers with more force than I've ever experienced. *I can pull myself through that whenever I want to. And I will. You were one of thirteen warriors, but twelve have deserted you.*

Shut up. Shut up. Shut up.

The plane jolts like a creature kicked and whipped and gripped by a deathly god. The sky is a dark fist around it. *Fuck. Oh fuck. This is all my stupid fault.*

There's a moment of calm. And my phone chirps. I look at the LCD: the schedule. Oh, no. Two hundred names. Lissa's is at the top.

It's too late.

"Steven—" Lissa's hand folds over mine.

The plane bucks, up and down, faster than I can adjust to. I feel the plane flash in and out of this world and Hell. My presence is causing this. The transition alone is killing some people. I'm weightless, then heavy. I smack my head against the nearest headrest. Lissa's hand slips from mine.

Time runs down here, bleeds away. Death is coming. I'm coming. This is all my fault. The air stinks of blood and piss and smoke.

"Hold my hand," I say to Lissa, snatching it anyway, just as the plane starts to tumble. There's a noise like the grinding of giant teeth, a dreadful rending. The plane is lit with a blue light. The pre-death light. Lissa's as bright with it as the others. I have seen her that way before, and I will not see it again.

The last fragment of the Hungry Death enters me. I feel it pushing against my flesh. The Orcus are dead, all but me. I am the last. And it terrifies me. HD loves it.

Lissa's not looking at me: her eyes are wide. The noise must be terrible but I can barely hear it. I snap my head around in time to see the back end of the plane split from the front, as though something has torn it off.

This plane falls tonight. Two hundred shattered lives. And it's but the beginning. All that ending ahead, and me/we at the fore.

I wish HD would shut the fuck up.

There are screams, guttural, terrified. Someone laughs. It's a peculiar sound; it cuts through me. And HD is joining in.

"I picked the wrong bloody flight, didn't I?" Lissa says.

"Jesus," I breathe. Every time I blink I can see the One Tree. I can hear it creaking. I force my eyes open. "Oh, Jesus."

Lissa holds my gaze.

"Don't be scared," she says, above all that noise.

Mr. D's words come to me: Sometimes terror is the only response. I'm not scared. I'm terrified.

She touches my face. "It's OK, Steven." Her hands do not shake, there is more strength in that touch than in all of me. We have been here before. I just never expected to be here again so soon.

"I love you," I say.

I grab Lissa's hand and try and shift. It hurts. HD

pushes against me. It's hard and toothed. The meat of me is screaming with it. I haven't felt this human since... since Morrigan cut me with the stony blade. The universe pushes. But I push back. I push back hard and it shrinks away. And this time I shift.

But Lissa doesn't come with me. I'm standing in my office. Alone. HD screams.

I shift back. Back to her.

This shift is not resisted. I see now that this is where I am meant to be, what I am meant to witness.

The plane crumbles and tumbles around me. People scream, and die. Their souls lash through me: bullet-quick and burning. It hurts, but I ignore it. I reach out for Lissa.

"No!" she says. I can't hear her, of course. The roar of a plane breaking, tumbling, dying, drowns her out. But I can read her lips.

I clutch at her. Wrap my arms around her, and shift again. Pain. A nest of needles jutting through every cell of me, and twisting. I'm shrieking in my office, blood running from my lips, my eyes, my ears, my arse. Every orifice bleeds.

No Lissa. She is not here.

I shift again.

The plane. The plummeting cage. Outside I see the One Tree looming and then a wing clips a branch. Metal grinds, windows crack and blow out.

"Sorry," she says, and squeezes my hand.

She shouldn't say that. This is my fault. All of it.

She touches my face. "It's all right."

"I'll follow you. I'll follow you to the end of fucking time if I have to." And then there is an explosion. The whole sky seems on fire.

I wrap my arms around her, shield her from the worst of it. I'm hit, but heal almost as fast as the wounds make their mark. There is so much strength in me. But not enough for her.

And there isn't a plane anymore. Just fragments dropping toward a black and perilous sea. The air roars and all around us, people fall. All around us is the death that I made.

She falls. And falls.

And I can't lift her up, so I hold her close. I whisper my love. I press my lips against her, and I fall with her.

We plummet toward water dark as slate in the storm. She holds my gaze with a strength that amazes me. An implacable acceptance. I can feel her heartbeat, like I can feel all their heartbeats, and it is racing. But she doesn't look away.

I am going to lose her.

Let me, the Hungry Death whispers, *Let me*.

And I do. I let it fill me. I make a void for it within my soul, and for the first time in my life I have an inkling of what real power is. I shift.

And this time she comes with me. We're here, in my office.

She belts her hands against my chest. "No! You shouldn't have, you shouldn't have!"

"Stay here. I'll be back. I promise."

"Where are you going?" Lissa asks, weeping.

"To bear witness. To pomp the souls of those lost."

There are bodies in the water, lifeless. Only their souls know motion among the flotsam, bits of plane, and pieces of people's lives. I hover cross-legged, shifting above them, and it is effortless. But the wonder has been sucked from it, by these dead: one hundred and fifty in total. Their souls thrash in the water, bound there, unable to do more than keep their essences afloat. Out here, if I don't do anything...

Long gray limbs slither from the sea. Water spills from narrow bald heads, beneath which beam mouths long and beakish. The ocean wants these souls for itself. It wants them restless and heaving in the depths. The gray shapes flash toward the souls of the dead. I glare at them. HD howls. And they hesitate.

"These are mine," the Water whispers. "Not yours. You have no dominion in my seas."

"This time I do."

"You would challenge me, Orcus?"

Orcus. I blink at the title, at the stupid formality of it. But it is true. It is what I am. I am Orcus, my region is the earth. I am the only one capable of pomping these souls to Hell away from the shore. Children! There are children here. Dozens of them. And, God help me, HD guffaws with pleasure.

"Yes," I say, "and you cannot stop me."

I close my eyes, and draw the souls within me. It's hard work pulling them from the suck and cold of the sea. I'm sweating and shaking by the end, with the effort of it. The Water was right. I have no dominion here, but I do have my power. Finally they are gone, sent to the Underworld, which is their right, no matter that it has come too soon for all of them.

The gray forms drop beneath the water. "Orcus, you do yourself no good in making an enemy of me."

"One more enemy. What does it matter?"

Then the Water beneath me is just water again, and the dead are soulless and drifting among the wreckage. I've done what I can here.

It's time to find Rillman. The bastard has to pay.

33

I can sense his heartbeat. It can't hide its secrets from me. I close my eyes and shift.

The Deepest Dark. Why here? Which is precisely the question Wal asks when he crawls out from under my shirt. I can sense Rillman circling around, shifting from space to space. I catch glimpses of him. A leg. A foot. A hand tight around a knife hilt. His feet send up clouds of dust. Closer and closer. I wait.

And then, through the dark to my left, two stony blades jab out at me.

I jerk to the right, though one of the blade points cuts through my suit, bites shallowly into my stomach. It burns. I resist the urge to crouch over it, as though to stop my guts spilling. But the wound is already healed.

"Out you come," I snarl.

A body takes form in the dark, arms and shoulders, then head, torso and legs knitted from all that cold shadow.

Solstice smiles. Who else would it be?

"So what do I call you? Rillman or Solstice?"

His limbs move with a jerky energy that Solstice never had. I wonder at the strength of will it must have taken Rillman to contain all that madness. He doesn't need to now, and it bursts from him as wild as any storm.

"I never really liked the name Solstice, but you take what the mask gives you. And he was such a good mask." Then he changes, becomes the Rillman I know. The Rillman in the tunnel. The dull, smiling bloke in Lissa's photo album. He shrugs. "You know, after I failed, I killed myself. Not once, but twice. And every time I came back. She helped me come back."

"Aunt Neti?"

"Yes, even when I didn't want to. And then RMs noticed. They tried to kill me, too, and each time I died, I came back, different, stronger."

Around him swings the tiny dragon, Smauget, its red eyes aflame. It darts toward my face. There's a blur of movement, a shrill yowl, and Wal has snatched it from the air. The dragon hisses and snaps, its tiny mouth going for Wal's jugular, but the little fella is ready for it. He catches it by the throat, and they tumble to the ground.

"Leave this to me," he says, from between clenched teeth. "You deal with him."

Rillman holds the knives at a distance from his chest, as though even he's afraid of what they are. I don't blame him. I understand their will intimately. The knives blur the air like light sticks waving in the depths of a cave.

They whisper and snort, *Hello, hello.*

"I am better armed now. These things kill RMs like you wouldn't believe. They're simplicity itself. And here, you don't have any Avian Pomps to protect you," Rillman says.

"Why did you kill them?" I ask.

"Who? The RMs, well, you know that they deserved it."

"Not them. This isn't about them."

I lift my hand. Dust shapes itself into a plane. Dust people tumble from it.

Rillman almost drops the knives. They shudder in his hands. "What?" The emotions that play across his face shock me. It's almost as variable as Mr. D's. Joy, sadness and a mad hunger mix and meld across his features, and it would almost be comedic if he wasn't waving knives in my face. Then I realize that Rillman isn't well at all.

I could almost pity him.

"Your Stirrer drones," I spit. "The ones with Lissa. I took them out, and then the Hungry Death came. I wouldn't have been there but for you. Its presence within me wouldn't have destroyed that plane."

Rillman snorts. "You RMs, always ready to blame anyone but yourselves. Lissa was meant to die. To make you understand. To teach you the mechanics of pain. And my attacks on you? That was their purpose, too. To hurt, to blind, to scare. I take it that you managed to save her. Too bad about the others, eh? They were your doing."

"I understand pain." HD snickers. It's intimate with pain as well.

"Ah, you only think you do. Maddie, I killed her. But I could have brought her back. And there he was, your Mr. D. Smug and useless. There he waited, in the dark that slides along the borders of the Underworld. And with a fucking grin on his face, he hurled her back. I was done, then. I was spent; no chance of another Schism. He had nothing to fear from me, but he hurled her back. And even now, dead, he is not dead. And you have made it so. The favored one, the fucking coddled one. The man who didn't want to be Death. How can you expect to do anything? How can you expect to hold back anything?"

"That's it," I say. "It starts and ends here. And the rest? The rest we will have to see."

A little calm returns to Rillman, a crooked smile. "That's what the Orcus said, and there's very little left of any of them."

"I'm something altogether different now," I say.

The knives flash toward me, but I'm ducking and weaving. It's motion absent of thought, fed on instinct. I've fought with these knives before. My movement is fast and sinuous. Something is hardening within me. A dreadful resolve, a chuckling vastness. The knives slice the air millimeters above my face, then to my left and right, never quite touching.

Rillman growls.

I gesture at the dust around my boots. It flashes up in a tight spiral between us—Suzanne would have been pleased—and into his eyes. My fist follows it. Rillman stumbles back. Wipes at his nose with his wrist. A knot of blood and snot stretches from his nostrils to his arm, then breaks.

His heart beats loud in my ears, and it's no longer that familiar steady rhythm. It's pounding, racing—160 bpms at least. His pupils are dilated. I know he's on something and it's raging through his body like fire. He comes back at me, fast. But something is burning through my body, too.

The knives dance figure eights before him. It would almost be beautiful, but I've no eye for beauty now. HD argues the point, but I ignore it.

More dust, a blinding burst. He staggers, his eyes stung. I kick him in the chest. He crashes backward, lands hard.

"Dust? Is that all you have?" he pants, getting to his feet, wiping at his eyes with his wrists. He's half blind, but it doesn't stop him. I'd almost respect that, but I am hatred now. I am blazing anger.

"It's all I need." I launch more dust at him. Rillman slices through it with the knives, but it's only dust, it doesn't bleed. Not like him. He doesn't even know that he's beaten.

He charges at me. And this time I don't care to obscure his run. No dust. Just him and me.

"I want you to know that you made this," I say. The blades whirr around me, jabbing toward me and away, and I weave in time with them in perfect synchrony. The poor bastard doesn't understand that they are dancing for me. "Your desire for revenge. To cause me pain. To bring down the Orcus. To hurt me and mine. All of it. The whole fucking concatenation of hate and fear. You made it all, and now..." I snatch the blades from his hands, one, two... "These are mine."

I kick him to the ground, easily. Rillman lies there, bleeding. "What are you?"

"You don't get it at all, do you? I'm Steven de Selby," I say, picking him up with one hand, as though he weighs nothing. And he doesn't. No one does now. "I am Death."

I backhand him casually in the face. Bone cracks. He drops to the ground, and I stand over him. I grit my teeth, and feel my face shift. It's agony and it's glorious. For a moment all I am is pain. All I am is Death.

The knives in my hand slide toward each other,

bind each other in their stony gravity, and then I am holding a scythe. It shivers with the deepest of hungers in my grip.

Mayhem. Murder. Death, it breathes.

And God help me, I swing the scythe above my head.

Wal rushes in between us. "Whoa, whoa!" He hovers there, his wings beating so fast that they lift up dust. His eyes are wide with a kind of terror that I'm unacquainted with, and they're directed at me.

"Go away," I say.

"If you kill him, you won't get answers."

I jab my finger at his face. "But that's just it. I am the answer, am I not?"

All I want is death. His death. The world's death. HD cackles, like a drunk crashing toward damnation.

Then a squeak of brakes alerts me to his presence. My old boss.

"Stop this now," Mr. D says, sliding off his bike. His face is pale; he's out of breath. Must have been riding since I entered the Underworld.

"You," I growl. "This is as much your fault as his. Letting them—letting *all* of them—do this to me."

But it is glorious!

Mr. D holds my gaze. "Yes... They were convincing, Steven."

"Convincing!" I swing the scythe above his head. It would be nothing to lop it off. Mr. D doesn't move. "Is that all you can say?"

"You didn't prepare him for any of this," Rillman says.

Mr. D glances over at him. "Good evening, Francis."

Rillman spits toward him. "Hell must be so hungry for you."

"It's hungry for all of us," Mr. D says. "It will have me in its own good time, believe me."

"I'd kill you if I could," Rillman breathes.

"You're not the only one." Mr. D places a hand on my shoulder. "Steven, I am so sorry."

I brush his hand away. "You should go now. You have no power here."

"None of us do, Steven. The rules that bind us do so tightly. You have choices, but what horrible, horrible choices. Leave this idiot. The other RMs are still on the tree; they won't be for much longer. Go to them, find out anything more you can."

"I don't need them anymore. I want you gone." My voice is barely a whisper, but there is a dreadful force behind it. Mr. D diminishes, nods.

"As you wish." He throws a glance askew at Wal, as if to say sorry. Then he picks up his bike and rides away into the dark. I watch him until the gloom swallows the flickering red of his tail-light.

Rillman coughs. Wal flits in front of him again.

"You want me to go, too? I swear I won't go so easily," Wal says. None the less I tap my arm and he is nothing more than a tattoo, his face twisted with a bunched zippering of cherubic teeth.

I fashion a chair out of dust, and drop Rillman in it.

He coughs, spits blood. He's not bound. I don't need to do that.

"You can run," I say. "But I will find you. Have no doubt of that."

He eyes the knives I've left resting on a nearby root tip of the One Tree. They're no longer the scythe. I raise one hand and that's what they become. I'm intuiting a lot, but I know I can call that scythe to me in a second, just as I know its name is Mog. In a breath, a single breath of that name, it will find me.

He looks shiftily from the scythe to me, and back again. I dare him with my eyes. But Rillman has had enough.

"Why did you do this?" I ask. "Tell me and I might be gentle with you."

"I hate you," Rillman growls. "You got what I wanted. While Mr. D was alive he locked me out. But you, you were so interesting. So naive. You were the only RM not like them. You were the one who I wanted to suffer, not just kill, because you didn't deserve what you had been given. I've been a long time in planning this, and when you won your Negotiation and changed the rules... Well, you have to realize that I had to make you pay." He sneers at me. "Is it any wonder that governments agreed to my requests, when I showed them what I was capable of, with but the merest sliver of an RM's powers? They've been frightened of Mortmax for a long time, the consequences of it. And they're terrified of you."

Yeah, they have a bloody good reason to be now. HD's pleasure radiates through me.

"I knew it would only be a matter of time until it fell apart, and the world's governments would be left picking up the pieces anyway. The Thirteen have lurched along for an age. But everything ends." He fiddles with his tie with his restless jerky fingers.

"Yeah, when you murder them."

Rillman's face darkens. "All of them were murderers. Every single one, and I know you're not stupid enough to believe otherwise. You want to become a murderer, Steven?"

"I'm Death. It's what I do." Mog quivers in its resting place. And the new and ancient part of me remembers its endless predation, its racing hunger. It would be easy to give in to that. After all, it's what nature intended. It's so like humanity to shape things into much more convoluted patterns. I've a chance to break them all, starting with the death of Rillman. One enemy removed. "And maybe it's your time," I say.

Rillman shakes his head. "I've read your files, Steven, it's not in you." He's waiting. There's a pulsing vein in his forehead and a slight smile breaks the line of his lips. Then he scowls and maybe, for the first time, I have the real measure of the man, and what I see is shocking. There is too much of my rage in there. "You're just not that kind of guy."

I grab him by his lapels and lift. "I am now."

This close, I can feel what it is that gives him power: the thing that Neti gave him that allows him to slip from the land of the living to the land of the dead, and back again. It shivers inside him like a second beating heart. This is a free pass between the gates of the two worlds, and it belongs to me! I don't know how Aunt Neti stole it, but I want it back. I yank him to his feet, touch his face with my hands, grip his skull hard, and draw that power from him.

It hurts. Because what he has is fed by pain and anger. I drag it into me; more power, more of the essence that is now so much of what I am. I understand the truth that is the Hungry Death, its persuasive presence, and the tiny thing that is the man before me. I close one hand around his neck, curious how that might feel, and then the other hand.

And I squeeze.

He grabs my wrists. He struggles. He kicks out at me, and thrashes. But I do not relax my grip. If anything I tighten it. HD laughs, and I laugh too, until I feel Rillman's spirit pomp through me. It bursts free, not toward the One Tree, but straight into the Deepest Dark. I watch it there, and then, something bright and eight-armed snatches out and grinds out the light within it.

I'm left staring up into the dark.

I drop Rillman's body.

Mog drifts toward me. I close a fist around its curving snath and back away from the corpse. Let the dust engulf the body.

I'm empty, weak. I can barely stand. My hands grip Mog so tightly that my knuckles ache. It's the only thing that is keeping me upright.

Wal pulls himself from my arm. "What have you done?"

The body is there, between the two of us. It's answer enough.

34

I shift to my office. It's late. Ten. I can hear someone using the photocopier. Such an everyday sound.

I'm sick, but it's not from the shifting. Mr. D was right, all I needed was practice. I smile, and spew into the bin, but it's not cathartic. There's no release in it. Just pain.

I slump into my throne. It's bigger now, far bigger, all encompassing. It dominates the room like the dark seat of some dark empire, and yet I hardly notice it. I settle in, and my pain ebbs, a little. But I have worse hurts. I put my head in my hands.

All the world's heartbeats rain down on me, all those clocks winding down, all that strength pulsing toward its undoing.

And that's the least of it. Every time I close my eyes they're there—those innocent deaths of which I was the cause, that final pomping of Rillman's soul.

I sit in my throne, sobbing, drowning in the world's pulse. Tim's is there. So is Lissa's. I can pick them out like threads. Mr. D once said that the sound becomes soothing—the cacophony a lullaby. Here I am, struck by those billions of heartbeats, and then I feel Lissa nearby. I drag myself from the comfort of the throne and Mog blurs, becomes the knives again. They rest, bound by sheaths knitted from evening, on my belt. I shift through the wall, and there she is.

"Steven, are you all right?" She's been crying, too. I should have sought her out straightaway, but I couldn't face her. I can barely face her now.

"Yes," I say. "Are you?"

"I think so."

Then I'm holding her and I can almost forget the pain and guilt I'm feeling. Finally she pulls from me.

"You shouldn't have done that," she says. A vein pulses in my head. Does she know? "You shouldn't have come after me like that."

"You know I had no choice. I've nothing left but you."

"I know you were trying to do the right thing. But Christ, you—"

"I should have told you about Suzanne. No more secrets, right? I promise."

She touches the knives at my belt, curiously.

"They're mine," I say, "and, to be honest, I don't want them out of my sight. I'm the only RM left standing. Mortmax International is my responsibility now."

"And HD?"

"It's under control, I think...I don't know. Rillman—Solstice is gone. He won't be a problem anymore."

In my office I can hear the unmistakable ring of the black phone. I ignore it. Lissa looks at me questioningly. "It can wait," I say. "We need to get out of here."

Lissa holds me tight, and it's all I can do not to crush her in my grip, so desperately do I need that contact. "Where do you want to go?" she asks.

"Home," I say.

I shift with her in my arms. And we are back in my parents' place, in the hallway, Mom's perfume as strong as ever.

"We're going to move out of here. It was always a mistake to live here," I say.

I can't bear my parents looking down at me from those photos. I know how they would judge me for what I've done, what I am.

"Are you sure?" Lissa asks, though I can tell she's pleased. This was never our home. I nod. "Then we need to find a place that Stirrers can't just stroll into," she says.

I can tell Lissa wants to talk this through, all of it. And I want to as well. But there's a weight of exhaustion pulling on her. She's worn out with worry, with the hell that has been this last week. And we have time. There's no Death Moot or Rillman to concern us now, and the Stirrer god isn't here yet.

"Try and rest," I say. "We have so much to do, but not now."

I walk with her to the bed. Lissa's fast beneath the sheets and even quicker to fall asleep. I stand there looking at the person I have risked all for, and for a moment I feel better.

I call Tim.

"Jesus, what happened to you?" he asks. "I came to the office, and you'd both just left."

I don't want to talk about it. Tim's going to have to trust me. "How are the Ankous?"

He's a while in answering. I can't tell if I've offended

him, which probably means I have. "They're all right. In shock, but that's understandable. Mortmax has suffered its biggest, loss...gain...Shit, I don't know, what's happened? What the hell do we even call you?"

"Steve," I say. "I'm your cousin, remember?"

"Steve. Solstice's offices, they were worse than anything Morrigan ever did. The rotting dead. Their rage and, God, their laughter. That's what's going to stick with me the most. They laughed as we stalled them, every single one, as though it didn't matter. I'm fucking terrified."

I'm more than familiar with that laughter. "Sometimes it's a reasonable response. Listen, Tim, we're going to have to start mobilizing," I say. "The Stirrer god is coming. But we will be ready."

"Are you OK? You sound—"

"I'm exhausted," I say. "Bloody knackered. I'll call you tomorrow. We both need to think, and to rest—that most of all. You can't do anything if you're tired."

"I thought you couldn't sleep."

"I can now," I say. "You should, too."

"One more thing," he says. "The black phone in your office keeps ringing."

"Don't answer it," I say. "I can deal with that tomorrow, too."

I hang up, and take a shower. But I can't wash HD or the thing I've done from me. Wal is on my biceps, and he looks frightened. When I'm done, I walk to the back balcony, the towel wrapped around my waist.

Another storm rolls in from the south, but this one's soft and earthy, and while it may hide a stir or two, it's just a storm. I watch it build for a while. Rain falls, light spatters at first, and then it's a real downpour.

Lightning bursts in the distance. I wait for the thunder to come rumbling through the suburbs, and when it does I turn to go inside.

Something catches my eye.

They must have been there for a while, silently waiting for my scrutiny: a shivering darkness spread across the lawn. Sharp beaks. Slick black feathers, glossy with the rain. A thousand crows, at least. And they have bowed down low, their wings extended.

"Awcus, awcus," they caw.

I dip my head.

HD seems pleased, all this laid out for it and me. I raise a hand, gesture toward the sky. As one they beat their wings into the angry air, and batter hard against the rain. The vast murder of crows breaks from the ground, finds the night sky and is gone. I could have dreamed the whole thing, but for the dark feathers fluttering down.

Awcus.

I walk into the living room and pour myself a drink, a big one.

Lissa's asleep when I stumble back into the bedroom. The rain hammers on the iron roof but it's ebbing. HD roils within me, grinning its ceaseless grin. But I force it down. I'm tired and on my way to being drunk. I can't stifle a yawn. I settle next to Lissa, slide my arm around her. So tired. She moans something in her sleep, then calms.

The dying rain and Lissa's breathing are the most perfect sounds in the world. I'm not sure when sleep claims me.

Death. Mayhem. Madness and blood. The metronomic sweeping of the scythe.

But I sleep soundly.

ACKNOWLEDGMENTS

So Book Two. Who'd have thought?

Once again, for the last stages (after the big grub of a first draft), a huge thank you to my publisher Bernadette Foley, my structural editor Nicola O'Shea and my copy-editor Roberta Ivers. This was foreign ground to me, and you've made the whole process a lot less scary than it could have been. If the book's a butterfly it's because of the chrysalis you lot wove...maybe I'm taking that metaphor too far.

Thanks again to everyone at Avid Reader Bookstore (and the cafe) for being amazing, and for still putting up with the least available casual staff member in the universe, and to Paul Landymore, my SF Sunday compadre who never lets me get away with much. Thanks also to the city of Brisbane, with whom I have taken even more liberties—particularly concerning her bridges—and to my Aunty Liz, who isn't going to like the swearing but switched me onto fantasy when I was a very young lad.

All those Greek myths and tragedies: you can't get a better gift than that.

Thanks to Diana, who has to put up with everything, and still loves me.

And thanks to you, who have followed me onto Book Two. I hope you liked it.

extras

orbit

meet the author

TRENT JAMIESON has had more than sixty short stories published over the last decade, and, in 2005, won an Aurealis award for his story "Slow and Ache." His most recent stories have appeared in *Cosmos Magazine*, Zahir, Murky Depths and Jack Dann's anthology *Dreaming Again*. His collection *Reserved for Travelling Shows* was released in 2006. He won the 2008 Aurealis Award for best YA short story with his story "Cracks."

Trent was fiction editor of Redsine Magazine, and worked for Prime Books on Kirsten Bishop's multi-award winning novel *The Etched City*. He's a seasonal academic at QUT teaching creative writing, and has taught at Clarion South. He has a fondness for New Zealand beer, and gloomy music. He lives in Brisbane with his wife, Diana.

Trent's blog can be found at
http://trentonomicon.blogspot.com.

introducing

If you enjoyed
MANAGING DEATH,
look out for

THE BUSINESS OF DEATH

Death Works: Book Three

by Trent Jamieson

So, I have two major issues, not counting the nearing End of Days—that's really too much of problem to be called an issue as such.

How do you make peace with the Death of the Water, and how do you ask a girl to marry you?

The first, well, I've got something of an idea. The second...

Lunchtime at a table on the footpath outside a cafe in West End waiting for Lissa to pay the bill because I forgot my wallet—perfect illustration of how distracted I am. I should be too busy to worry about this, but I can't help it. Can't say that it was the best of lunches. Don't really remember what it was I said, or even what I ate: felt a little too sick. Waiting for the moment to present itself.

It never did.

Now, here's the thing—Is she going to think I'm asking because the world's end is nigh and it isn't much of a commitment?

Ask, then save world?

Save world then ask?

Problem is what if I don't save the world? What if I ask and she says no, and I don't feel like doing the savior thing after that? It's the kind of work you have to put your whole heart into.

Bugger, it would be easy (I guess) if I had another job. But I'm the guy that got to be Death.

Trust me, you don't want to be following my career path. For one there was a lot of blood and slaughter involved. Before I came along, those that wanted what I have sacrificed their friends and family willingly—even excitedly.

Not me. Not at all. In less than a week I had everything blown out of my life in a burst of gunshots and explosions. All of which sounds exciting unless you're living it.

Friends, family—with one or two exceptions—gone.

To say it sucked is somewhat understating the case.

And that was before I became one of the Orcus—the thirteen Deaths that run Mortmax industries.

And then, when I was getting used to it—as much as you ever can can. The nightmares, natural and supernatural alike. The lack of sleep. The constant cumulative pulse of a nation's hearts. The rising deathlust. Just as I was getting all that under wraps, it got a hell of a lot worse. The only people that really understood me, my fellow Orcus, all went and sacrificed themselves because they thought I had the best chance of stopping the End of the World.

I certainly wasn't consulted in that instant promotion from Regional to Global.

Still I took it all in my stride, partly because I'm not completely me anymore. Try living with a fairy tale madness inside you, that takes a great pleasure in mocking your every move and wishing for wholesale slaughter. I've indulged it only once. And I regret that indulgence… sometimes. It was a stupid and mad act, and but for two witnesses, not even Lissa knows. I should never have strangled Francis Rillman. Not that he gave me any choice.

Should I tell her? Should I divulge…repent…whatever it is I need to do? And how does that factor into her response to my proposal? Gotta be a tick in the negative column certainly. HD is rather keen to see me come clean. It would, HD loves it when the shit hits the fan.

I look up. Look for Lissa.

Lissa who is taking forever to come back out of the cafe. I do my best to ignore the smell of someone's herbal cigarette, even if it's making me cough. There's an engagement ring in my pocket. It's been slipped from jacket pocket to jacket pocket for three weeks. Can't forget that, but I can forget my wallet.

I glance at my watch. Two-thirty, I need to be back in the office soon, so much to do, and Lissa has a soul to pomp on the Southside around three-thirty. We hold off too long, and she'll be stuck in traffic. Death waits for no one—the M3 motorway leading out of the city on the other hand…

The world's pulse thump thumps away within me. HD rattles the bars of his cage. A typical day, these days. As is that question.

How do you ask a girl to marry you?

All the problems besetting Mortmax, the world, and my sanity, and my mind keeps coming back to that.

I peer into the cafe.

How long does it take to pay a bill?

Lissa's chatting away with the barista. I've never known a person who makes friends so easily. She says something and the guy laughs—a little too heartily. Would he take as long to ask her to marry him? HD suggests we kill him.

No. No. We do not kill cute guys that laugh at my girl.

The barista laughs again, even reaches out a hand to touch her arm.

It's never too late to make an exception. A single breath and I could call the scythe of Death into being.

Lissa turns from the laughter, and looks in my direction, for a moment I think she's read my mind, but she's smiling and the smile is directed at me.

Who wouldn't want to laugh with a girl like that? She made my heart beat faster from the moment I saw her. And that first time she was dead, a soul come to warn me, to tell me to run. Fell in love with her before she opened her mouth. And it's been a constant falling since.

She's in her standard get-up. Black and black. Black skirt ending a little above the knees, black long-sleeved blouse, dark hair, cut messy and short. She's wearing one of her favorite brooches of Mickey Mouse, classic mid-fifties Mickey stomping along merrily. For a touch of variety she's wearing purple Doc Martin boots—she has a green pair at home, but she favors the purple. There's a knife hidden up her left sleeve, strapped to her wrist, another in her left boot. She blinks as she leaves the dark of the cafe for the street. Her eyes, green flecked with gray, focus on me. There's something challenging and wonderful in the gaze. I feel at once mocked and loved at the same time.

How does she do that?

Lissa grabs her handbag from the chair beside me, slips her purse into the bag's cavernous interior.

"You were laughing a lot in there."

"I know, he's cute, huh."

I can't help but pout. "Cute? Mr. Barista?"

What about me? I'm wearing my best suit here. And I know that my hair looks good—I only had it cut yesterday.

I take her hand and she squeezes mine. That contact shocks me as it always does, even now. Just over six months ago, touching Lissa would have sent her to Hell, literally. It's what Pomps do. It's what Death is all about. And me, back then, so unprofessional, so immediately in love, I couldn't do it.

It saved my life.

And it saved hers, too. I pulled an Orpheus Maneuver and brought her back from the Underworld. A complicated start to our relationship but better than no start at all.

We walk out from under the awning of the cafe and into the most perfect sort of Autumn day. The sky is clear and luminous, an utterly stunning blue. It should take the breath from you, put everything in context, except I can feel the weight of the ring in my pocket like it's a bowling ball, and my context involves enemies avid for the world's ending.

There's a lump in my throat. My mouth's dry. I glance back longingly at an untouched glass of water on our table.

I want this over with.

But I shouldn't want this over with. The fact that I do is irritating. Christ!

Lissa stops, considers me then frowns.

"What?" I ask.

"You look a bit off color."

"I'm fine."

"Are you sure?"

"Really, I'm fine."

She's parked the car around the corner on Vulture Street. We're standing on a crossroads. Now that's gotta be symbolic. I scan the road. Nothing peculiar. There's plenty of people about. Someone's playing a Harmonica very much out of tune down the street, they're getting a good rhythm though. I swallow, take a deep breath. It's time.

"Well there is something. I've, that is to say.... Will you—"

Lissa's hand clenches around mine.

"Run," she says. "Now."